THE SUMMONING

BOOK ONE OF THE CAMNOEL TRILOGY

D1416052

HANNAH SHOOP

DEDICATION

To the One who gave me the passion to write.
May it be all for You.

CONTENTS

ACKNOWLEDGEMENTS

I have the best family. Thank you for always supporting my writing and for your editing eyes. You make my books better. Gram, thanks for informing me about cornfields. Even small details count. Twins, thank you for letting me talk things out with you and for all of your fabulous ideas. Sarah, you are the heart and soul of Camnoel and know these characters better than I do. This book wouldn't exist without your idea of three teenagers entering a medieval world. Josh, your encouragement was invaluable. Thanks to my Fullness family and my Simmons Middle School students who were test readers. I am grateful to everyone who has rallied around this novel, believed in it, and promoted it. And lastly, thank *you* for taking the time to read this story. May it be a grand adventure. Much love.

~Hannah

PART 1

1

NIGHTMARES

Wesley jolted awake with a start. His heart hammered. Sitting up in bed, he took a quivery breath. *"Another nightmare."*

The clock displayed red digits, telling him it was 5:03 a.m. Damp with cold sweat, he reached for the hoodie at the foot of his bed and shrugged into it.

He shoved the covers aside and sat on the edge of the bed. The room was dark.

Wesley stood and made his way to the bathroom. He stared at his reflection in the mirror, his eyes dark.

He leaned forward, bracing his hands on the sink. His gaze caught the photograph wedged in the frame of the mirror.

In the picture, his parents had their arms around him and his sister. They were standing on a red dirt road in front of a blue house. All four of them were smiling.

Wesley gave a slow blink.

"Why can't even sleep be restful?"

Nowhere, not even in his dreams, could he escape the reality of what had happened three months ago.

In his memory, he could see the day clearly. It had been deceptively normal, and then everything had changed.

***

3 months earlier…

Fifteen-year-old Wesley Haddon Connor lounged in a chair at the kitchen table, the bangs of his brown hair touching his eyes.

His fourteen-year-old sister, Anna, was sitting next to him. Her face was round, and her dirty blond hair was long and straight. She had inherited their mom's tan skin. While her brother's angular face was passive, her round brown eyes followed the movements of their mother with a smile. Wesley wondered how she was perpetually in a good mood.

Wesley's dad, Benjamin Connor, sat with hands folded on the table. He was a lean, well-built man with close-cut brown hair, who looked younger than his 40 years.

Their mom, Kate Connor, carried the candle-covered birthday cake and placed it in front of his dad. White teeth flashed against a bronze face that was framed with dirty-blond waves hanging below her chin.

She rubbed his dad's back as she and the two teens finished the last line of "Happy Birthday."

His dad blew out the five candles and glanced up at his mom. "Five candles?"

"One for each decade of your life and one for our year in Ecklebridge."

It was hard to believe that a year ago today their family had left the village in Africa where they were missionaries to come run the orphanage in this little European country. Some U.S. humanitarian program had started the crumbling orphanage twenty years ago, and the missions' board asked Wesley's parents to take it over.

Within six months of accepting the position, his parents had staffed a new team of workers and had already started the process of several adoptions for the children housed there.

At the time, Wesley hadn't wanted to leave Africa. He had been comfortable with the simple lifestyle and daily dusty soccer matches. But this place, with its pale people and green mountains and dairy farms, was starting to become familiar to him.

His dad rubbed his hands together with a grin. "Well those are some good causes to celebrate!"

After downing the frostingless lemon cake and clearing their plates, Wesley and Anna excused themselves.

"Be back for dinner," their mom called. "We'll head into town around five."

"We will," Anna said.

Wesley let the screen door of their small white house slam shut.

The two-story orphanage building was at the top of the hill. Next to it, across the playground, was the red brick structure where the kids, including Wesley and Anna, attended an English prep school.

On this Sunday afternoon, the grounds were quiet. One of the staff members had taken a group into town and the other kids were probably hanging out inside.

Wesley kicked up the soccer ball and juggled it between his knees. He dribbled it to Anna.

"It doesn't feel like it's been a year, does it?" Anna passed the ball back to him.

Wesley kept his eyes on the ball. Anna was maybe the only person who knew how much he missed Africa and how hard it had been for him to leave.

"I wonder how long we'll stay here."

"Do you hope we'll go back?" she asked.

Wesley kicked the ball harder than he meant to, but Anna caught it with her foot and returned it to him.

"I don't know. No place quite feels like home." He kicked it hard. "How do you feel so at ease?" He didn't mean the statement to sound so accusatory.

Anna shrugged. "I have Mom and Dad and you."

She was right. So why did he still feel so restless?

"You never would have met Drew if we hadn't come."

That was just like Anna. Always looking at the bright side. She was right on that score though.

The same age as him, Drew had been the first real friend he made in this town. Wesley had been trying to convince his dad to let them take a two-day camping trip in the mountains. So far he hadn't been successful.

As if reading his thoughts, Anna said, "I think Dad will let you go camping. He's just waiting for a time when he can go with you."

"When is he going to have time?" Wesley kicked the ball and muttered, "He's too protective."

"You should talk to him."

Wesley glanced at her, not voicing the thoughts coming to his head. To appease her, he said, "I will. Just not on his birthday."

Anna looked at her watch. "We should go back to the house."

When they entered through the screen door, his parents weren't in the kitchen. Wesley was surprised. He figured his dad would be working at the kitchen table on accounts for the orphanage.

Anna poked her head down the short hall to the bedrooms. "Mom? Dad?"

They made a quick search in the house and met back in the kitchen. Wesley checked the backside of the house, the garden, and the chicken coop.

He walked back into the living room to find Anna staring at the floor. The lamp had been knocked down and several books were tossed on the floor. Highly unusual for his scrupulous father.

His blood chilled, and for a reason he could not explain, a sick feeling surged in his stomach.

"What happened here?" asked Anna.

"The car was still outside," said Wesley, his voice faint in his own ears.

Anna turned to him. He could hear the fear leap to her voice. "Wesley," Anna's voice faltered. "Where are they?"

***

Present time...

Wesley tightened his grip on the sink as he fought a wave of nausea. He had called the police. There were sirens. There was a search. And then...there was nothing.

Police officials called it a crime scene but found no evidence besides the torn up room. At first, his parents were declared missing. Then the case seemed to be forgotten.

"Dead. Everyone thinks they're dead."

Wesley bit the inside of his mouth until it bled.

"We were missionaries. We came to help the orphanage. We weren't supposed to become one of their projects."

Wesley hit his fist against the sink. His fingers dug into the rim as tears filled up his vision.

What he would give so that none of this had ever happened. He could still feel every raw emotion of that day sitting in the orphanage office...

***

Wesley tried to stop his hands from trembling. *"I won't cry."*

His eyes already had creases pooling below them from sleep shortage. Instead, he clenched his teeth. *"I'm going to be strong for Anna."*

His sister sat close to him, and he could feel her body shaking from stifled sobs.

She had barely said anything since the disappearance of their parents.

Wesley ached for her. He ached for himself. It had been three days since they had come home to an empty house.

Wesley hated not knowing what happened to his parents. He wished the police would find something, anything that would give a clue to what occurred.

He wondered if they were alive.

Looking around the office, agony gripped him. His parents had saved this orphanage, and Wesley had met his best friend here. Sometimes he pitied Drew's orphan status, but he never imagined that he would be like him.

Wesley wished he could see Drew. Since the disappearances, the police had kept his and Anna's contacts limited.

"What are we going to do, Wesley?" Anna's broken voice pierced Wesley's thoughts.

Wesley didn't know how to answer.

Finally, he rasped, "We're going to be okay."

The encouragement sounded hollow. He looked across the room where a lady spoke on a phone behind a glass window. He turned his head again at the brush of the waiting room door.

Drew Vincent strode toward them, a contorted expression on his face. Wesley stood up, and Drew put his arms around him in a strong embrace.

"I came as soon as I could."

A lump caught in Wesley's throat. Anna stood, and Drew hugged her.

"The police won't tell us anything," Wesley said. "They can't find any information. It's like they vanished into thin air."

Drew shook his head. "They have to find something. Your parents are strong. They'll make sure that they get back to you."

Wesley stuffed his hands in his pockets and stared at the carpet.

"Hey," Drew's deep voice commanded his attention, "you're not gonna stay here."

***

Wesley blinked. Drew had been right. They hadn't stayed there.

They had been put in a foster home.

He splashed water on his face and walked back into the bedroom, looking around the unfamiliar surroundings. Instead of sleeping in his own room, with his parents down the hall from him, he was now in the care of Josiah Smith.

"At least we can all be together," Anna had said when the staff members announced that Mr. Smith would be taking in all three of them. Originally, Mr. Smith was going to be the foster parent to Drew. But when Wesley's parents' disappeared, the man arranged to take in all three of them.

"All together and parentless."

Across the room, Drew was still asleep in the twin bed by the window. Anna was in a room down the hall.

Wesley wondered how Anna was doing her first night in this new place. He was only a year older than her, but he had always been protective of her. Now he felt an even more urgent need to look after her.

Anger swelled inside him. Anger that she had been put in this situation. Anger at the police for not finding his parents. Anger at whoever had taken his parents away from him. Anger at God for allowing this to happen.

He sank back onto his bed as hot tears slid down his cheeks.

"How could You let this happen?" he whispered hoarsely.

A quiet snore from Drew called Wesley out of his thoughts.

More than ever, Wesley was thankful for him. Stocky and confident, Drew had been a rock for him and Anna. He kept reassuring them that they would find their parents.

When Mr. Smith had agreed to take all three of them, Wesley was glad he would remain with his two closest friends.

Still, Wesley hated being the objects of charity, and he didn't understand why the elderly man would want three teenagers running around his house, especially a house like Mr. Smith's.

When they had pulled into the driveway the night before, Wesley was surprised at the size and style of the house. It reminded him of the old English manors from the late 1700s. The inside wasn't any less antique.

Gazing at the numerous book spines that lined his bedroom walls, Wesley straightened his back. *I'll make the best of this.*

His thoughts were interrupted by a shuffling sound at the door. He turned and saw Anna's face through the cracked opening.

She entered quietly and whispered. "I couldn't sleep."

"Me either."

Wearing one of Wesley's old sweatshirts, she curled up on the foot of his bed. Her eyes were red.

"Do you think we'll ever see them again?"

Wesley's throat tightened. "I don't know."

"I don't think I'll be able to fall back asleep," said Anna.

"Me either," said Wesley.

Drew echoed that, "Me neither if you guys won't shut up."

Anna laughed quietly. "I didn't know you were awake."

Drew rolled over to face them. "I am now. What time is it?"

"6:15," answered Wesley.

Drew rubbed his face with his hand and muttered something about it being summer. He was pretty sure he swore too.

Drew sat up in bed and glanced at the large bookshelf that lined the back wall, and said, "You and Mr. Smith will be good friends, Wes."

Drew often picked on Wesley for his love of information, but Wesley didn't mind. Wesley was the better one at school between the two. Drew was an athlete. Though he was a couple inches shorter than Wesley, he was every bit as strong. Wesley wouldn't want to be standing on the wrong end of his tackle.

Ever since he'd met Drew, Wesley had thought him an oddity in the little dairy community. His short brown hair and tanned skin made him stand out against his pale countrymen. He'd also picked up an American accent from the orphanage workers and had affinity for American football. He was smart, but he made no pretense of loving school.

"Maybe you can find a book that you like enough to finish," Wesley said.

Drew laughed. "That'll be the day."

When they walked into the kitchen, Mr. Smith was already there. He was pouring boiling water from a kettle into a teacup.

Wesley guessed the man was in his sixties. He had short silver hair and blue eyes. He was tall and fit, making Wesley wonder if he once played sports.

Despite how much he didn't want to be here, Wesley found himself regarding the man with esteem. His house not only had hoards of books, but maps and old paintings also adorned most of the walls.

As he poured a cup of the strong black tea for each of them, he asked, "Did you sleep well last night?"

"Like a baby," said Drew as he helped himself to the eggs and sausage.

Mr. Smith smiled and handed a mug to Anna. "I am glad to hear it."

As they were eating, Mr. Smith spoke, "I'm afraid I will have to leave this morning for a meeting. I was hoping we would be able to spend the morning getting to know one another better, but that will have to wait until noon. Feel free to explore the house. What sorts of things do you like to do?"

Once again, Drew was the first to speak. "Sports. Futball, American football, basketball."

Mr. Smith nodded slowly with a curious smile. "And you, Wesley?"

"Sports. I like to read and camp and that sort of thing."

"Perhaps you can find some books of interest from my collection," Mr. Smith smiled.

When Mr. Smith looked at Anna, she said, "I usually helped my mom with the cooking or helped with the younger kids. She was teaching me how to sew. But," she looked at Wesley and Drew, "I like to kick the Futball with them or play basketball."

Mr. Smith asked them more details about their hobbies, and looked interested in every word they said.

Wesley knew he should feel grateful, but right now, he really wasn't in the mood for talking.

When they finished eating, Mr. Smith glanced at his watch and frowned. "I must go, but I shall be back by noon and we can pop into town for lunch if you'd like."

Once he left, they exchanged glances.

"I guess he trusts us," said Anna.

Wesley agreed. He thought it was strange though.

"Well," Drew stood up, "he said feel free to explore the house so that's what I'm gonna do."

2
THE MIRROR

Mr. Smith's house was old, with creaky wooden floorboards and aged wallpaper. A History professor at the local university, he kept textbooks and classics on coffee stands, shelves, and tables. From the assortment, Wesley gathered he specialized in European medieval history.

Wesley liked the large fireplaces and paintings of castles. Since they had moved to Europe, he had yet to visit a real castle.

"He doesn't have any photographs of family," Anna commented.

"Maybe he doesn't have any," said Drew.

"Even if they died, you'd think he would keep up their pictures," said Anna.

"Maybe it hurts him too much," Wesley thought, identifying with how Mr. Smith may have felt.

They came upon another spare bedroom. It was plain, with embossed wooden paneling on the walls, and a few framed paintings.

What caught Wesley's attention was a small door on the back wall. It was half covered by a chair and blended with the rest of the room to easily go unnoticed.

"I wonder where that leads."

He jiggled the door for a moment. It wasn't locked, but was difficult to open.

Drew grinned. "Careful, Wes, you don't want to break the door."

When Wesley pushed it open, he looked at Drew. "Still in one piece."

Anna smiled teasingly. "Barely."

Wesley had expected it to lead to a storage room, most likely an attic, but it opened into a very tight space, with stairs to the left.

Anna peeked at the stairs, "Can we go up?"

"I'm going up," said Drew, taking the lead.

At the top of the stairs was a square landing and another door to the left. Drew swung the door open and let out a breath. "An attic."

Wesley wasn't so quick to lose interest. He observed the nearly empty room carefully. A cardboard box sat against a wooden table. On the table, leaning against the wall, was something that looked like a picture. It was covered with a canvas.

Anna walked first to the box and knelt beside it. She was about to open it, but stopped. "I feel weird about prying into his personal things."

"Why?" asked Drew. "He said we could explore the house. Open it."

Wesley was curious too. He crouched down by Anna and lifted the flaps of the box.

"What's in it?" Drew asked impatiently.

Wesley reached in and pulled out a piece of leather.

It was an old-fashioned tunic.

"Costumes?" Anna asked.

"I bet their real," Wesley said softly.

"How do you know?" asked Drew.

"If Mr. Smith is as passionate about history as his house suggests, why wouldn't they be?"

"What else is in the box?" asked Drew.

Anna reached into the box and pulled out more articles of clothing. There were leggings, a cloak, a belt, and a pair of boots.

"I just wonder why he'd keep them tucked away up here," Wesley said almost to himself. There were plenty of other artifacts on display. Why keep these hidden?

Drew stood up. "Well, what's on the table?" He took away the canvas.

It was a mirror.

Oddly, the mirror seemed to be covered in mist, like a foggy bathroom mirror after a shower.

"Is it dust?" asked Anna.

Drew wiped the mirror. "No." His mouth hung agape.

As he wiped away the fog, Wesley stared at the mirror. It wasn't a mirror at all. It was a picture. It was like an ancient painting, but too life-like. The scene depicted a sylvan setting, with thick green grass and a dense forest. There was a still pond in the background.

Drew continued to wipe away the fog, and as he did, the fog didn't disperse on his hand—it spread around them, tendrils reaching out like a cloud.

The mist that floated around them grew thicker and moister, first making their clothes damp, then growing so thick that they could no longer see each other. It felt as if they were being immersed in liquid.

"Wesley, what's happening?" Anna panicked.

Wesley tried to call out for his sister, but when he did, his mouth filled with a nasty tasting liquid. He was no longer standing on a hard surface, but was waving his arms and kicking.

He was swimming.

He opened his eyes and saw murky green water around him.

His first thought was to get air. Instinct told him to swim upward.

"What's happening?"

Finally, his head broke through the water's surface. He gasped for air and tried to find his bearings. Was he near land? He saw green grass a few feet from him and swam towards it. A strong arm reached for him and helped him to his feet. Wesley looked up.

"Drew!" He spun around looking for his sister. "Where's Anna?"

He was about to dive back into the water when he saw a blond head pierce the mossy surface. Anna swam towards the bank, and Wesley and Drew pulled her out.

Wesley caught his breath as muddy clothes clung to his body.

Standing on the bank, he took in his surroundings. They were in the middle of an extensive wood, with towering trees all around. The forest floor was a thick carpet of grass and leaves. The tree trunks were expansive, with aged bark garbing their sides. Rays of sunlight pierced the forest canopy, casting shadows on the ground.

Wesley stared, turning in a slow circle, a sinking feeling in his chest.

Drew let out a low string of repeated curses in fright.

"Are we..." Anna said slowly. "Did we just enter that picture?"

The question didn't need answering.

"How did that just happen?" asked Anna.

"Can we get back?" asked Drew.

Wesley looked at him but didn't say anything. He sucked in some air and dove back into the water.

Beneath the surface, he opened his eyes. It was murky green with tangled roots and moss. He swam farther, looking for any kind of window or opening. Anything that would suggest a portal back into Mr. Smith's house.

He found nothing.

When he came up for air, Drew tried to talk to him, but he plunged back under.

After several tries, his lungs burned. He swam to the bank and pulled himself out.

"Anything?" asked Drew.

Wesley shook his head. He felt dizzy, colors and pressures around him spinning. A hundred thoughts stampeded through his brain. How did they get here? Did they travel in time—or place? How many worlds had God created? Would they ever get back? Were there humans here? How would they survive? Had Mr. Smith known his mirror could do this? Who was Mr. Smith? Was he to be trusted? And if they could suddenly be transported to another realm, perhaps so could...

"Wesley," Anna said.

He looked at her and nodded. "Mom and Dad."

Anna looked at him with wide eyes. "They might be here."

Drew's eyes were wide as he nodded. He spun around, cupping his hands to his mouth. "Ben! Kate! Are you here? It's Drew. Your kids are here!"

Wesley stiffened. If his mom and dad were here, who was to say they were right around the next tree? Or that there weren't more sinister forces behind their disappearance? He wasn't sure shouting was the best method.

"Drew, shh..." he didn't finish, thinking he had heard something.

Drew stared at him. His wide eyes belied the fear that was just barely being contained.

"What the heck is going on here?" he pronounced each word slowly, begging Wesley for an answer.

Wesley shook his head. "I don't know." His heart was racing. His thoughts felt fuzzy. He forced himself to take a deep breath. "I don't know. But we have to stay calm."

"Brr!" Drew gave a violent shiver.

Wesley wasn't sure if it was from shock or cold. Probably both. Their wet clothes and the late afternoon sun did pose a problem. "We need to find a place to get warm."

He glanced at Anna. Her shoulders were hunched, arms crossed against her chest. Her jaw quivered, and she blinked. Wesley knew they could all possibly come unhinged.

Drew cursed again, and Wesley spun on him, about to command him to stop.

Drew ran a hand through his hair and rubbed his forehead, taking in deep breaths. "Dude. Wes. We're in another...we just...holy crap...what's going on here?" his last question sounded almost accusatory. "Did you know about this? Did you know Mr. Smith? Your parents had contact with him before they disappeared. *Did they know about this?*"

"Of course not! Drew, snap out of it."

"Drew, they didn't know," Anna said, "They couldn't have."

Drew pointed to the pond. "Then how are we in an attic one minute and in freaking woods the next?"

Drew grabbed his hair again, pacing.

Wesley planted himself in front of him. Drew swatted him away.

"Drew," Wesley commanded. "Get it together."

Wesley grabbed his arms, holding him in place. Drew stared at him for a long moment.

He took in a breath and nodded.

Wesley waited before releasing him, unsure of what he would do.

Drew turned his back to them, hands on his hips.

"We're going to be okay," Anna said. She looked at Wesley, then Drew.

Drew turned around, looked at her then Wesley. He nodded.

"Go no farther."

Wesley stopped, his pulse working overtime. He slowly turned his head to see where the voice had come from. Ten yards away, a man stood with a bow, the arrow drawn and aimed right at them.

3
A NEW WORLD

Drew cursed under his breath.

Wesley put up his hands in surrender.

The man held his position for what felt like five agonizing minutes. Finally, he relaxed. He was dressed in mostly black. A vest covered a dark shirt and hung over britches. He wore soft boots that made no sound as he walked towards them.

The man came to stand in front of them, his bow and arrow still ready at a moment's notice. His hair was dark, and Wesley guessed he was in his low twenties.

"I have hunted in these woods for over ten years and never have I seen anything like that. What devilry is this? I was here long before you could have entered that pool and come out with breath still in your lungs."

Wesley was lost for words, and from the silence that surrounded him, he knew Drew and Anna were too.

The man waited. When no answer was given, he looked at Anna. "And you—do you always dress as a man?"

Anna glanced at Wesley. "I," she stammered, "I'm not dressed like a man."

The man relaxed his bow a little. "I was beginning to think we did not speak the same language."

Wesley wondered if he hadn't heard them speaking to each other earlier.

The man eyed them. "Have you no words?"

"You wouldn't believe us if we told you," said Drew.

He narrowed his eyes. "Whom were you calling out for?"

"Where are we?" asked Wesley, changing the subject.

The man eyed him. "In the forests outside of Vladoc. Where are you from?"

Wesley's answer came out barely above a whisper.

The man took a step closer. "Is that in Camnoel?"

Wesley dropped his eyes and shook his head. "No." His mind reeled with the implications of this man's words.

"Devilry indeed," he marveled. "How did you get here?"

"There was a mirror," said Drew. Wesley glanced at him.

"A mirror?" The man raised his eyebrows. "Well then...intriguing days are upon us."

It didn't escape Wesley that the man hadn't pressed for more information. Was he aware of something they weren't? Were there some mirrors in the world that acted as portals to this place? Drew's words haunted him. *Had* his parents known about all of this? Drew was right; his parents had been speaking with Josiah Smith months before they had disappeared.

He blinked. *"No way."* Still, while his mind said one thing, his emotions spoke another. Feelings of anger and betrayal dripped into his subconscious.

"I am Drail, knight of the Citadel...although I suppose that means little to you."

Wesley gave a curt nod. "Wesley."

"Drew."

Drail looked at Anna.

"Anna. I'm Wesley's sister," she managed, her voice still a low rasp.

He gave them one last cursory glanced and returned his arrow to the quiver strapped to his back. He slung his bow over one shoulder as his eyes flickered to the sky.

"You will catch cold in those wet clothes. We will make for the city to get there by dark," He eyed them, "unless you have other plans."

Wesley shook his head, sure that his befuddled expression conveyed that they were lost, innocent travelers.

"Very well." Drail turned and started walking south. "You ruined my hunt," he called over his shoulder.

"Sorry," Drew called back as he yanked Wesley's arm.

Startled, Wesley turned to face him.

"What are you doing?" Drew whispered. "Are you going to trust this guy? He just tried to kill us!"

Wesley shrugged out of Drew's grip. "We don't have a choice. It sounds like he's going to take us to shelter at least."

Drew's eyes were wide.

Drail paused up ahead. "The longer we tarry the later we will arrive in Vladoc."

Wesley met Drew's eyes. "It's okay," he mouthed.

He hurried to catch up with Drail. Anna stayed close to his side.

"So you're from Vladoc?" asked Wesley.

"I hail from Aloehan."

"Aloehan. Where's that?"

"A journey eight days north of here. And do not assume I forgot you have not yet answered my previous question."

Wesley answered with a question of his own. "Have you seen a man and a woman come through here? They'd be dressed similarly to us. In their late thirties."

Drail stopped and stared at him, clearly wanting more information.

Wesley exchanged glances with Anna and Drew. He shrugged helplessly. "Our parents. They disappeared three months ago. It's like they vanished into thin air. We thought, if we could be whisked here, then maybe they could be too."

"I have not seen them. Perhaps, though, you had better tell me your entire tale."

Wesley ignored the looks Drew kept shooting him. He didn't think they had much choice but to trust this man; he was the only one they had met. He gave Drail an abbreviated history of his parents' disappearance, their stay at Mr. Smith's, and their discovery of the mirror.

Drail shook his head. "You speak of fantastical things. I would not have believed you had I not seen with my own eyes your appearance in the water. We shall ask Sir Kaden about your parents. He is the captain of the guard where I come from."

"Aloehan?" Wesley verified, trying to keep track of the new names.

Drail nodded.

"Captain of the guard...Citadel," Wesley's brain was spinning. He watched the ground beneath his feet, the cracked leaves, twisted roots, and crawling insects. That much, at least, felt familiar. He had done this before. He had left America for Africa and Africa for Europe. *"But at least they were in my world..."*

"You said you're a knight?" Drew asked.

"I was the last time I checked."

"What do you do?" asked Drew.

"Are you thinking of becoming one?"

"I was just asking."

"We do whatever we are commanded to do...which is mostly train and keep peace," he said flatly.

"What were you hunting?" asked Drew. Wesley marveled at his ability to make conversation when he was about to blow up earlier. But he was thankful; he felt like they should learn as much as they could about this man.

"Deer."

"Will you go back out tonight?"

Drail simply cocked his eyebrows at him as if that were a foolish question. "No," he said at last.

Drew shrugged.

They walked on in silence, Drail seeming content with the quiet, and the others not comfortable enough to speak in his presence.

Wesley was aware of his wet clothes, the cold, and the setting sun. A sudden weariness struck him and he felt fatigued, though they had only been walking a half hour. *"It's like jet lag. I wonder if traveling through the mirror caused it."* He fought to stay alert, trying to pay attention to the smallest sounds in the forest, from the birds to the squirrels, always glancing at the knight.

Although both Wesley and Drew were athletic, he hoped their self-defense skills wouldn't be tested if Drail proved untrustworthy. Wesley noticed, in addition to the bow slung across his back, the knight wore two knives belted at his waist.

Drail glanced back, and Wesley tried to act like he hadn't been staring.

"Vladoc," Drail said.

Wesley looked up. They reached the edge of the forest and were standing atop a ledge. In the distance, he could see flickering lights from the city and the reflection off a large body of water.

"If we have any manner of luck a shop will be open and we can procure you some clothes. You will turn every head wearing those garments. Especially you," he flicked his eyes at Anna.

Anna didn't say anything.

Drew gave her arm a squeeze and bobbed his chin up.

Though Wesley was the one who had agreed to this venture, he didn't feel as comfortable as Drew looked. How little Drail talked unnerved him, how little they knew of their guide, and how little they knew of this world.

The trek to the city was longer than Wesley expected. Night had fallen, and their clothes were dry by the time they reached the outline of the city wall. The gates were open, which gave Wesley a measure of reassurance. Perhaps times were not so evil here that the locals felt they needed to enclose themselves behind stone boarders.

Inside the walls, buildings were made of wood and stone.

"This is real," he told himself. Was it? Or was it all just a dream and he would wake up in Mr. Smith's house? Maybe he'd wake up in his own house, his parents chatting in the kitchen, the smell of sausage and eggs wafting through the hallway. *"Don't be an idiot. This is reality. Stay alert."* He couldn't afford to be daydreaming right now.

The streets were dark, with sparse flickering lanterns lighting their paths. Some streets were cobbled, but most were dirt. They had to skirt several puddles and ally cats that darted in front of them. Some windows were shuttered, but the firelight exposed other house scenes. In one house a woman was sitting by a fire, needlework in hand, while her husband smoked a pipe.

They emerged from an ally to a main cobbled road. On the side opposite the shops was a stone walkway that outlined the lake. It was better lit here with flickering torches that reflected in the water. If he weren't so on edge, Wesley might have enjoyed the quaint lake town.

The streets were quiet, with few pedestrians. Though Wesley didn't know what time it was, he assumed people here rose and went to bed with the sun.

Drail took one look at a shop across the street and shook his head. "Closed. You will have to wait until the morning."

He led them farther along the lake sidewalk until they came to the side of town that had not retired to bed. Warm light and noise spilled out of a large wooden building. A swaying sign read *The Silver Knob Inn and Tavern*. Outside, horses that were hitched to a post flicked their ears lazily.

Inside, the air was thick with pipe smoke and human sweat. Wesley scanned the room. He saw only men, except for a lone woman behind the bar drying mugs. They were dressed more or less the same as Drail, and most wore beards.

There was one loud table of young men playing some kind of game of dice. Wesley noted that they were all dressed the same, wearing black armor. One of the men called out a greeting to Drail. He nodded in return.

"How'd the hunt go, Master knight?" a round man with a thick mustache called.

"Unsuccessful," Drail replied.

The man opened his mouth to speak, but no words came out. Wesley was uncomfortably aware of the inspecting look with which the bartender regarded them. They were catching stares from others in the tavern as well.

"Do you fellows need a room?" the bartender asked.

Walking straight ahead, Drail answered. "They are with me."

"That'll be—"

"They are not staying the night," Drail spoke over him, pressing right on ahead.

Wesley followed Drail, hoping no one else would stop them. Anna and Drew stayed close by.

"We're not?" Wesley asked.

"You are, but if I told him, he would charge me three times extra."

Wesley didn't respond. He didn't know how he felt about trusting a man to whom lying came so easily.

Drail led them around a corner that widened into a wooden lobby. They cut right, scaled three flights of stairs, and came before a door for which Drail produced a key.

"I would offer you another room, but rooms are not cheap, and knighthood is not the path to trod if one is seeking riches. Not Citadel knighthood anyways." He swung open the door, allowing them to enter first.

Wesley couldn't see anything until Drail lit two small lanterns. The flickering light revealed a small, simple wooden room with a desk, chair, and twin bed.

"You may have the bed," he said to Anna. "There is a rug over there one of you may use. I shall fetch more blankets from my horse. He is in the stables next door." Before shutting the door behind him, he added, "Lock the door. Do not open it until I return."

When he was out of earshot, Drew gave Wesley and Anna a wide-eyed look.

"Dude," he said. "This is real. Like this is really, really real." He swore again.

"Would you cut it out?" asked Wesley.

"Sorry. This is just...I mean...this is crazy!"

"I don't trust him," said Anna.

Wesley glanced at her. "I don't either, but we don't have much of a choice right now."

"The man can hold his own," commented Drew. "It's not bad to have a guy like that on your side."

"We don't even know what the sides are," Wesley said. "If he can take us to this Citadel, maybe a place that important would have heard something about our parents." Wesley looked down. It felt strange to be speaking about them again. Since they had been put into the foster care system, he had shut down most mention of them. Thinking they were dead was less painful than considering other possibilities.

Drew caught his hesitation. "Hey."

Wesley met his eyes.

"If they are here, we'll get them back. I swear it." He held out his hand. Wesley clasped it, and they clapped each other on the back.

When they pulled apart, Drew looked more settled than Wesley felt. Drew sat on the bed where Anna sat with her knees drawn to her chest.

"You okay?" Drew asked her.

"I'm fine," she said softly.

Drew looked from Anna to Wesley. "You know what? This is going to be good. We're gonna be okay."

Just then, the lock jangled, and Drail entered carrying several more blankets. He tossed a bundle to Wesley. Wesley unwrapped it and saw a loaf of bread.

"Thank you." He tore off pieces and handed them to Anna and Drew. When he offered the remainder to Drail, the knight shook his head.

"Keep it."

Wesley nodded gratefully. "What do you plan to do with us?"

Drail leaned against a wall and slid into a sitting position, arms propped on his knees. "We should find clothes first thing in the morning. We shall need horses and supplies for the journey. Then, we make for Aloehan."

"We don't have any money," said Wesley.

"Convenient." Drail regarded them wryly. "Why are you here?"

Wesley stared back at him. "I wish I knew."

4
VLADOC

Wesley wasn't sure he slept that night. The even breathing around him told him the others probably did. Since he had known Drew, the boy didn't seem to have a problem sleeping. He was glad Anna had found rest and wondered how she was doing. He knew she wouldn't open up while Drail was around.

The knight slept closest to the door, with Drew next, and Wesley closest to the bed. It was difficult to get comfortable on the wooden floor, and Drail's thin blanket did little to shield against the damp air.

Knowing he would never fall back asleep, he sat up, his back against the wall. His eyes traced a crack in the wooden shutter. The sky was just starting to lighten. Somewhere outside, a waterfowl called.

The mattress creaked, and Anna raised her head. She shifted into a sitting position, her back against the wall. Wesley joined her, leaning against the adjacent wall.

"Did you sleep?" she whispered.

He shook his head.

She nodded at the bed. "Do you want to try to get some rest?"

"I don't think I'd be able to."

"How are you?" she asked, keeping her voice low.

He shrugged, aware that Drail could be awake any minute if he wasn't already. "It's crazy," he whispered, knowing his answer was not articulate. But he couldn't figure out how to put into words what he was thinking. Less than twenty-four hours ago, he wouldn't have even agreed that something like this could have happened. Yet here he was, in a world real as anything he'd ever known, his body's fatigue a familiar sensation in an otherwise unfamiliar setting.

"God has a big imagination," Anna said with a trace of a smile.

Wesley couldn't manage a smile. Not now. He wasn't sure he had smiled since his parents had disappeared.

"You should rest," she said in a voice that reminded him of their mom's. She stood, crossing her arms in the cold and stood in front of the window.

Wesley did not argue. He stretched out on the bed, which held no match to his bed back home, but was loads better than the floor. He barely had time to acknowledge his surprise at the sudden pull sleep had on him.

The next thing he knew, he was blinking in the mild light of the morning. He raised his head from his stretch on his stomach. Anna was still standing by the window, and Drew was still asleep, but Drail was not in the room.

Wesley got up and made no effort to be quiet. "How long did I sleep?"

"A half hour maybe."

"When did Drail leave?"

"Ten minutes ago. He said he was going to see about getting us some breakfast."

"Well, he's taken care of us," said Wesley.

"He's been respectful enough."

"Drew," Wesley said, sticking a toe in his side.

Drew jolted awake. He grunted, sat up, and rubbed his eyes. Looking bleary-eyed at Wesley and Anna, he said, "Morning."

Anna smiled.

"Drail is getting us breakfast," said Wesley. "We should talk about what we're planning to do."

"What's there to plan?" asked Drew. "He's going to get us clothes and then take us to some castle place."

"Should we stay with him?" asked Wesley.

"What else would we do? At least he's given us food and a place to stay."

Wesley couldn't argue with that. Still, he hated not knowing anything about this man while blindly accompanying him. But Drew was right; they didn't have much of a choice. Wesley had said as much himself last night. The lack of control in this situation was maddening. It was too unpredictable. He looked at Anna. She nodded, agreeing with Drew.

He inhaled. "Yeah. Okay."

No sooner had he spoke when Drail reentered. He tossed them each an apple and small loaf of bread. The simple fare comforted Wesley.

"We will attract attention in the town. Do not attract any more than necessary. It is better to not get caught in conversations," said Drail. "Stay close. Walk tall."

Wesley saw Drew smile.

Drail was right. Men, women, and children walking on the street glanced at them. Especially Anna. All of the other women wore long dresses.

He knew Anna was accustomed to being stared at when they were in Africa, but it always made him want to tell people to mind their own business.

There was a trio of men wearing the black armor Wesley had noticed in the tavern the night before. Swords were belted at their waists. Wesley wondered if they were the law enforcement of the town.

He asked Drail.

"They are Ratacin's men, ambassadors from his kingdom from the West."

"Is that kingdom separate from the one you mentioned yesterday—Aloehan?"

Drail snorted. "Quite separate. They are not on the friendliest of terms, but I have found conversing with them to be helpful. His men have given me no trouble thus far."

"Drail," one of them called out.

"Carloc," Drail answered.

Carloc looked about Drail's age. He eyed Wesley, Drew, and Anna. "Friends of yours? Can you hold a sword?" he asked Drew and Wesley.

Drew shrugged. "If you want to give me one."

Wesley said nothing. He wished Drew wouldn't have said anything. They had no idea of the nuances enclosed in that question.

Carloc shrugged. "Ratacin is always looking for men."

"As young as these?" asked Drail.

Wesley felt Drew bristle beside him.

"Never too young to start training, eh?"

"I shall convey to the Citadel he is in want of men," said Drail wryly.

Carloc gave him a quizzical look.

Drail tipped his head and kept walking, leaving Wesley to wonder at the exchange.

"Do a lot of the guys here know how to use a sword?" asked Drew.

"Here in Vladoc? Nay. Most are merchants. Every man likely has lay to some means of defense—knives mostly—but swordsmanship will only be found in those trained as knights."

"And in Aloehan?" asked Wesley.

"Most are farmers, more comfortable with pitchforks than broadswords."

"Were you a farmer?" asked Wesley.

"Farmer, tracker…School runt."

Somehow, Wesley had trouble believing that.

"How old do you have to be to start training to be a knight?" asked Drew.

"Those in the royal families train from their youth. Others enter their training at twelve, fifteen, eighteen…the Citadel takes whom they are able to acquire."

Drail led them to a stone shop with a wooden sign that read *The Tailor*.

Inside, there were shelves of cloth of varying fabrics, patterns, and colors. Wesley saw no ready-made clothes.

The tailor was a thin man with hunched shoulders and spectacles.

"Good morning. Can I help you?"

"We need a dress for the girl."

The man's eyes widened when he saw Anna, but he quickly regained his composure.

"And trousers and shirts for them," said Drail with a nod towards Wesley and Drew. "As quickly as you can spare them."

The man eyed Drail but gave a nod. "All right. Let us see about the lady first. Your name, ma'am?"

"Anna."

"And what type of dress are you looking for today?"

Anna looked at Wesley and then at Drail.

"A simple traveler's dress," Drail informed.

"Very well," the man said, "We have an assortment of fabrics over here." He led Anna to one wall and held up various stacks for her to see.

Anna regarded the fabrics and pointed to a blue one. "I like this one."

"How much?" asked Drail.

The man named the price.

Drail offered a counter sum.

"I am sorry sir; I have got to make a living. I cannot be haggled."

"And I have a specific set of needs. If you cannot allay them I am wont to look elsewhere."

The tailor held up his hands. "I am sorry sir. You'll not find new garments for less than that price in this town."

"Understood." Drail walked out the door, leaving Wesley, Anna, and Drew to follow.

They walked several more blocks and took a turn down an alleyway until they came to an outdoor market. There were vendors with booths, tables, and tents selling their wares.

Drail ducked inside one such tent hosted by a plump woman. He exchanged words with her, and then she peered around him to look at the teenagers.

"Dearie me," she tsked. "I've got just the thing."

She rifled through a chest of clothes until she pulled out a long green dress. She held it up to Anna.

Wesley guessed it was second-hand clothing, and there was little chance of getting it washed before wearing, but then, he thought, they might as well get used to being uncomfortable.

The woman dug some more through her collection until she found two pairs of trousers and two shirts.

Drail seemed content with the price, paid, and led them back to their room.

"You can change first," Wesley told Anna. He, Drew, and Drail waited outside the room.

"What is your plan next?" asked Wesley.

"I shall stop by the livery, gather supplies, and then meet you here. We will be on our way before midday." He regarded Wesley and Drew. "Can you ride?"

Thankfully, there were stables not far from the orphanage in Ecklebridge where they had ridden on more than one occasion. Still, none of them had been on rides that lasted more than a few hours. "We've never ridden for very long," said Wesley.

"We know how to ride," Drew added, his voice exuding a lot more confidence than Wesley's.

The door opened and Anna came out. The dress seemed to fit her fine. It looked a little strange to Wesley, as if she were dressed up for a medieval play.

Drail nodded approvingly. "Better." He looked at Wesley. "Meet me in front of the tavern in an hour."

Wesley nodded. He and Drew went into the room and slipped out of their twenty-first century, Westernized clothes. Surprisingly, the trousers and shirt fit well. Both had a soft, lived-in feel. The boots were a little big but would work well enough.

Drew ran a hand through his hair. "My hair's too short. All the guys here have longer hair and beards. Maybe I should grow it out."

Wesley glanced at him. "You say that as if we're staying here for a while."

Drew shrugged. "Do we know how we can get back?"

Wesley didn't answer. Maybe someone at this Citadel place would know.

"What's the hurry to get back?" asked Drew.

Again, Wesley couldn't give an answer. He just wished things could go back to the way they were. He felt a pang of homesickness, wishing his parents had never disappeared...wishing the four of them could be on a carefree outing to the mountains. Wishing he could take that camping trip with his father. He blinked. Thoughts like those wouldn't help him. Right now, he could only think about the step right in front of him. For now, that meant waiting for Drail.

5
HUSTLED HORSES AND
BLUE WOLVES

An hour later, Wesley, Anna, and Drew stood in front of the tavern as they waited for Drail.

Even though they had changed clothes, Wesley still felt out of place. All the people seemed to know what they were doing or where they were going. He tried to assume a relaxed air.

Drew was leaning against the rail of the tavern's porch, absently dribbling his fingers on the rim as he curiously watched the streets. He seemed to fit in.

Anna stood by, reserved, quiet, her eyes scanning the city.

From what Wesley gathered, they were in the poorer part of town. The people didn't seem particularly well-kept, with dirty skin and greasy hair.

Still, the lake in the distance brought him a certain amount of serenity. Its calm rippling seemed to be something that was predictable in his otherwise baffling environment.

He noticed that Anna kept reverting her eyes to the water and the birds that flew overhead.

He saw Drail walking towards them. Drail's eyes also constantly scanned his surroundings. He walked confidently, but he didn't look like he trusted those around him.

"The horses are ready."

Wesley jogged to catch up with him and match his quick stride. "How are you paying for this? Aren't horses expensive?"

"Ask me when we are out of this city," was the crisp reply.

Wesley glanced at Drew. He arched his eyebrows and shrugged.

The livery was an old barn with chipped paint. As soon as they stepped inside, the earthy scent of animals and straw accosted him. Next to him, he felt Anna relax. She stepped up to one of the stalls, stroking the face of a bay. She smiled.

Drail's movements were quick as he led a bridled horse out of a stall. He handed the reins to Drew without a word. Though the horse stood taller than him, Drew held his ground, tightening his grip on the reins.

Drail retrieved another horse and gave the reins to Anna.

"He's observant," thought Wesley, realizing that Drail had immediately assessed who in their company was most comfortable with the animals.

"You will have to ride with someone," he said to Anna as he mounted his own horse. The action looked effortless.

Anna looked at Wesley and he nodded. He waited for her to mount, took a deep breath, and climbed into the saddle behind her.

Drew mounted his steed, and Wesley caught the grin that spread across his face.

Was he the only one who felt uneasy?

Without any more words, Drail steered his horse through the door and set out at a canter. Anna and Drew matched his pace.

"Say farewell to Vladoc," said Drail as they retraced their steps from the day before.

As uncomfortable as he was in the city, Wesley felt a knot thread in his stomach as they left its boarders. The wild lay ahead of them.

"You said to ask you once we were outside the city. How did you pay for these horses?"

"The man's price was the all the fortune I had. I paid and picketed his pouch as he was readying the horses."

Wesley kept his face blank, but the knot in his stomach did a flip. He was riding on a stolen horse. He felt his face flush. "I thought knights were supposed to be chivalrous."

He saw Drail's face contort in a wry grin. "If you would prefer to walk, be my guest. I am continuing to Aloehan with or without you."

Perhaps Drail wasn't as hospitable as he had first thought. "Or perhaps he knows his leverage. We would never be able to find Aloehan on our own, so he knows there's nothing we can do about it."

Still, the thought of riding thieved horses was distasteful to Wesley. And if those in Aloehan followed Drail's code of ethics, he wasn't so certain it was a place he wanted to be.

Their horses fell into a steady gate. Drail proved to be not only a competent rider, but a good leader as well. He found paths through the forest that, while needing to be traversed single-file, allowed them passage.

The quiet hum of the forest did little to calm Wesley's nerves. And the repetitive up-down of the horse's hindquarters only made Wesley uncomfortable.

Again, the victual of anger simmered inside him. Why did any of this happen? What madness existed that orchestrated two worlds and ripped parents from their children?

"What are You doing?" Wesley mentally spat with vehement accusation. It was the first time he had prayed in longer than he could remember. He didn't care to continue the conversation.

When they broke midday to water the horses and eat some bread, Drew asked Drail, "May I see your sword?"

Drail turned a hooded gaze on him. Wesley watched him.

After a moment of thought, Drail unsheathed the silver at his side, flicked it so the hilt faced forward.

A smile crossed Drew's face as he took the weapon. He held it, eyes admiring the length of the blade. He held the handle loosely and took a fluid dry swing. It swooshed as it sliced through the air.

Drew grinned. "Can you teach me?"

Drail arched his eyebrows. "How to fight?"

Drew nodded.

Drail snorted. "Apply to be a knight." He took the sword back and sheathed it, preparing to mount his horse.

"Who taught you?" asked Drew.

Drail did not answer.

"Have you ever been in a battle?" Drew continued as they returned to their mounts.

"Not with humans."

"With what then?" Anna asked. It was her first attempt to join any of their conversations.

Drail shrugged. "Skyrogs mostly."

"What-rogs?" asked Drew.

"Woodland creatures. They have a nasty bite and attack even when   unprovoked."

"Do you think we'll see one?" asked Drew. He sounded like he actually hoped they would. Wesley rolled his eyes.

"Not in these woods."

"Good," Anna said under her breath.

"Here you need only worry about bears and wolves."

"That makes me feel better," said Wesley.

Drail cast him a wry grin. "Bear is a fine meal if you can catch one."

Wesley had no desire of finding one. "Who is the captain of the Citadel?" he asked, changing subjects.

"Sir Kaden."

"Is he your king?"

"Kaden is a knight. Aloehan has no king. There is a steward—Sir Rowan. And he is far from kingly."

"Why don't you like him?" asked Drew.

"He hides in his castle and knows nothing of the world's events outside his halls."

"Did the city ever have a king?" asked Wesley.

"Aye. When I was but a boy. They say tragedy took the king and queen."

Wesley wondered what had happened. Had they disappeared too…like his parents?

"But I think it matters little whether there is king or steward on the throne. Aloehan is not an *ambitious* city."

Wesley tried to interpret the scorn in his voice. Was Drail disappointed in his city?

"Do you have a family?" Anna asked.

Though he could only see his back, Wesley saw the impatience in Drail's posture. "Does everyone from your world ask so many questions?"

Anna was quiet.

They rode the next hour in silence and showed no signs of stopping, until Drail pulled quickly on his mount's reins. "Whoa." He listened to the forest then uttered a word Wesley did not recognize, but took from his tone to be a curse.

"Wolves," he said.

"Are you serious?" asked Drew.

Drail looked at him with annoyance.

"We're not exactly from here," Drew snapped.

"Which is why you would be wise to listen to one who is," Drail retorted. He lowered his voice. "We must ride. Hard." He kicked his heels into his horse's side, "Yah!"

A howl pierced the wooded twilight, sending a shiver through Wesley's body. With one hand still on the saddle's horn in front of Anna, he twisted and looked behind them. His heart pounded.

The only wolves Wesley had seen were in zoos. Those resembled dogs and were not much bigger than foxes. What he saw prowling towards them were as large as tigers, with a bluish cast to their fur, hackles raised.

"They're following us!" he yelled.

"I know! Keep riding!"

Wesley hung on to Anna, hoping she knew how to steer this horse better than he would have.

"Great. We come to another world and get eaten by overgrown wolves."

"To the rocks!" Drail barked.

Interspersed among the woods were large gray rock formations. Wesley didn't see how horses would stand a chance against more agile creatures in this location.

Drail charged his steed up a narrow path until it stood on a rock plateau. The others followed him.

The tracker quickly dismounted and handed the reins to Anna. "Keep them steady."

He fetched something out of his saddlebag. He tossed one to Drew and one to Wesley.

Wesley glanced down. It was a sheathed knife. How was he supposed to fight a wolf with that?

He looked over the ledge. The wolves were surrounding them. One leapt effortlessly to the rock right below them. The horses reared and Anna worked to keep them steady.

Drail nocked his bow and let one arrow swoosh through the air. The nearing wolf let out a yelp and collapsed.

"There, you blue-back jackals!" Drail yelled. "Let that be a lesson to you!"

Wesley swallowed hard. The rest of the pack seemed to take the hint.

There was a snarl behind him. He spun around.

Drew yelled and reacted first. A wolf leapt toward him, but he stuck it with the knife. The force of the beast knocked Drew to the ground.

"Drew!" Anna screamed.

Drew rolled the beast off him, and stood, breathing hard. He and Wesley made eye contact. Drew yanked the blade from the creature's matted hair. It was soiled with blood and gore.

Drail fired several more arrows, killing one, and scaring the others. They scattered.

He turned to face them and nodded at Drew.

Wesley and Drew were both panting. "You okay?" Wesley asked.

Still catching his breath, Drew nodded. "Yeah. Just killed a wolf. No problem."

Wesley's eyes fell to the dead beast. *What have we gotten ourselves into?*

"Will they come back?" asked Anna.

Drail shook his head. "Not tonight. We will camp here though. On high ground."

6
IN THE WOODS

Wesley was thankful for the small campfire Drail built. Wolves didn't like fire, the tracker said, but Wesley had a hard time not being chary of the shadows and sounds in the forest around them.

Night enveloped them, and Wesley felt lonelier than ever. Drail was from this world and reacted with natural instinct. Drew had thought fast and killed the wolf. Even Anna had managed to keep the reins of three frightened horses three times her size.

He had stood there. What was wrong with him? He had adapted to other cultures. Why was this different? *"I'm not being brave enough. Or strong enough. I'll have to do better."*

He blinked as Drail handed him some bread. He wasn't sure he would be able to eat it; his stomach was in knots.

"Do we need to find shelter?" asked Anna.

Drail glanced at the sky and shook his head. "It will not rain tonight. We shall camp here on the rock." He looked amused. "Have you never slept on rock before?"

Anna didn't answer.

"Should we take turns keeping watch?" asked Drew.

"Be my guest," said Drail. "I intend to get some sleep."

Though he had barely slept the night before, Wesley wasn't sure how much rest he would find on the cold stone. When they finished their meal, he tried to get comfortable lying near the fire. The others did the same. Apparently, Drail didn't think a watchman was necessary.

His head pressed against the ground, he stared at the smoldering sticks, their orange ripples seeming content in their death. How could some things in life seem so peaceful? So confident of their role in the realm of nature?

Unbidden memories of his dad taking him camping skipped to his mind. Fires. Marshmallows. Laughter. Fresh trout.

Wesley's vision watered, and he blinked. He was back in the forest.

Somehow, he knew he couldn't let his thoughts wander there.

When he woke, the forest was cast in blue light. His clothes and skin were damp with dew, and when he moved, his body ached. He blinked. He had slept.

Moreover, he was the last one to wake, which annoyed him. Drail was rolling blankets and putting them back on the horses. Anna was feeding one of the horses. She had braided her hair. Drew was throwing pebbles at an invisible target on a tree.

Wesley rubbed the sleep from his eyes. His stomach growled, a good sign. He picked up his blanket and joined Drail.

"Morning."

The tracker glanced at him. "You were able to sleep."

"Surprisingly."

Drail grunted with a smile. "It becomes easier with practice."

"I'm hoping I won't need that practice."

Drail shrugged. "Perhaps once we reach the Citadel they will have you back on your way. You might even return to your own world."

Wesley didn't know how to feel about that. On one hand, the idea thrilled him. He would love to escape this place that his brain couldn't explain. At the same time, he thought he would be disappointed to return home with no word of their parents or no indication of purpose as to why they had been there.

Anna brought Wesley a mug of porridge. "Drail made it this morning."

"Thanks." There was no spoon, so he gummed the thick substance down.

"Dude, this place has creepy sounds at night. I don't know how you slept so much," said Drew.

"I don't know either."

"I can't wait to get to this Citadel place. Maybe they have some decent food and a decent bed."

Wesley rolled his stiff shoulders. "Look who's talking. Usually you can sleep anywhere."

"I know," said Drew, shaking his head, "but this…This is crazy. I mean, to think this place has always existed and nobody on earth knows about it. How'd we get to be the ones to come here?"

Something Wesley's parents said jumped to his mind. Something about God having purposes for everyone and Him having their days already written in His book. But he didn't say that. He simply shrugged. "I don't know."

Finishing the porridge, he rinsed the mug and joined Anna by the horses.

"How are you doing?" he asked.

"I'm okay," she said, stroking the horse. She gave him a small smile. "They have pretty sunrises here. Looks kind of like the ones back home."

Wesley snorted. Home. Where was home? What did he consider home? The U.S.? Africa? Europe?

"Wesley," Anna spoke slowly. "Maybe we shouldn't wear ourselves out searching for answers. Maybe we should just enjoy this."

How was his younger sister able to arrive at that conclusion before he was? Wesley depended on answers. Always, he was trying to figure things out, whether it was helping Dad with the budget, learning a new language, or reading a new history book. He didn't know how Anna was able to dismiss things so easily. Sure, she had cried hard when their parents disappeared, but had she already gotten over them? Were they that forgettable to her?

Drail came up beside them. "We should be off."

The ride was uneventful, if not uncomfortable. Wesley wasn't accustomed to sitting hours at a time in a saddle. Drail didn't seem to be in the mood to talk, and there was little conversation among the four of them.

Wesley was hoping they would stop soon. His joints were stiff and breakfast had worn off, leaving his stomach rumbling. But he wasn't about to say anything. He was thankful when Drew did.

"Dude, I have to stop. My butt is numb and I'm starving. Man, I could go for a cheeseburger right now." He looked at Wesley, and when he saw the consent in his eyes, grinned.

Drail nodded. "There is a stream up ahead. We will stop there."

Wesley dismounted gratefully, but even though his feet stood on solid ground, his body still felt the up-down motion of the horse's canter. He went to the stream and splashed water on his face and drank deeply.

Drew lay on his belly on the grass.

Drail eyed them. "Do you not use horses for transportation in your world?"

Drew laughed. "You have no idea."

Wesley was careful not to utter a complaint because he felt like Drail was already thinking them weak. "Can the horses go all day?"

"Rest will do them good," said Drail. "Besides, we should hunt. Unless you want bread for your next meal."

The knight retrieved his bow from the saddlebag. "Drew and Anna, make a fire. Wesley, come with me."

Wesley started to follow, and Drail pushed something against his chest. He looked down. It was the dagger. He grasped it, wanting to prove himself in the hunt, but having a hard time envisioning a successful one with this tool.

He and Drail wordlessly walked deeper into the woods. Drail found a thicket of bushes and crouched behind them, facing the stream. Wesley followed his lead.

"Squirrels will work. Rabbits will be better." He glanced at Wesley and down at the dagger. "Do you know how to throw it?"

Wesley nodded, figuring he could figure it out.

Before long, a squirrel scampered into view. Drail nocked his arrow, but must have decided against it. "Too small."

A quarter of an hour later, a rabbit hopped along.

Drail gave a single nod to Wesley.

Wesley's brow knit in a frown of concentration. He drew the dagger back, poised for a throw. He could visualize it, the knife spinning and lodging right in the hare's neck. He was confident he could make the shot. The rabbit perched frozen, its nose twitching.

Wesley paused. It wouldn't be wrong. It wasn't pointless killing. He would learn a valuable skill in how to skin and cook a rabbit; he was sure Drail knew that in and out.

But there was something frail and innocent and blissful about the creature. For a split second he saw his mom. He saw their living room. Lamps shattered and books scattered. He lowered his hand, and the rabbit skipped away.

Drail eyed Wesley. "You have never hunted before."

Wesley could have told him about the doe. It was a perfect shot with a 6.5 mm. His dad had to help him drag it back to their truck.

But he didn't say anything.

Before Wesley could blink, Drail nocked and released an arrow. Wesley jerked his head to see another rabbit—this one brown—lying dead. He hadn't seen it approaching. Drail didn't even seem to be looking in its direction.

"You have," he responded to Drail's earlier statement.

"I am fond of eating."

Wesley and Drail walked back to the campsite to find Drew and Anna next to a small fire. They were playing tic-tac-toe with charred sticks on stone.

"Who's winning?" asked Wesley.

Anna grinned. "Who do you think?"

"She thinks because she's won the first three that she's pretty good. But it's best out of ten," said Drew.

"Batting 300 is still pretty good," observed Wesley.

"Not compared to someone who bats 700," volleyed Drew.

"That doesn't happen."

"Anything can happen."

Anna turned away from their game and saw the cony in Drail's hand. "You were successful?"

"Not as much as we could have been."

Anna looked at Wesley questioningly.

Wesley shrugged.

Drail sat a pace away, but Wesley didn't miss the crack of the animal's vertebrae. He didn't watch as Drail removed the skin.

"Would you?" asked Drew. "If you had to?"

"Would I kill?" asked Wesley.

Drew nodded.

Wesley stared at the fire. He pictured himself in their house in Ecklebridge. If an intruder had come in, his parents and Anna at risk, of course he would. He would grab their gun from the safe and shoot without a thought. But if it were only his life at stake? Maybe. "I hope I don't ever have to," he said.

"I don't know that I could," Anna said, her brow furrowed.

"Even if someone was about to kill someone you love?" probed Drew.

"If they were about to kill my family," Anna said slowly, "I know that I would see them again one day. Death wouldn't be so bad. But if I killed the other person…they probably wouldn't know the Lord and…well," she left the rest of her thought unvoiced.

Drew shook his head. "I'd pull the trigger in a heartbeat." He was quiet for a moment. "Would you kill the people who took your parents?"

Wesley looked at him. They didn't even know if people *had* taken his parents. Wesley assumed that's what had happened; his parents wouldn't have simply left. But they didn't know for sure.

He was angry at Drew's brazenness. How could he ask such a question? Because if Wesley were honest, the anger inside him was most definitely strong enough to pull a trigger.

His Christian beliefs told him it was wrong, but if he were given the chance to kill to bring them back? Yes. He would.

He could feel Anna watching him. He was mad at Drew for bringing this up around her. Why bother upsetting her? What was the point in asking that question?

He glared at Drew, stood up, and walked away without answering.

Standing up stream, he was so lost in his thoughts he didn't hear Anna walk up beside him. He jumped.

"Sorry."

"He shouldn't have said those things," said Wesley.

"I think he says those things because he cares. He wants us to know that he would do whatever he could to stand up for us. He would even kill the people who took Mom and Dad."

"Well he can't!" Wesley said louder than he meant to. "He can't, all right? None of us can. So why bother talking about it? This is a stupid conversa—"

"Because we don't have to forget!" Anna raised her voice. "We don't have to stop talking about Mom and Dad and pretend like nothing happened."

"Right! Let's stop pretending like nothing happened. At least I don't laugh and make jokes all the time."

"You don't do anything anymore! You shut everyone out. You never talk about Mom and Dad. You never talk about God—"

"Well excuse me if I'm a little mad at Him right now. You think He couldn't have stopped this? Of course He could have. But He didn't. So there. Yeah, I'm a little ticked off at Him right now."

"We could at least talk about it."

Wesley just stared ahead.

He could hear her crying, but she wasn't going to make him feel guilty by getting emotional.

"Fine," she said quietly, her voice raspy. "We don't have to talk about it." She backed up a couple steps, then turned and walked away.

Wesley picked up a stone and hurled it into the stream.

7

MEMORIES

Wesley had waited as long as he could before returning to
camp. He avoided both Anna and Drew, wagering she told him
about their conversation. He was annoyed at both of them.

They ate the cooked cony in silence.

Wesley ate in defiance.

He slept farther from the fire, not caring if it was chillier. His
argument with Anna made his face hot. He uttered some choice
words in his head. He tried to wrench his mind from the
memory, but it came like a horse breaking from the gate that
couldn't be stopped.

*"I'm just saying, you call me a man, but you don't treat me like one,"
Wesley said, his narrow shoulders shrugging, palms upward. "I mean, why
not trust us?"*

*"Wesley, it's not a matter of trust. We don't know this place. We just
moved here. Give it some time. Let's get to know the people. The culture."*

*"So let me get to know it. Let me experience it. I'm not asking to go
alone. Drew would be there. He says teens go camping all the time."*

"And do you know what goes on during those camping trips?"

"Dad, we're not going to do something stupid."

"We don't know Drew that well."

"We're missionaries. Aren't we supposed to get to know people?"

"We're to be wise as serpents."

Wesley grabbed a fistful of hair, frustrated at his lack of progress. His dad could be so stubborn. "Then come with us."

"I would love to. And we will. We just can't go now. It's the busy season. Son, you know that."

"Dad, it's always the busy season. When will you ever have time to go camping with your son?"

Wesley could see the hurt in his dad's eyes. "Wesley, can't you see the value of this work?"

"Yeah, it's real important work. I can see that. More important than your family." He knew the comment wasn't totally fair. He knew his dad loved him. And he knew if he had stayed in the room, his dad would have voiced that. But he didn't want to give him that chance. He wanted him to feel the sharpness of his jab. So he walked out of the kitchen.

And it was the last time he talked with his father. Hot tears spilled out, trickling into his ears. He kept his cries quiet, not wanting the others to hear if they were still awake. Why couldn't he and his dad have talked? Worked things out? Why did that have to be their last conversation? The next day had been his dad's birthday, and he had told him happy birthday, but they hadn't spoken beyond that.

Wesley wished he could have talked to him again. He wished he could have taken back his words. He wished they could have gone camping and fishing and played catch.

His mom had always been there. Sure, she was busy, but she always had time for him. When he complained to her about Dad not letting him go camping, she had listened and sympathized, but had taken Dad's side. Predictable.

Maybe he was fifteen. Maybe he was becoming a man. So why did he still feel the need so strongly for his dad?

Anna was the only family he had left. He knew he couldn't leave things the way they were with her. He thought about waiting until morning, but wasn't sure they would have a chance to talk privately before setting out on the road.

As quietly as he could, he sat up, padded over to where she lay curled by the fire, and tapped her shoulder. She turned over, still awake.

He nodded for her to follow him and waited until they were far enough away that they could talk without waking Drail or Drew.

He wasn't sure how to start. "I'm sorry for what I said earlier. I didn't mean it. I know you care."

"I'm sorry too." Her voice was quiet. "Wesley, I don't want you to be mad at God."

Wesley wasn't sure how to respond. "I'll be okay. I still believe."

He looked at her and saw she was crying.

"I need my brother, Wesley. We lost Mom and Dad. I can't lose you too."

He was surprised at the lump that caught in his throat, and when she hugged him, he didn't pull away.

She pulled back and wiped her face. "I don't know what to make of all this."

"We just take it one day at a time, I guess."

She inhaled. "One day at a time. I can do that."

"Sure you can." He nodded back to the campsite. "We better get some sleep."

As Wesley was about to reclaim his spot under his blanket, he saw Drail shift. The knight was awake.

"Not much gets by him," Wesley thought as he drifted to sleep.

8
HOSPITALITY

The next two days passed with little excitement. They rode. They stopped to eat. Drew tried to keep conversation going, and while Drail wasn't reticent, he wasn't overly talkative.

One day, while they were riding, Drail pulled the reins on his horse, and held up his hand for them to do the same.

The knight glanced back at them. "Someone is in the woods." Speaking louder, he said, "You can come out."

Wesley's heart pounded a little harder as he imagined a band of knights emerging from the surrounding trees.

He felt an internal sigh when it was only a gangly teenager who looked to be his age. The boy was tall and thin, with a brown ponytail tied behind his head. He held a bow, but it wasn't drawn. He seemed embarrassed that he had been discovered.

"Austin," Drail nodded.

"Drail," the boy's voice cracked. "How did you know I was there?"

"You will have to get a lot quieter if you want to sneak up on people."

"I was not sneaking up on you," Austin protested.

Drail didn't seem convinced. "Is your family home?"

"Do you mean is my sister home?"

Drail gave an amused smile that seemed to irritate Austin. "This is Wesley, Drew, and Anna."

Austin stared at them. "I've not seen you in these parts before. Are you from Aloehan?"

"It's a long story," said Drew.

"We would be grateful for lodging. We shall be on our way in the morning," said Drail.

Though Austin didn't appear thrilled at the idea, good breeding must have won out. "Mother will be preparing dinner. I shall tell her to make extra."

They dismounted and led the horses by foot, following Austin.

"Austin's father is Sir Orson, captain of the guard," said Drail. Austin glanced back. "Austin has begun training to be a knight."

"Can you swordfight?" asked Drew.

"Aye," the teenager replied as if it were obvious.

"That's cool," said Wesley, trying to cover what may have been taken as an insult. "Not a lot of people where we come from can."

"Where is that?" asked Austin.

"Wait until we get to your house," Drail told Austin.

They walked several miles before Austin led them down a slope that gave way to a small valley. As they were walking, the gray sky yielded to a gentle rain. Soon their clothes were wet and their shoes soggy.

A brook trickled over stones to their left. They followed it until the valley broadened and finally defused into flat forest grounds. The trees remained dense except for a small clearing where a cottage was nestled in the distance. Smoke rose from the stone chimney.

There was a wooden hut with stick fences surrounding it, which Wesley guessed was the stable.

Austin came to an abrupt stop while they were still thirty feet away from the house. "I had better only take one of you in; then the others can come a few minutes later. My mother may react better that way. Seeing three strangers at once may not bring a pleasant reaction from her. Plus I am late for dinner," he added. He looked at Anna. "Ladies first?"

Wesley stepped forward quickly. "I'll go first." He glanced at Anna who shrugged at him. Maybe she wasn't concerned, but he wasn't about to let her go into an unknown house without him.

Austin shrugged and led Wesley to the house. Wesley glanced back at Drew and felt him understand. Drew wouldn't let anything happen to her.

Wesley stepped into the house behind Austin and scanned the place. The door opened into a large room, part of it serving as the kitchen and the other part as a sitting and eating area. Three doors led to other rooms in the cottage.

A woman wearing a floor-length dress bent over a stone fireplace oven. Her hair was tied in an untidy bun.

When they entered, she spoke without turning, "Austin, I told you to be here half an hour ago." Before Austin could explain, she pulled bread out of the oven and turned around. Her eyes widened when she saw Wesley, but otherwise showed no emotion.

"I am sorry I am late, Mother. This is Wesley. He is a traveler and needs a place to stay."

Austin turned to Wesley and said, "Wesley, this is my mother, Sairla."

Wesley nodded to the woman.

The woman acknowledged him with a nod, and then returned her gaze to her son. "Austin, will you bring the extra meat from the storehouse?"

"Yes ma'am." Austin shuffled his feet and then added, "There are two more guests as well, Mother. And Drail."

Her eyebrows arched, but she nodded and said, "Well, hurry; bring them in. And fetch your sister."

Austin smiled and nodded. He ran out the door to get the others. Sairla continued to busy herself with the meal.

"Sit by the fire so your clothes may dry," she calmly ordered.

Grateful, Wesley obeyed. A moment later, Austin reentered with Anna, Drew, and Drail trailing him. Sairla greeted them briefly and made room for them by the fire.

"Drail," she acknowledged.

"Sairla, how are you faring?"

"Well enough. Were your travels successful?"

"Successful enough."

Wesley wondered at the stilted interaction.

Anna smiled at Sairla. "Thank you for opening up your home to us."

"You are welcome here, Anna," Sairla replied. Her eyes scanned them. "Where have you three come from?"

After a pause, Drew stood from his seat by the fire and said, "You probably won't believe us if we tell you, but we'll explain where we're from. It's a heck of a story."

9
CROSS-CULTURES

As they sat down to the table, Sairla placed steaming meat, vegetables, and bread before them. She kept glancing at the door. Just as she was seating herself, the door opened and a young woman entered. She resembled Sairla, but had sharper features.

Wesley guessed she was a few years older than himself.

Surprise crossed her face when she saw Wesley, Drew, and Anna. Her eyes landed on Drail and a smile touched her lips.

He grinned as well, stood, and kissed her on the cheek.

"I did not know you were coming. Who are your friends?"

"This is Wesley, Drew, and Anna. This is Miraya."

Miraya smiled pleasantly at them.

When everyone had food on his or her plate, Sairla said a prayer and then looked expectantly to her three guests. "Please, tell us your story."

Drew looked at Wesley with arched eyebrows.

Wesley took a deep breath and launched into their story, glossing over his missing parents, but including the details of Mr. Smith's home, the mirror, and their meeting with Drail in the woods.

When he finished, the silence that followed was dense.

Finally Sairla broke the stillness.

Her gaze was unwavering, and her tone solemn. "What was the name of the man who took you in?"

"Josiah Smith." Then he added with genuine surprise, "You believe me?"

"There is no reason not to. My only surprise is *your* confusion; did not Josiah tell you of the mirror?"

Wesley shook his head. "No. How do you know of it?"

Sairla frowned. "I am not the one who should be telling you this, however, I will tell you enough. Someone else will have to explain more later."

"The mirror you found is a portal from your world to Camnoel, which is the name of our world, the one you have entered. You are in the city of Aloehan. Josiah is a Keeper of the mirror. He has been guarding it for some years now. Your entrance," she said, looking from Wesley, to Anna and then to Drew, "to Camnoel is rather significant because it has been anticipated for some time now."

Drew leaned in, his eyes narrowed. "How could people have been anticipating us? We didn't even know we would come here."

Sairla chose her words carefully. "There has been...expectation, a hope that one would come from your world to help Camnoel. Our city and many others wait under the threat of evil."

"Expectation," Wesley probed, "what do you mean? How would we be able to help your world?"

Sairla pursed her lips. "I cannot say anymore."

"How do you know this much? And how do you know Mr. Smith?" questioned Drew.

"Through my husband, Orson. He is Captain of the Guard at the Citadel. You should speak with him or someone else from the Citadel. It is not my place to disclose anything. Presently, he is away on business. Still, you must go to the palace where the knights may speak with you. Austin can take you there if Drail cannot."

"I will travel ahead on horse and tell Kaden what has transpired," said Drail. "Have Austin lead them on foot. Then the Citadel will be expecting them."

A wide grin crossed Austin's face. "You will not be disappointed with the Citadel. Wait and see."

Once they finished eating and clearing the table, Austin sat back at the table.

"I should like to hear more of your world," he said. "I have only heard about it from my father, never from one who has been there, let alone one who is from there."

"What do you want to know?" Drew asked. He, Anna, and Wesley had joined Austin at the table while Sairla sat by the fireplace with some sort of knitting. Miraya and Drail had excused themselves for a walk.

"Do all of the people wear those types of clothes?"

Drew grinned at Wesley and Anna. "It sort of depends on where they are in the world."

"Do they all talk like you?"

They went on to explain accents and different languages from earth, noting that, in some countries, there were people who had similar accents to Austin's. They patiently answered all of his questions regarding everything from their clothes to the kinds of food that they ate. All the while, they eagerly waited to hear more about Camnoel, and its culture.

This kind of conversation was familiar to Wesley. In Africa and Europe he had talked with other teens about their respective cultures.

"Is all of Camnoel covered in forests?" Wesley asked once Austin had relented from his questioning.

Austin shook his head. "There is much variety in the landscape, so I hear, and from what I have seen on maps, though I have never traveled anywhere very far. Speaking of woods, I shall show you ours."

"That sounds great," Drew eyed Wesley and Anna brightly.

Wesley did want to learn as much as he could, but he also felt jetlag-like fatigue creeping into his bones.

Austin jumped from his chair and reached for his bow and quiver that he had set in a corner.

"Be sure you do not stay too long out after dark," Sairla cautioned.

Austin gave the three of them cloaks before they left, warning that the evenings could be chilly.

"So where are we going?" asked Drew.

"You will see."

Austin continued to lead them deeper into the forest in the opposite direction of where they first entered. In the light of dusk, the tree bark was a burnt brown and the leaves scintillated like fire. The myriad trees cast shadows on the wood's floor. A slight breeze accompanied the forest sounds. Nearby frogs and crickets chirped. The branches rustled as squirrels darted overhead.

Yet even the forest's serenity could not distract Wesley from questions that burned in his mind.

"Austin," he said as they came to a stop in front of a gentle waterfall, "Do you believe the same as your mom—about us being here to help Camnoel?"

Austin was looking at the waterfall and shrugged. "I know not. There are some people who have been hoping and praying for help to come to this land, but I did not think it would come in the form of three youth." He turned to face them.

Drew scoffed. "Ever heard of the young and brave?"

"My point is," continued Austin, "that if you are hoping to go to war against the lord Ratacin, then you will have to undergo the most vigorous training, so harsh that many men would rather not train altogether."

Wesley tilted his head. "War against him? Drail made it sound like Aloehan and him just weren't getting along. He didn't say anything about a war."

"I would not put stock in what Drail says. A war has not yet begun, but my father says one will."

Wesley frowned. How were they supposed to understand this world's political system when the only people they had met couldn't seem to agree?

"You don't seem to like Drail very much," Wesley observed.

"He is courting my sister."

"Why don't you like him?" asked Anna.

"He tolerates my whole family, feigning courtesy, but the only one he really cares about is Miraya."

Drew must have been bored with the topic, because he asked, "When do we leave for the castle?"

"Tomorrow."

"How often do you go to the castle?" asked Anna.

"As often as I can. When Father is gone, I usually must stay home with Mother and Miraya. But sometimes Father takes our whole family to the palace and we stay for several weeks. During my time there, I have been training to be a knight."

Wesley wondered if it were the same type of training they would be expected to undergo to help save Camnoel from this Ratacin.

Before he could mention it, Austin said, "Come, it is dark. We should be on our way home."

By the time they reached the cottage, the sun had set, and the first stars lit the night sky. The cottage windows glowed with the warm light of the fire. Austin entered without bothering to knock, and they followed him. Drail and Miraya were standing next to the fire, and Drail gathered his things to leave. Sairla sat at the table with some fabric and a needle.

Drail kissed Miraya's cheek, and muttered something in her ear. She smiled. He nodded to Sairla, "Good night, ma'am."

On his way out, he acknowledged Wesley. "I will see you shortly. Good luck in your travels."

Wesley shook his hand. "Thank you for your help."

Without looking up from her mending, Sairla spoke to them, "We have made your bedding arrangements. There are two mats in Austin's room where Wesley and Drew will sleep. Anna, you will share Miraya's room."

Anna said goodnight to Wesley and Drew before retiring to Miraya's room. As she moved to go to her room, Drew muttered something to her. She nodded and shut the door behind her.

Wesley glanced at Drew, and Drew said lowly as they walked to Austin's room, "We'll meet outside tomorrow to talk."

Wesley nodded in agreement. He wanted to talk. But right now, all he wanted was sleep.

They didn't get to sleep right away though.

Austin asked questions for what felt like hours.

Finally Drew said, "Dude. I want to sleep. Enough with the questions tonight, okay?"

Austin may have been offended, but he stopped talking.

Drew rolled over on his mat to face Wesley. His eyes widened and he gave a bright smile.

Wesley knew that face. Aside from being giddy that he had convinced Austin to be quiet, Drew was ready for an adventure. To his surprise, Wesley was beginning to feel ready for one too.

10
A QUESTION OF PURPOSE

The morning came much too quickly for Wesley, who had stayed awake another two hours after they stopped talking. He awoke to a firm shaking and gruff whispering in his ear.

"Wake up, Wes," Drew urged. The room was still dark.

Wesley opened his eyes. "What time is it?"

"Time to get up," Drew replied in a hushed tone.

Wesley sat up on his mat and looked around the room. Austin was snoring loudly. He reluctantly stood and stretched his arms. Though he was still tired, nearly as soon as he did so, adrenalin rushed through him.

"Is Anna up?" he asked Drew.

"We gotta get her."

They quietly exited Austin's room. No one was in the main room, though he could hear the shuffling of feet on the other side of Sairla's door.

"Go get Anna." Drew kept his voice at a whisper.

Wesley hesitated, then cracked open their door. They were both asleep. He treaded softly on the floor and knelt beside Anna. She stirred at his gentle shaking.

Anna rolled over and opened her eyes.

He put a finger to his lips and stood, nodding for her to follow.

She followed Wesley out of the cottage where Drew was waiting and rubbed her arms in the cool morning air. "Good morning."

"Morning," said Drew. He looked wide awake.

Anna stifled a yawn.

"We need to make this meeting a short one," said Wesley. "I don't think we have much time. Because they don't have electricity, they probably get up when the sun does, which is pretty soon."

"Yeah, and I think Sairla is already up," said Drew.

"Well?" asked Anna.

Wesley took a deep breath. "Okay, they know Mr. Smith and said that he knew of the mirror's power."

"Which makes sense," said Drew, "because he kept it hidden."

"Right," said Wesley. "But Sairla thought that Mr. Smith would have told us about it."

"He didn't have time," said Anna. "We found it on our first day in the house."

"But why would he have even wanted to tell us about it?" asked Wesley.

"Because he thought that we could help save this place," said Drew.

Wesley ran a hand through his shaggy hair. "Yeah, but why would he think that three teenagers could help save some country? I mean…why us?"

The question lingered in the air; none of them had an answer.

Finally Wesley broke the silence and replied to his own question, "Maybe it's a mistake. Maybe he never meant for us to come here at all."

"Well what if it is?" asked Anna. "We don't know how to go back. All we can do at this point is go with Austin to the Citadel."

"I'm with Anna on this one, Wes," said Drew.

Wesley wasn't convinced. "How do we know who we can trust? Drail and Austin have told us different stories."

Drew shrugged. "We'll figure it out as we go along."

"I guess we don't have any other options, do we?" asked Wesley.

When they entered the cottage, Sairla and Miraya were in the kitchen. Sairla stood over the stove, scrambling eggs with a wooden spoon. Miraya was wrapping loaves of bread in cloth. The two women looked up when they entered.

"You are awake early this morning," commented Sairla.

"We needed to talk about some things," Drew explained curtly. Changing the subject, he added, "Breakfast smells good."

"It is almost ready," she replied. "You may have a seat."

They obliged, and Drew asked, "When do we leave?"

"As soon as we can manage. Miraya is packing your food and Austin is gathering your packs."

Not long after the mention of his name, Austin appeared through his doorway carrying several bundles. His face brightened when he saw them. "Good morning! Are you ready for our journey?"

Wesley glanced at Drew and Anna. Drew looked eager and Anna looked peaceful, ready to go along with whatever lay ahead. He couldn't say he felt either of those emotions.

Their hosts had loaded a horse, Fendar, with supplies, but each traveler still had to carry a bundle. They left the horses Drail had stolen in the stables. Wesley didn't mention the part about them being stolen.

When Miraya turned to say goodbye to Wesley and Drew, she said, "It was nice to meet you both. I am sure you will make excellent knights of Camnoel."

Drew raised his eyebrows and was about to speak, but Wesley beat him to it. "Thank you."

Sairla placed her hands on her hips. "May your journey go smoothly. You have a good guide." She smiled at her son, and then returned her gaze to them. "Remember, though you do not fully understand your purpose here presently, it will become clearer."

"Only clearer?" asked Drew.

Sairla smiled. "It will become clearer. In the meanwhile, do your best to accept what you do understand." Then, with a piercing gaze, she added, "I have faith in you."

Wesley wondered why her words felt so weighty.

"Well then," she said briskly, "you should be off. Farewell Austin." She enclosed her son in an embrace and for an aching moment Wesley missed his mom. Releasing all but his head, she said, "Guide them well."

"I will, Mother. Farewell." He looked brightly at them. "Shall we be off then?"

11
ON THE OUTSKIRTS

The sun rose higher in the eastern sky, casting rays of light through the forest canopy, though shadows still covered most of the wood's ground.

They strode farther away from the cottage. Once they had scaled a small hill, Wesley looked back. The cottage looked small and distant. He turned his head forward, toward the dense forest ahead of them, wondering if he'd ever see the cottage again, or his own world again.

The four of them walked in silence for several miles, respecting the tranquility of the forest around them. It was Anna who finally broke the quiet.

"Austin," she said as she fingered the leather straps on her backpack. "I've been wondering...Your mother prayed at the meals to the Maker, and I was wondering who that was."

"Oh," said Austin with a rather confused expression. "Why, He's the Maker of all of Camnoel." He arched his eyebrows a little. "He created your world as well." He squinted. "Have you never heard of Him?"

Anna smiled. "I have. But," she continued curiously, "how do you know about Him?"

Wesley watched Austin.

"Well," he started, "people from your world brought holy writings with them. I don't know much beyond that. "

When the sun was directly above them, they made a brief stop to eat and to water the horse at a nearby stream. Then they resumed their journey, following the winding waterway.

The warm searing air of the afternoon gave way to a cool breeze of evening. Shade filled the halls of the forest again and crickets sang. The gentle gurgling of the stream had crescendoed to a steady gushing. As the sunlight waned, Austin called them to stop.

"We will make camp here," said Austin. He handed Fendar's reins to Wesley. "Will you take him to the stream and water him? I will search for kindling."

When Wesley rejoined camp, Austin had a small fire going. "Have you enjoyed the journey thus far?"

Drew gave a short laugh, and then tried to cover it with a cough. "It'll be nice to get to the palace," he said, a smile still lingering in his eyes.

"Tomorrow's journey will prove nicer," Austin reassured. "'Tis only a half day's journey and much of it is through the town. We will pass through the fields first, which can be a bit hot."

"I've liked this part of the journey already," Anna reassured. "This forest is beautiful."

Austin grinned. "Wait until you see the forest of Ellwood."

"What forest is that?"

"The forest of the elves."

"Elves?" Anna cast wide eyes at Wesley and Drew. Turning back to Austin she inquired, "Will we get to meet them?"

"Not many humans have that privilege. But who knows? Perhaps fortune will smile upon you."

They finished their meal and unrolled their blankets. The guys let Anna sleep closest to the fire while they claimed spots for themselves away from the warmth.

The ground wasn't comfortable, but Wesley's thoughts weren't on the sleeping conditions. *How many nights have we slept in this world? There doesn't seem to be much chance of getting back.* Lying on his back, he stared up at the stars peeking through the treetops. *Please just let this take us to Mom and Dad.*

Wesley awoke with a start, sitting up and darting his head around, his breathing labored.

Drew eyed him with a frown and Wesley realized Drew had kicked him in the side to wake him. "You okay?"

Regaining his bearings, he replied, "I'm fine."

He could tell Drew wasn't convinced, but he didn't press Wesley.

Wesley squeezed his eyes shut, shuddering. Opening them, he searched for Anna. Drew was waking her with a gentle shake of the shoulder.

Austin gave them a cheery greeting, and the four of them ate a quick breakfast.

"What will happen when we reach the castle?" asked Wesley as they trekked the remains of the forest.

"You will meet my father, if he has returned from Revowen—that is the Elvin city," he explained with a glance at Anna. "He says it is the loveliest city in all of Camnoel. A shame that Ratacin is from there."

"So," said Wesley, "Ratacin is an elf?"

"Yes," said Austin. "But he betrayed both elves and men when he committed that act of treachery."

"What was the treachery?" asked Wesley.

"He forsook the elves to build his own power. But," Austin said with a lighter tone, "let us not speak of this now. You will also meet some of the other knights, I am sure."

He went on to explain about the different persons of prestige at the palace. "There is Sir Kaden, the Second of Guard, a noble man. None can match his defense skills, and I hear he is a fearsome warrior. Sir Rowen, the steward, is a fat old man," this earned a snort of compressed laughter from Drew, "but nice enough. His daughter, Charmaine, is probably the bravest girl I know, but a good deal too self-important if you ask me."

"How are we supposed to act around these people?" asked Anna. "Do we bow and curtsy or say 'your majesty'?"

Austin chuckled. "There is no one you will need to address as that, unless you go outside of Aloehan. The king and queen are referred to by that, I suppose, but Camnoel is kingless presently. As for bowing and curtsying, well that would be proper to pay to Sir Rowen, but they will not be necessary for anyone else."

After a few more instructions on civility had been given, Wesley broached the subject that had been occupying his mind for the last several minutes. "You said that Aloehan was kingless. Why is that?"

"Well," Austin faltered a bit, "That is difficult to explain. The king and queen passed away. There is no more to this story that I have the heart to tell you."

Wesley frowned. What were Austin and Sairla not telling them?

The four travelers maintained a good pace, reaching the edge of the forest where the trees gave way to open fields. Untamed meadows yielded to stretches of green crops. They had to walk single file through narrow paths among the towering stalks where the earthen scent of mature corn enveloped them.

"We are on the outskirts of Aloehan," Austin informed them. "Farmers raise all kinds of crops here that they sell in town."

They continued to trek through the fields, brushing pesky insects out of their way.

When the path widened for two to walk abreast, Austin struck up a conversation with Anna about customs from their world.

Wesley was trailing the company, and Drew slowed his steps to match him.

He let Austin and Anna get farther ahead before asking, "So what's up? You were weird when I woke you up this morning."

Wesley's stomach clenched. "I had a dream."

"About—?"

"It was you and me, and Anna. I couldn't tell where we were, but there was trouble."

"What kind of trouble?"

Wesley shook his head. "I don't know." He paused and lowered his voice. "Anna was in danger, and we couldn't get to her. She cried out for me to save her…but I couldn't."

"What kind of danger?"

"I don't know." Wesley sighed. "The dream was vague, but also clear. I can see her expression vividly." Wesley looked ahead to his sister. "There was fear in her eyes. It was a horrible feeling, Drew—knowing that she needed me and not being able to do anything about it."

Drew frowned. He lifted his shoulders. "Wes, it was just a dream. Nothing's going to happen to Anna. We'll look out for her."

Wesley didn't say anything. *"I wish I had more faith."* He thought to himself.

"Lord" he started to pray and stopped short. Why should he speak to God about this?

"Why don't we focus on finding what's already lost," said Drew, "not worrying about losing what you already have."

Wesley inhaled. "You're right."

Austin let out a joyful whistle. "We are almost there!" He nodded at the hill that rose in the distance. "Just beyond that hill is the city."

They crossed several bridges, spanning gushing brooks before reaching the incline of land. It was a steep climb, but with every step, Wesley became more anxious to see what lay on the other side.

When they reached the top, he stopped and stared at the view.

A city spread across the range of land. It was hemmed in by a dense forest to the west and a glistening sea to the east. To the north, rising above the city, were mountains. And there, protruding from the rocks was the Citadel.

The sight made Wesley catch his breath. The castle was cast of creamy stone and white marble, forming turrets of all shapes and sizes. Layers, ramparts, bridges, and balconies escalated above the villages, reflecting the midday sun.

Wesley now understood why Austin boasted of it.

Drew whistled. "Let's go."

12
ALOEHAN

They descended the hill at a brisk pace until they reached the fringes of the city. Other dirt paths fed into the one they traveled upon, eventually widening into one main cobbled road that ran through the city.

People walked on foot or rode on horseback. Many drove wagons or hauled carts. Some children led sheep or goats along the road. The men were all dressed in similar clothes to what Wesley, Drew, and Austin wore. The women wore long dresses.

Wesley felt a surge of familiarity. Though it looked completely different, he knew this: town life. The muscles in his face relaxed, and he felt a surprising gladness to be here.

Though close-knit, the homes and shops were rustic. Built of wood and stone, the houses on the outskirts had thatched roofs. Wooden fences used for animal pens bordered many homes. As the teens traversed farther in, the structures grew taller. Austin explained that the two-story buildings were people's homes and shops combined into one.

"There," he pointed to a wooden home with gables embellishing its frame. A small balcony projected from the upper level. "That is the shoemaker's house. On the first floor is his shop, and on the second is his home. Most of these buildings are built in the same fashion."

Wesley looked around with fascination as Austin pointed out the blacksmith's shop, the mill, and the bakery.

By the afternoon, they had reached the castle. A thick wall spanned before them. The buzz of the town had faded, but they were nearer to the sea and could hear the lapping of the waves against the rocks and the wind whipping the flags that were posted along the castle.

Wesley noted the flag; it was white, trimmed with green, with two tails and the emblem of a rising sun stitched in gold over a shimmering sea.

They stopped in front of large doors. Two guards, fully armored, stood watch at the iron doors. The guards knew Austin and granted them admittance.

It took both guards to open both doors, and when they did, a loud grinding noise erupted.

Austin boldly entered, and looked around with pride. Turning to the others with a wave of his hand, his said, "Welcome to the Citadel."

Wesley took in the courtyard paved with grass and stone walkways. A bubbling fountain sprouted from the center of the lawn. To the west and east sides, archways breached the stone wall, leading to other wings on the grounds. Directly ahead, broad steps spanned several yards leading to the palace.

Austin led the way, leaving Fendar in the courtyard. Wesley admired the huge structure.

At the top of the stairs, arched wooden doors with golden latches towered above them. Two more guards stood at its hinges. They cleared the doorway for them, opening the passageway to the Citadel.

Wesley's heartbeat quickened. What lay beyond these doors could affect their entire future.

The inside was made of cream-colored stone, but was embellished with royal green tapestries hanging on golden rods on the walls. The ceiling soared above them.

Austin pointed to another set of double doors straight ahead. "Through those doors is the throne room."

"This is incredible." Wesley could hear the awe in Anna's voice.

Austin grinned. "Indeed it is." Then facing them briskly, he said, "Please wait here; I will see if my father is here." He strode to a doorway and disappeared down a hall.

Long minutes stretched before he returned. Drew picked up a vase in the lobby, and Wesley inwardly willed him not to break anything.

Austin returned, accompanied by several others. There was a girl who looked about Austin's sister's age, and a man who Wesley guessed to be in his low thirties and who was dressed as a knight, and a middle-aged man with a brown beard peppered with specks of white.

The knight had blond hair that hung around his bearded face. Even with his armor on, Wesley could tell he was muscular. A long sword hung at his waist. Wesley was impressed and he knew Drew was too.

The young woman stood straight, her shoulders back. Her coppery hair was partially tied back in a braid. Wesley got the feeling she wasn't happy to see them.

The older man was short and round. He wore rich colors of velvety green and blue. Hazel eyes peered at them from over a bulbous nose.

They stopped a few feet in front of the teens.

Wesley wondered how much Drail had told them. He hoped that they hadn't gotten themselves into trouble. His mind was racing, calculating how best to talk to these people.

The knight bowed his head. "I am Kaden, Second of the Guard, Knight of the Citadel. Welcome to Aloehan." His voice, though quiet, carried authority. He gestured to the older man, "This is Sir Rowen, Steward of the Citadel," then to the girl, "and his daughter, Lady Charmaine."

Wesley nodded respectfully and hoped Drew and Anna followed suit.

Kaden spoke again. "Austin's father, Sir Orson, is not here presently, so I meet you in his stead. Drail told us you would be coming. He said you are not from Camnoel."

"No sir," said Wesley before Drew could say anything, "we're not. I'm Wesley," he extended a hand, which Sir Kaden shook. Drew and Anna did the same.

Kaden nodded. "You are welcome here, Wesley, Drew, and Anna. I imagine recent events that have befallen you have been rather confusing."

Drew snorted humorously at the understatement.

"Austin told me what he has explained to you. You already possess some knowledge of our history, but I presume you are at a loss as to why you are here."

Again, they nodded.

He gave a slight tilt of head. "Even I cannot tell you that. But...I do believe that you are here for a purpose. And, now that you are here, I ask you, will you join us?"

Drew lifted his chin. "What do you mean, join you?"

Kaden didn't bat an eye. "With your consent, I would train you both," he said looking at Drew and Wesley, "to be knights. And you," he looked at Anna, "would learn under Charmaine."

There was a heavy silence. Wesley could feel the others looking at him.

Kaden said softly, "We will not force you into anything against your wishes. You will be granted welcome here. You will be our guests."

Sir Rowen and Charmaine watched them carefully. Austin looked upon them with curious interest. Wesley averted his gaze from the onlookers. He tried to quiet his pounding thoughts. He looked at Kaden and nodded. "We'd appreciate it if you'd allow us time to think about it."

Drew cast Wesley a sideways glance.

Kaden nodded understandingly. "Austin, show them to the guest quarters. Give them clothes from the tailor and show them around the palace." Looking back to the other three, he said, "We will talk later."

Minutes later, they had been led through corridors and doorways weaving throughout the extensive palace hallways. Austin obviously knew his way around.

Wesley was impressed. The Citadel was composed of one chief structure, with many wings branching from it, and smaller buildings lined along walkways. They had seen bridges linking one building to the next, indoor and outdoor landings, and stairs winding from the numerous levels.

Now Wesley stood in the room Austin assigned to him and Drew. Anna's room was next door. Both rooms opened to a joining balcony that overlooked the Eastern Sea.

They changed into the fresh clothes Austin collected from the tailor. They were similar to the ones Drail had given them, but more regal in appearance. White collars, blue velvet vests, and black britches. The clothing felt stiff.

They met Anna out on the balcony. She was wearing a floor-length green dress.

"What are we going to do?" asked Anna.

"I say 'what are we waiting for?'" Drew said.

Wesley looked at Anna. "What do you say?"

Anna leaned on the stone rail, watching the water. "I think we should do it."

Wesley nodded. "Me too. As crazy as it is, I can't figure out a reason why we'd have come here to just turn around. And since we don't even know how to get back to our world, I guess we have one option left."

Drew grinned and clapped excitedly. "All right!" Then he backhanded Wesley across the chest. "Hey, did you see how big that Kaden was?" Drew nodded with a half-grin. "That could be us. When we train to be knights we're gonna get ripped!"

A small smile threatened to tug at Wesley's mouth.

"Let's go tell him our decision," said Drew.

"Just one problem," said Wesley.

"What?" asked Anna.

Wesley smiled grimly. "Finding our way back."

***

This is the second highest level of the Citadel," said Austin as they scaled the top step and walked into the fresh evening air. He had brought them a meal and led them from their quarters to talk with Kaden. They were now on top of the Citadel. It had high walls, with sentries stationed around them. There were buildings in the center, which Austin informed them were the blacksmith and armory. Another roofed turret rose above this level and housed a horn. That was the highest level.

Kaden stood with his back to them and his hands clasped behind him. When he turned and saw them, he greeted them. "Come, this is a view you will not want to miss."

He led them to the edge of the southern wall. From that vantage point, they could see the town. There were structures with thatched roofs and fields with cattle.

Then Kaden took them to the western wall that looked over green plains and forest. The northern wall faced mountainous terrain into which the Citadel was built. Then he took them to the eastern wall. The view was breathtaking. It overlooked the Eastern Sea as far as the eye could see. It was even better than the view from the balcony of their bedroom.

"There is no better place in all of Aloehan to watch the sunrise," said Kaden. "That is why this castle has been given its name: the Citadel of the Dawn."

"All if this is awesome," said Drew. "But you promised that we'd talk."

"And I shall keep my promise." Kaden sat down and motioned for them to do the same.

"Long ago, in your world, during the time of what your world calls the Dark Ages, there lived a man named William. His wife's name was Elizabeth. His son's name was Cole. When they entered Camnoel, they chose to stay. They built this castle and became the first king and queen of Aloehan." Kaden paused and met each of their eyes.

"They gave this city its name." He tipped his head and continued his story. "More men entered this world and thus the race of men began to form cities. But that is getting ahead of the story. The story begins one day when William and his youthful son Cole were hunting.

13
THE FIRST MIRRORS

The woods were still save the occasional chirp of a bird and patter of a squirrel's scamper. The dense trees provided plenty of hiding places.

As Cole tightened his bowstring, he feared that his breathing would give him away. A steady hand on his shoulder relaxed his tense muscles. He would have looked up at his father's face where he knew he would find a reassuring nod, but he did not want to lose focus on his target.

Yards away from Cole, a buck grazed on the vegetation of the rich forest, unaware of the hunters that stalked him.

Cole inhaled and paused. He released his string. The arrow sprung from the string with confident force, but a less assured aim. It swerved aside, inches from the buck. The creature, alerted with fear, bounded away.

Cole spiked his bow into the ground with frustration. He frowned and shook his head. "I was incredibly close."

"You are getting better, my son, very surely. One day you will be a fine hunter. Now, you had better retrieve that arrow."

Cole jogged over to the arrow with a natural athleticism that few of his friends could match. He kneeled to pull the arrow from the dirt, but a beam of light glared in his eye. Caught off guard, he blinked, searching for the source. It had come from the ground. He brushed away leaves and saw a smooth glass. His father had now joined him.

"What is it, Cole?"

"I know not." He continued to sweep the leaves away with his hand until he saw a mirror. It was what had reflected the sunlight and caused Cole to blink. Cole lifted it from the foliage and held the large mirror bordered with a golden frame. He and his father looked at it with intrigue.

"What is it doing all the way out here?" His father wondered aloud. "A keepsake this fine must belong in the king's palace."

"How do you think it got here?" asked Cole.

"I have not the slightest idea. We should return it. It is too late now. Soon it will be dark. Come, let us return home, and we shall dispatch this mirror in the morning."

Cole nodded. The two of them set foot towards home.

At their home, Cole's mother had prepared dinner. She stood at the small table preparing the last trimmings of the meal when they entered the house. She flashed her husband and son a warm smile, and then saw what they carried.

"Goodness, son, wherever did you get that?"

"I found it while hunting."

His mother's smile disappeared. "But that does not belong to us. We mustn't keep it."

"We will not, dear," his father reassured her. He laid a large hand on her shoulder. "We will attempt to find its owner in the morning. We merely brought it home for safekeeping."

His mother nodded. "I am sorry Cole."

Cole accepted her apology and sat down to the table. He leaned the mirror against the wall.

His mother ladled stew into their bowls. "How was the hunt?"

Cole started to answer, but a flicker of light caught his attention. He darted his head toward the mirror and saw that it had grown misty. With cautious fingers, he touched it and wiped the mist. Colors appeared behind the film. They grew crisper until an image appeared. The mirror now displayed a beautiful picture of pastel and forest colors. There was an elegant room with blowing curtains against ivory walls and a doorway to the outside.

Cole fastened his eyes upon the scene, not releasing his hand from the mirror. His mother and father stood and joined him. Just then, Cole felt a pull on his hand, a force drawing him towards the picture. The mist that had covered the mirror now filtrated into the room, surrounding the three family members. The force grew stronger. He tried to pull his hand away but could not.

"Father!" he cried. His father tried to grab his shoulder, but could not see it. The fog was too dense. The force grew stronger, and wind blew past their faces as they were drawn to the mirror. A blur of misty colors enveloped them, and the surface on which they stood changed. Distant voices spoke excitedly.

Then everything went silent.

Cole and his parents regained their balance. Their eyes adjusted to the different light. Cole's eyes grew wide as he looked around. They had traveled through the mirror and stood in the room of the picture.

An elf stood before him. The elf smiled. "Welcome to Camnoel."

***

Kaden looked at Wesley, Anna, and Drew. "And that is how the first humans entered Camnoel."

"The mirror," said Drew. "That's the same thing that happened to us, except we were surrounded by water and entered through a pond." He looked expectantly at Kaden. "How does it happen?"

"The elves created several mirrors, just like the one you three entered. They sent one of the two mirrors through the other one, just like you went through a mirror. You see, the elves have a power to manipulate the mirrors, since they are the ones who created them. The mirror they sent appeared in some woods in what your world called Europe, I believe.

That is where Cole and William found it. At the time they were eating dinner, the elves were experimenting with the mirrors to see if they could pull something back through it, using the mirror they kept with them. Cole happened to be touching the mirror at that moment when the elves exerted their power. It pulled all three of them through."

"And the room they saw?" asked Drew.

"Was the room that the elves were in. When someone views an image and touches the mirror, and another person, that is, an elf, is extracting power, that elf pulls the person to the image they see. But the elf must also be using a mirror for the transmutation to occur. When an elf draws someone, it is called a summoning."

"So, someone pulled us through? I mean, someone summoned us?" questioned Wesley.

Kaden stroked his chin. "That we are uncertain of. It appears that way, but there has been no communication or indication from the elves that such an action was performed. There are other elves that could have done it without our knowing, but it seems doubtful."

"Then…how are we here?" Anna scrunched her forehead in puzzlement.

A smile traced Kaden's mouth. "That is the mystery."

14
TRAINING BEGINS

These are what you will be using to train." Kaden handed Wesley and Drew each a wooden sword. The sun spilled morning light over the Citadel, creating shadows on the green lawn where they prepared to train. They stood on the western side of the castle designated for such purposes. A few other knights trained in the distance across the span of the extensive field.

Wesley gripped the wooden hilt. It felt good in his hands. He glanced at Anna, who was standing next to Austin and Charmaine, watching. She smiled encouragingly at him.

He looked at Sir Kaden, who was fully armored. Wesley would have liked to try on a suit of armor, but Kaden said he didn't want them to be burdened by armor just yet, as they were only beginning to train.

Drew took the weapon and frowned. "Wooden swords?" his disappointment seeped into his voice.

"You will be using real ones in no time," Kaden assured. "For now, these will help you become comfortable with the movements."

Austin nodded in agreement from his stance next to Anna. He stood with his arms crossed, viewing the boys with a fastidious eye.

Wesley sliced his sword through the air. He nodded with satisfaction.

Drew took a few swings himself. Impatient to begin, he urged, "Let's get to work."

Kaden smiled. "You shall, but I will not be the one training you."

Drew cocked his head. "Then who will?"

"That would be me."

Wesley turned to see another knight treading towards them. He stopped in front of them and gave a polite bow of the head.

"Always on time," said Kaden approvingly. "Gentlemen, meet Sir Adius."

Sir Adius gave a half grin. He was young, probably in his low twenties, with blond hair tied behind his head and lively blue eyes. He was smaller of frame than Kaden, but still muscular. "A pleasure."

"You're our trainer?" Drew confirmed.

"He and Austin," said Kaden.

Wesley could feel Drew stiffen beside him.

"Drew, Wesley," Kaden looked at them, "I want you to watch Sir Adius and Austin fight a round. Observe all you can. Then, you will begin your instructions. Good luck." He turned to Anna. "Charmaine will work with you." He smiled. "I hope all goes well."

Anna smiled back. "I'm sure it will."

"Are you ready?" asked Charmaine.

Anna nodded.

"Follow me then."

Wesley watched Anna hurry to match Charmaine's brisk trot. She waved goodbye to Wesley and Drew as she strode across the lawn. He could tell she was nervous.

Drew let out a holler, "Have fun, Anna!"

She looked over her shoulder. Drew smiled at her. She grinned back. "You too!"

Wesley watched with fascination as Sir Adius and Austin sparred. Though he knew nothing about sword-fighting, he could tell that they were skilled swordsmen, especially Adius. Their adept movements came in triplets as each would strike a blow and defend it with a block and return attack.

As Adius carved his blade through the air, his advances looked effortless. Even his footwork held perfection.

Austin worked more laboriously, striving to keep up with Adius's pace. Though he was able to defend the knight's blows, he stumbled a bit and was slower to attack. He lunged at Adius who parried the strike with a graceful slash. The knight then performed an involved string of attacks that bested Austin. He knocked the sword from Austin's hand and held a blade to his chin. They broke their routine, sheathed their swords, and faced their audience.

"That was awesome!" exclaimed Drew.

Wesley nodded vigorously.

The two swordsmen looked pleased.

"How long will it take us to learn that?" Drew asked eagerly.

"You will be the judge of that," replied Adius. He casually walked over to a barrel that held more wooden swords and drew one.

Stepping back to Drew he started coolly, "The most effective way to learn, though, is by doing!" He thrust his wooden sword at Drew with such suddenness that Drew stepped backwards, nearly stumbling. But Drew had quick reflexes and, though slightly delayed from surprise, he raised his sword quickly enough to block Adius's.

Adius grinned and nodded. "You have quick reflexes. That is good. But I wonder, how are the reflexes of your friend?" and with that said, he spun and slashed at Wesley. Wesley parried it with a clumsy movement.

Adius withdrew his sword and nodded with satisfaction. "You two will do well, but you have much to learn. First, assume the fighting stance. Let your shoulder face your target, your weight evenly balanced, and your nose lined with your navel."

Wesley and Drew obeyed.

"Now," said Adius, moving in front of Wesley as Austin stood before Drew with a wooden sword, "if I come at you from a high left," he raised his sword and Austin mirrored him, "then you must block with the same." He demonstrated and Wesley blocked as Adius told him.

"Good," said Adius. "Do it again."

They effected the movement a second time, and then a third. Then Wesley lost count.

"Now do it from the right," he commanded.

Each time they performed an advance, they increased the velocity of the attacks.

Wesley relished the fight. For the first time since his parents' disappearance, he was able to hit something. And he hit hard.

15

LEARNING THE ART OF WAR

Wesley turned over in his bed as sunlight poured in through his bedroom window. He sat up, feeling tension in his muscles. It was a good soreness, reminding him of the progress they had made.

Then his muscles tightened in wary anticipation. Slowly, he relaxed. *"I didn't have any nightmares last night,"* he realized. He let out a slow breath.

Maybe that's why he had so enjoyed training yesterday. It had given his mind a rest from the anxieties that plagued his thoughts. As he lay in bed, though, he felt his mind racing again.

"Did someone summon us? And why did they do it? Why us? Did You bring us here?" Then Wesley's countenance darkened. *"Why, God? Why did you take them away—with no explanation whatsoever? It's not like we saw them die—they just disappeared. It's not fair. At least the kids at the orphanage never knew their parents, or they knew what happened to them. But You gave me great parents...and You took them away."*

He bit the inside of his mouth until it bled. His mind wondered to former days. He saw himself playing catch with his dad. People said he looked like his dad, with a lean and muscular build, having brown hair and a narrow face with keen blue eyes. He remembered the camping trips they took in Africa and longed for the ones they never got to take in Europe. They talked about everything—sports, hobbies, girls, faith.

His dad had led his son through books of the Bible, unraveling their insights with a clarity that always made Wesley proud.

They memorized verses together. A verse pierced Wesley's thoughts in his father's voice, *"Trust in the Lord with all you heart and lean not on your own understanding; in all your ways acknowledge him, and he will make your paths straight."*

Wesley scrunched his brow. *"My path isn't straight. I have no idea what's going on. I thought I understood Him. I thought I trusted. Now I'm not so sure."*

***

Today you will be practicing with the Rope," Adius announced as they stood on the same green lawn of the day before.

Wesley, Drew, and Austin followed as Adius walked to an oak tree near the stone wall that bordered the field. It had several lower branches protruding from its trunk, and tied to one of the branches was a rope that dangled just above the ground.

"To sharpen your reflexes," said Adius as he handed Wesley and Drew their wooden weapons. "A rope's movement when struck is unpredictable until you have mastered the skill of battling it."

Austin nodded and said, "That's right. Believe me, this practice is most difficult; I still have not yet mastered it."

Adius looked at him. "Which is why you will be practicing with them."

"But sir," Austin objected, "I may not have mastered it, but I am sure I am far beyond their skill as mere beginners."

Adius crossed his arms and replied coolly, his blue eyes looking amused, but holding enough confidence to silence the young knight-in-training. "It will help Drew and Wesley for you to train with them, as it will help yourself to review."

Austin lowered his head and mumbled an apology.

"Now," said Adius, moving on, "allow me to demonstrate what you will be doing." Using a wooden sword himself, he slashed at the dangling rope, aggravating it to fierce convolutions that nearly tangled around him. He avoided it easily, ducking and spinning when necessary, all the while applying more blows to the rope. He stepped away from the cord, and gestured to it with his hand. "Who is next?"

Drew stepped forward.

"Do not let the rope touch you, and apply ten hits to it."

Drew assumed the fighting stance, waiting for the rope to settle before attacking it. He hacked at it with a one handed blow and jumped back at its quick response. It licked around and hit him behind the knees.

"It's quicker than I thought!" Drew marveled.

"Try again," said Adius.

Drew took hold of the rope to still it and slashed it with less force than his previous blow. Its reaction was not as violent, but still hard to judge. It coiled vertically while flopping sideways. Drew sidestepped it and affected another hit, grunting as it came near him. He amassed three hits before the rope hit him.

Wesley tried next and had similar results. He had the advantage of having observed two people battle the rope, and made mental notes of how it behaved. He applied gentler strikes and was swifter to dodge its course. He reached four blows.

Adius turned to the lanky youth lounging against one of the other branches. "It is your turn, Austin."

Wesley took a seat next to Adius on a log as Austin battled the rope with much ferocity. Drew remained standing, his arms crossed against his sweaty shirt. Wesley watched Austin, trying to garner any pointers that he could. But he also wanted to speak with his mentor.

"Sir Adius, what does Sir Kaden have in mind for us? I mean, why does he want us to train?"

Adius leaned forward, clasping his hands and leaning his forearms on his thighs. "Times have been hard, and our knights are scarce. We need more men."

"So that's all we are? Reinforcements?"

Adius eyed him and said, "Kaden believes you three will serve a special purpose, though he has not revealed to me what that is."

Wesley nodded. "He hasn't revealed it to us either." He returned his attention to Austin. He noticed the corners of Drew's mouth twitching, and knew he was up to some sort of mischief. He waited.

Drew spoke up to the young knight, "You're doing good, Austin."

Austin turned his head to the source of the compliment. "Why, thank you…" but before he finished speaking, the rope caught him off guard and whipped against his face, knocking him off balance. He turned red.

Drew turned away to hide his smile, but grinned at Wesley.

Wesley kept himself in check, but felt a small smile on the inside.

16
HERITAGE

Wesley awoke as the cool morning air caressed his face. He turned over in bed, pain shooting through his body. Every muscle ached. *"This is worse than after the well-digging days in Africa!"*

For the past few weeks, he, Drew, and Anna had undergone vigorous training. Sir Adius was friendly, but he wasn't afraid to work them. From sunup till sundown, the boys sparred, battled the rope, ran the streets of the Citadel, rode horses, and learned archery. They exercised by push-ups and crunches, and lifted iron bars that served as weights.

Anna worked with Charmaine on the bow and riding, but gained a few sword-fighting skills as well. Wesley already felt his endurance increasing, although by nightfall, he was always ready for a hot bath and sleep.

Adius has told them to take today off, insisting that rest was an integral part of training.

He sat up in bed and noticed that Drew was gone. When he checked Anna's room, it was empty. A fear reflex grabbed his stomach. There was a knock at his door.

When he opened it, a boy dressed in a courier's uniform said, "Your sister wished me to leave you the message that she and Sir Drew went to town for the morning."

Wesley realized this message was the Camnoel equivalent of a text message. He appreciated Anna's thoughtfulness. "Thank you."

His fear subsided, knowing that Drew was with her.

Left alone in his room, he decided to visit the palace library.

He was reading one of the scrolls he'd borrowed from the library when Drew and Anna found him three hours later in the boys' bedroom.

"I guessed you would be reading," said Anna as she and Drew joined him. She was wearing a floor-length dress instead of her typical leggings and tunic training uniform. "We checked the library first."

"There were too many other people in there reading," said Wesley.

Drew grinned. "Nerd."

Wesley looked up from the scroll he was reading. "You just get back?"

Anna nodded.

"You been reading all morning?" asked Drew. He pulled out his leftover coins and shoved them in the pockets of his jeans that hung over a chair. Wesley silently acknowledged it as a smart move. Drew wouldn't be wearing those anymore in this world and they would be a safe place for them.

"You should try it sometime," Wesley said with a straight face.

Drew smirked. "You can keep on reading. Anna and I have been hitting up the town."

Anna smiled and said quietly, as she slipped for the door, "I'm going to walk around the palace and let you two finish your debate."

Drew picked up a decorative rubber ball that sat in a basket on their nightstand. He tossed it against the stone wall and let it roll to him, fielding it like a ground ball.

"Like the town?" Wesley rolled over onto his back and crossed his hands behind his head.

Drew nodded as he continued his pastime action. "Yep. It made me wonder though."

"Wonder what?"

"Every kid in this town learns their parents' trade. I don't know how many shops we passed where a son or daughter was learning from their mom or dad. It made me wonder if I'd been born here, what my trade would have been."

"The candy-maker."

Drew cocked a smile. "Maybe. I was thinking more along the lines of a carpenter or blacksmith. You know, jack these up," He flexed a bicep and grinned.

Wesley watched Drew as he hurled the ball against the wall. He knew more was on his mind, despite his flippant attitude. "You think you'd like to live here?"

"I don't know about that, but I do think it's cool how the people here talk so much about their parents."

"What do you mean?"

"Everyone introduces themselves as so-and-so, son of so-and-so. I mean, it's just cool how everyone knows who their parents are and they carry that around as a part of them."

Wesley continued to listen as Drew talked. He had an idea where the conversation was headed.

"I mean, I'd give a lot just to know who my parents were, even if I can't know them." He frowned. "All I know is that some woman dropped me off at the orphanage." He grunted. "She could have been just a girl that got pregnant and didn't want me. And who knows who my dad is."

"You don't know that," Wesley objected.

"Yeah," he shrugged. "At least she decided to have me."

"Maybe she just didn't have the means to take care of you. Or maybe whoever dropped you off at the orphanage wasn't your mom at all."

Drew glanced at him. "If she wasn't, I'd like to know who was."

17
LESSONS

The next day, they resumed their training. After eating a morning meal together, Anna left with Charmaine as Wesley, Drew, and Austin followed Sir Adius.

"Today," said Adius as they stood once more on the open training field, "you shall begin using real swords."

"Yes!" Drew pumped a fist.

Adius handed Drew and Wesley each a blade. Austin already had his own sword. He wore a frown on his face.

"Sir Adius," he said with a grumble in his voice, "Think you it a wise idea to give them real swords so soon? Most knights-in-training complete many months of wooden swords before receiving real ones."

"We do not have many months, Austin," Adius answered matter-of-factly. "Drew and Wesley will do fine using these if they are careful." He redirected his attention to them. "These blades are blunt, but they are dangerous nonetheless. Use caution. Give extra attention to your footwork and to where you apply your strokes."

Wesley and Drew nodded seriously.

"And you must wear armor."

Drew flashed Wesley a smile.

Wesley took a few dry swings once he was fully armored. The extra weight burdened him, but he still liked the fitted plates.

Adius gave an approving nod. "All right then. Shall we begin?"

After an hour of training, Wesley's attention diverted as Austin called out to someone.

Then he saw what had arrested Austin's attention. Sairla and Miraya were walking towards them.

The sparring ceased, and the mother, sister, and brother greeted one another. Wesley felt a stab of pain.

Anna and Charmaine walked over and joined them from where they had been watching from the stone patio.

Sairla saw Anna and received her with a hug. "Look at you," she surveyed Anna's array of training clothes—leggings, a long sleeve top, and a sleeveless, fitted dress that loosened at the waist into a skirt that cut off above the knees. "You look like a true citizen of Aloehan."

The moment felt weird to Wesley. That should be *his* mom saying those things.

While Anna was gracious in her reception of the complement, he saw her smile falter and knew she was thinking the same thing.

Sairla turned to him and Drew, "And are you enjoying your training?"

Drew launched into an answer until finally Austin posed the question Wesley had been wondering.

"Why have you come here? Have you news from Father?"

"Yes," replied Sairla, looking happily at her son. "We received a letter two days ago saying that he had finished his work in Revowen and would be returning to the Citadel. He asked us to meet him here. He should arrive here in a week."

Sir Adius cleared his throat and said politely. "Austin, you are released from the rest of the day's lessons, but you two," he looked at Wesley and Drew, "should come with me."

Wesley nodded without any disappointment. He wasn't sure he could handle witnessing a reunion between the father and son.

Charmaine and Anna also excused themselves to resume their practicing, and the three parties each went their separate ways.

Wesley and Drew followed Adius out of the Citadel boarders into the western forest beyond the stone wall.

Vines dangled from the trees and formed twisted shapes.

"The vines you see," said Adius, "are your next training tool."

Wesley stared up at the earthen cords that stretched high above ground.

"Arm strength is important for a knight. This exercise, grueling as it is, will develop that. Your assignment is to climb the vines as far as you can, using only your arms. Aim for the top. Come back to the palace when you are done."

Wesley nodded. He bet it was harder than it looked.

"Oh, and I brought you a lantern—it can get dark out here at night. Good luck." He sauntered away.

Drew scoffed. "He better be walking pretty fast if he hopes to beat us to the palace."

"Come on," said Wesley, "Let's just get started." He stretched his arm across his chest and held it for a moment.

"Bet it's not that hard."

Wesley clasped the vine and pulled himself off the ground. Placing one hand over the other, he scaled several feet of the vine. He grunted. "It's harder than it looks."

Drew smirked. "Weakling."

"You try!" Wesley heaved.

Drew hoisted himself onto the vine.

Wesley's arms started to burn. He bit his lip as he lingered in one place, trying to go farther. He glanced back at Drew, who was silently concentrating. His pride and competitiveness urged him to call out, "How's it going?"

"Fine," was the curt reply. Drew took a sharp breath.

"Going a little slow, aren't you?"

"Pacing myself," he growled.

Wesley almost laughed. Drew wasn't one to pace himself; he exerted all he had right from the start. "Weakling indeed," Wesley called back.

Drew gave an exasperated breath. His started to slip, and slowly, he began to repel downward. He let out a frustrated groan.

Wesley chortled, but the laughter weakened his own strength, and he slid downward. The friction on his hands stung, and finally he had to release his grip. He and Drew both tumbled to the ground with a thud.

"That," Drew panted, "is much harder than it looks."

Wesley panted in agreement.

The lantern that Adius had left with the boys proved useful. Illuminating the immediate perimeter, it served their purpose for continuing the excruciating drill. By nightfall, they had gotten beyond the playful banter, and were determined to reach the halfway point. An hour ago, they had concluded it would be impossible to reach the top today.

Wesley released his right hand to put it higher, and his body weight tugged upon his other arm. Sweat drenched his shirt, and his hands were torn with blisters. He grunted loudly.

"Come on," urged Drew. "Don't let go." He was even with Wesley.

Wesley inhaled and heaved himself upward, using all of his energy. By now, his body was being driven solely by the will of his mind. "Almost there," he muttered.

"Don't let go," Drew coached. "Just another foot."

Drew beat Wesley and hollered with relief. Wesley was a moment behind him.

They both let go and landed on the ground, feeling like noodles.

Drew clapped Wesley on the back. "We did it."

Wesley bent forward, digging his hands into his knees, and caught his breath. "Uh-huh."

When they reached the Citadel, the stars were bright in the sky. As they headed to the west door, a voice stopped them.

"I guess I was walking fast."

Wesley saw Adius's shadowing figure lounging against the wall.

Drew nodded. "Point taken."

Adius pushed himself away from the wall and clapped the boys' backs with a smile. "I am proud of your tenacity."

Wesley nodded briefly.

"How far did you get?"

"Half way," Drew replied.

Adius's eyebrows shot up. He nodded, admiration in his eyes. "Indeed."

Wesley stared at him. "You said to aim for the top."

"I spoke that for your mind's benefit. Most beginners take weeks for that feat."

Wesley inhaled and felt a proud warmth. He glanced at Drew, who was nodding.

"We're gonna make it to the top."

18
HERALDS

Over the next several days, they continued their training. Everyday they added distance to the vines. Sir Kaden frequently checked on their progress and observed their practice.

One day, Wesley noticed him out of the corner of his eye as he sparred with Sir Adius. The senior knight quietly watched the two knights-in-training.

Wesley tried to ignore his presence and focus on the task at hand. He had to devote great attention to sword fighting, especially against one as skilled as Adius.

He blocked a high right side slash and dodged a cut to his side. Most of his previous sparring sessions had been against Drew or Austin who were more equally matched with him. This fight was no easy feat.

Sweat beads formed at his hairline. He ducked from a lunge.

"I need to get on the offensive."

Mostly, he had been concentrating on blocking Adius's blows. He swung his sword at the knight's shoulder, which was narrowly blocked.

"Very good," Adius praised.

Wesley hardly took in the compliment, not having time to let down his guard. He spun out of the way of a left side advance.

Once again, he saw Kaden watching him. The knight's eyes went back and forth between him and Drew, who was sparring with Austin across the lawn.

"What does he think of our skills? Are we ready to be knights—to fight in the service of the Citadel?" He wondered why they hadn't seen much of Drail. Was he busy with his own training? Wesley was distracted by his thoughts and Adius had soon knocked his sword from his hand.

Snapping back to reality, Wesley sighed and retrieved his sword. Once again, he had lost. *"One of these days I am going to beat him,"* he promised himself.

"You fought well," Adius encouraged. "You are getting better." He squinted slightly. "But you were distracted."

Wesley lowered his eyes, embarrassed that his mistake was that obvious.

"Stay focused," Adius said.

Wesley nodded. He turned his attention to Drew's skirmish with Austin. Drew was executing a string of complex advances, which threw Austin on the defensive. He backed up, and Drew used his lack of balance to his advantage. With a final heavy blow, he knocked Austin off his feet.

Drew and Austin strolled over to where Adius and Wesley waited. Wesley spotted that Sir Kaden had gone.

He hadn't even seen him leave.

"Good work today," Adius addressed them all and then looked at Drew and Wesley. "To the vines with you."

The boys grudgingly obeyed.

"Let's make it to the top today," said Drew as he and Wesley stood before the gnarled vines. It was the end of the week and they were both tired of the daily exercise.

Wesley nodded. "Let's do it."

He pulled fingerless leather gloves from his trouser pockets and fitted them on his hands. Drew did likewise. After their first attempt at the vines, they decided to visit the palace tailor. They had already received more than their share of blisters and determined that the next time would be better.

Taking deep breaths, the boys started the climb. They quickly reached the halfway point. As they advanced, their speed decreased. Pressure built up on their arms.

"Come on. We're making it all the way today," Drew reminded.

Wesley nodded.

Wesley paused. He was at the point he'd reached yesterday. His body felt weak. *"I'm not so sure we'll make it all the way today."*

Drew must have noticed that he had stopped. "Look, Wes; you're two feet from the top. You can make it."

"I can't," he breathed, shaking his head.

"Yes you can," Drew barked. "Now come on!"

Wesley looked at Drew's firm gaze, and then at the remaining distance. He released his hand and locked it inches above. With renewed resolution, he climbed with greater speed.

Drew matched his pace. Wesley closed his eyes as he hauled upward. His head hit something. He opened his eyes and saw that it was a branch. He grinned and welcomed the nock.

They had reached the top.

They pulled themselves onto the branches high above the ground and let their feet dangle.

"Whoo!" Drew hollered.

"Yes!" Wesley shouted.

Drew grinned. "Good job."

"You too."

Drew looked at the ground below and whistled. "Now, all we have to do is get down."

When they returned to the training field, Adius and Austin had just finished a sparring round. Adius turned aside to talk to another knight and Austin greeted the boys.

"How fared the vine training today?" he asked, unaware of the progress they had made. "Did you reach very far? I've made it beyond half way," he said proudly.

Drew casually rubbed the back of his neck. "Yeah we didn't make it half way today."

Austin started to smile. "That is understandable..."

"We reached the top today," Drew cut in. He tipped his chin goodbye and strolled over to Adius.

Nodding goodbye to Austin, Wesley followed after Drew, leaving Austin standing with his mouth agape.

As Wesley walked towards Drew and Adius, a voice turned his line of attention.

"Austin! You father is back!"

Wesley turned and saw Sairla calling excitedly to her son from the stone patio of the palace. Austin forgot his wounded pride and ran after her.

Adius turned away from the other knight he was talking to and said to Drew and Wesley, "Come, you will want to meet Sir Orson."

They followed him into a room in the palace where Kaden, Sir Rowen, Charmaine, and Anna were already waiting with the family.

Sir Orson was a large man plated in armor that bore color accents of Aloehan: green and white. His brown hair and beard were peppered with gray. He was broad chested and had deep-set hazel eyes edged by many lines. Sairla and Miraya stood at his side.

When he saw his son, his eyes lit up. They shook hands and for a brief moment, and Wesley envied Austin.

Sir Kaden introduced Drew, Anna, and him to the First Guard of the Citadel.

After the greetings, Orson sank into a plush chair. He leaned his elbow on the arm and rubbed his creased brow. Sairla rested a hand on his shoulder.

"What news from Revowen?" asked Sir Kaden.

Orson cast a wary glance at Wesley, Drew, and Anna.

"They are friends," Kaden assured.

Satisfied, Orson began, "Ill news, I am afraid. Reports have come saying that Erion has joined with Ratacin."

"What?" exclaimed Adius.

Wesley looked at him. He had never seen his mentor so ruffled.

"Erion has always been our ally. How could they join Ratacin?"

"They have been persuaded by his hollow promises," Orson replied wearily. "Ratacin's knights also roam the southeastern border. Few major cities remain where he has not established headquarters."

Kaden looked troubled. He crossed his arms. "What about Revowen? Do they fare well?"

"The elves are continually secure, but they leave their own lands less frequently. Ratacin cannot enter the fair city but no protection aids elves that leave its boarders. Any wanderers are becoming strategic targets for Ratacin's men."

Wesley glanced around the room and noted their disheartened responses. Charmaine's brow knit in concern. Sir Rowen sat down wearily. Sir Adius's expression grew fiery. Miraya and Austin watched their father with unsettled expressions. Sairla's hand on her husband's shoulder moved to his neck where she proceeded to rub as if to wash away his weariness.

"What about the Forsvárerne?" asked Kaden. "Is there any news of them?"

Orson nodded slowly. "Yes... there is news. A scout arrived at Revowen just before I returned. He had set out with three other members of the Forsvárerne. The company was en route from Erion to Revowen to deliver some news of importance, but were intercepted by vuls and captured. Only the one, Ralphan, escaped. He was seriously injured, though. Two days after reaching Revowen and delivering his message, he died."

Anna gave a faint gasp.

"We believe the others are being kept in a fort in the foothills of the North Worrin Mountains, just south of Erin Dule. It is called Kurgon Fort, and is a secret base of Ratacin's, recently built. That was the news that the Forsvárerne had come to inform the elves of, along with blueprints of the fort."

"They are alive?" Adius probed.

"We believe so," Orson answered, "but for how long I do not know."

"What's the Forsvárerne?" asked Drew.

Kaden looked at him. "It is a resistance group, formed to oppose Ratacin. They are allies of Aloehan and Revowen. They travel the country seeking alliances against Ratacin and working to thwart his plans by any means they may." He turned to Orson. "Who were the ones captured?"

"An elf maiden from Miershire, a dwarf lord from Kalegon, and a man from Clavilier."

"Now that we know where they are," began Charmaine, "will we not send help?"

Kaden looked from Sir Rowen to Sir Orson, and replied. "We will discuss that." Looking around the room again he said, "We will announce our decision in the morning. For now, all training should continue." He glanced at Adius and Charmaine.

Everyone but the two senior knights and steward was dismissed from the meeting room to go their separate ways.

As they were walking with Adius and Charmaine, a knight intercepted them and spoke to Adius.

"A messenger, sir," the young knight said respectfully. "He wishes to speak to someone in charge."

"The steward and first two guards are meeting. I will speak with him. Where is he?"

"In the courtyard, sir."

Adius nodded. "Thank you." He beckoned for the others to follow him. "Come, this could prove to be a useful learning experience."

They followed him through the doorway onto the platform overlooking the courtyard. A lone figure stood wearing a dark cloak that clouded his face. Adius slowed his pace as he approached the hooded stranger. The others remained on the platform.

Unease rose in Wesley's stomach. *This isn't a friendly visitor.*

"Show yourself," Adius's commanding voice pierced the heavy silence. He was now standing two feet away from the stranger.

The man lifted bony hands to his hood. Wesley's eyes widened. He had never seen a human with such hands. The skin was a sickly gray with tints of green that stretched thin over nimble fingers with long black nails. He lowered his hood.

Anna gasped.

"He is a vul," Charmaine informed in a low voice.

Wesley felt Anna tense up next to him.

The creature looked like a man, but his facial skin matched that of his hands and his nose had a pronounced hook. Even his lips possessed the same greenish-gray color. He had a receding hairline that yielded to stringy black hair. His eyes were narrow with beady black pupils that stared from under a hairless brow.

Adius remained unwavering. "Why have you come to the Citadel?"

"I come on behalf of the Prince of the West, from the great city of Racin Dor. I am Hoshith, messenger of Hadis Shale. I seek an audience with the lord of this castle." His voice was low and raspy.

Wesley resisted the urge to wince.

"They are busy presently," Adius responded. "But I will hear you."

Hoshith reached into his long robe and pulled out scrolled papers. "I have come with a treaty. I am sure it is known in Aloehan that members from the unauthorized alliance known as the Forsvárerne have been detained due to their unseemly acts against the standing societies."

Charmaine frowned.

Adius's jaw tightened. He continued to listen.

"The lord Ratacin, merciful prince, is willing to release them and pardon their offenses if the Citadel will comply with the terms in this treaty."

He held up the scroll.

"And the terms?" asked Adius.

"An agreement not to send any persons south of the Greyback Mountains, or west of Erin Dule."

"And if we choose to not sign the treaty?"

"The members of the Forsvárerne will remain in detainment and may be subjected to… unpleasant circumstances."

Adius extended his hand. The vul handed him the papers with a pleased bow of his narrow head.

Adius looked down at the parchment in his hand and without hesitation ripped it in two.

Handing the torn pieces back to the vul, he replied with bite, "The Citadel will sign no such treaty. Now if you desire my advice, I suggest you fly out of this city as fast as your forked wings will carry you. Before unpleasant circumstances follow."

The vul's eyes flashed. He stuffed the discarded treaty into his robe. "The lord Ratacin does not accept rejection lightly," he hissed.

"Oh I am sure he does not," Adius responded coolly.

A sound similar to a growl gurgled in the vul's throat. "You will regret this." He spun on his heel and strode out of the courtyard.

Adius watched him leave, and turned back to the concerned comrades waiting for him.

"What was that?" Wesley demanded in a low voice as Adius scaled the steps.

Adius cast his pupil a long look. "Let us go to the library. There are some things that you need to know."

19
ENEMIES

The whole company followed Adius into the library where he spent a moment searching the shelves. Once he found the book he wanted, he laid it on a table and flipped through its pages.

Wesley, Anna, Drew, and Austin gathered around him.

He stopped on a yellow page with black sketches. The drawing depicted the same type of creature that they had witnessed moments before, but this one wore no cloak. It had on only breeches and arm bracelets. Protruding from its back were two bat-like wings.

"It is a race called the vuls," explained Adius. "They are in service to Ratacin."

"Do they fight?" asked Drew.

"Yes. They obviously can fly, but are also very fast on foot. They are wiry and cunning. Their deadliest weapon is a poison-dipped arrow, probably what Ralphan, the fallen member of the Forsvárerne, died of."

Wesley felt an involuntary chill run down his arms. *Please don't let them have Mom and Dad.*

"I had heard about them," said Austin, "but had never seen one."

"Not a lovely sight, you have learned by now," Charmaine remarked dryly.

Wesley stared at the picture. "Are there any more creatures we should know about?"

Adius skimmed through the pages and came to a stop. On the right side of the page, a short, furry animal was drawn.

"Skyrogs," said Adius. "Though they are only about three feet tall and are not very intelligent, they have sharp teeth and long tails which they use as weapons."

Wesley studied the picture. The creature had tusks like a walrus, beady eyes like a rat, and a long, furry tail with spikes at the end. He looked at the opposite page that hosted another drawing. "What's that?"

"That is a yorgon," said Adius. "They are just as dangerous as vuls. Where vuls are cunning, yorgons are strong. Towering seven feet at least, they wield axes and broadswords."

Anna frowned.

"But do not be afraid," Adius reassured. "You are now being equipped with proper skills to fight them."

Later that evening, after they finished their practices, Wesley and the others sat with Austin's family in one of the palace lounges. A large fireplace doused the room in a warm glow. Adius, Austin, and Miraya spoke with Austin's parents.

Wesley sat with Anna and Drew by the fireplace.

"How about those creatures?" asked Drew.

"They're very pleasant looking," Wesley answered with a straight face.

Drew chuckled.

Anna shuddered. "They're terrifying."

Wesley glanced at her, a pang of guilt in his stomach. He had not been able to protect his parents. Nor was he certain he would be able to protect her.

"Don't worry about them, Anna," said Drew. "You heard Adius."

Anna stared at the fire without answering for a moment. Then she looked up at Drew and Wesley.

"But they're real," she said, her voice raspy. "The evil is real."

They stared back at her for a moment without speaking.

"You've always known it's real, Anna," said Wesley. He wasn't sure where the words came from. "But so is the good. You saw Adius stand up to the vul today."

"That could be us soon," Anna said quietly.

Wesley glanced at Drew. He could tell that the possibility excited him. But Wesley didn't feel so jaunty. "We'll worry about that when the time comes."

A voice at the door turned their attention. A knight entered. Miraya stood. "Drail."

Wesley didn't know why, but he was glad to see him. It was a familiar face. But when he scanned the knight's face, he felt like something was wrong.

Drail greeted those in the room. He nodded to Wesley, Anna, and Drew. "Are you tired of this man yet?" he asked, clapping Adius on the shoulder.

"He's all right," Drew grinned. "You should come out and join us sometime," said Drew.

"Perhaps I will." He spoke a few more words as required by courtesy, but departed quickly, Miraya at his side.

When the evening drew late, Wesley, Anna, and Drew excused themselves from the lounge.

As they were taking the long way back to their rooms, traversing through the outdoor passageways, Drew stopped. "Listen."

Wesley and Anna stopped and tuned into the silence. They heard muffled voices. Drew followed them, taking a road that branched off the stone walkway. It led to a courtyard garden.

He stopped behind some tall shrubs and peered through the branches. Wesley and Anna followed him. The voices were clearer now, just beyond the bushes.

"I encountered some black knights while I was in Dradoc." It was Drail's voice. So that's where Drail had been. No wonder they hadn't seen much of him at the palace.

"Did they give you trouble?" came Miraya's voice.

"No."

Wesley squinted to see more clearly.

Drail tore up a leaf in his fingers.

"They inquired about my skill as a knight." He lowered his voice and spoke slowly, "Miraya, they asked me to join their ranks."

Miraya gasped. "Did they hurt you when you told them no?"

He hesitated.

Wesley's heart thudded.

"Miraya, I did not tell them no."

Her eyes widened.

"I am going to join them."

Miraya gave a short laugh. "You are not serious."

He looked evenly at her. "I am quite serious." He took her hand in his.

Miraya lowered her eyes to where her white hand was held in his. She withdrew it and stepped back.

"I know your father is not allied with them, but—"

"Not allied?" Miraya repeated in a sharp whisper. "He is their enemy! And they are his!"

"But that does not make them your enemy." Drail stepped closer. "Miraya," he whispered.

"Drail," her voice broke. "You are not thinking clearly," she said firmly.

His eyes flashed. Then his gaze grew serious. "I am leaving tonight."

"Do not do this," she said through clenched teeth. "Please." A tear slid down her cheek.

Drail squared his jaw. "I have made my choice. I am leaving." He lowered his head, but kept his gaze fixed on her. "Will I be traveling with a companion?"

Her bottom lip trembled, but finally she spoke, "You will be riding alone."

Drail stiffened. He took a step back, looked at her one last time, and then turned away.

Miraya stood looking after him, her shoulders shaking in quiet sobs. Then she turned and strode past them without even noticing them.

For a moment, none of them spoke. Wesley was frozen in shock. How could Drail betray them?

Then Drew said, "We gotta tell somebody before he gets away."

They ran back to the lounge. Sir Orson, Sairla and Adius were just leaving.

Drew skipped the details and spilled rapidly, "You have to go after Drail. He's a traitor and he's leaving!"

They stared at him. Sir Orson laid a hand on Drew's shoulder. "Slow down a bit. What seems to be the matter?"

"Drail is joining Ratacin," Drew said. "He was headed for the stables. If you want to catch him you need to go now."

That was enough for Adius. He tore off in a sprint in the direction of the stables.

Sairla looked at Wesley. "Is it true?"

"We overheard him talking to Miraya," said Drew. "He tried to convince her to leave with him tonight and join Ratacin. She refused and then he ran away. We came to you right after that."

Sairla steadied herself on her husband's arm.

Sir Orson drew in a deep breath to maintain his composure. "Thank you for bringing us this news."

Moments later, Adius reappeared, breathing hard. He shook his head. "He is gone. The stable boy was asleep and Drail's horse was nowhere to be found."

"Can you go after him?" asked Drew.

Adius shook his head. "We have no idea where he went."

"I will speak with Miraya," said Orson. "I must know everything that she told him."

20
THE MEETING

Have you had any more dreams?" asked Drew as he buttoned his cotton shirt. He and Wesley had just gotten up and were preparing to attend Kaden's meeting.

Wesley shook his head. "No." He rolled his shoulders, easing out tightness. "Some days I forget I ever had that dream about Anna." But whenever he did think about the dream, a knot formed in his stomach.

"Sorry. Didn't mean to bring it up."

Wesley shrugged.

"It's just a dream, Wes. It's not real."

"That's what I keep telling myself."

"Well just keep on telling yourself that." Drew slapped Wesley on the back. "Come on—or we're gonna be late."

***

Thank you for coming," said Kaden as they entered the council room. Sir Rowen, Sir Orson, Adius, Charmaine, Sairla, and four other knights whom Wesley did not know were already there.

Once everyone was seated, Sir Orson stood and addressed them.

"Sir Rowen, Sir Kaden, and myself have discussed what advances should be made toward rescuing the Forsvárerne. We have agreed upon sending five knights. They sit before you now."

He turned towards Adius and the other four knights and motioned to them one by one. "Sir Adius, Sir Delmore, Sir Cleven, Sir Castonir, and Sir Narin."

Facing the others again, he said, "It is a small but able party. We believe their small number will be to their advantage, able to penetrate the enemy's base with little notice."

Wesley surveyed the chosen knights. They looked around Adius's age or older. Delmore was broad and short with a stubby brown beard and looked older than Kaden. Wesley guessed he was pretty strong.

Cleven looked to be closer to Kaden's age and was tall and fair-haired. Castonir had shaggy black hair and a stern expression. Narin was small-framed—probably Wesley's size or smaller—with copper colored hair. Wesley wondered if they had all gone through the same training he and Drew were now undergoing.

"The questing party will stop in Revowen," said Sir Orson, "which is on the way to Kurgon Fort and will retrieve the outlines to the fort. I would like to ask you three," he looked at Wesley, Drew and Anna, "if you would consider accompanying these knights and Sir Kaden to the city of the elves."

Wesley's eyes widened. In his peripheral, he saw Anna grin. She looked at him with hopeful eyes.

He looked at Sir Kaden cautiously before asking Sir Orson, "Why do you want to take us there?"

Orson nodded to Kaden, inviting him to reply.

Kaden addressed Wesley. "This was my request. I believe you can further your training under the elves. Sir Adius and Lady Charmaine feel that they have taught you all they can."

Wesley was surprised. He felt that they had years ahead of them.

"We would now like you to learn from the elves. Does that sound agreeable to you?"

They exchanged glances. Anna nodded with a smile. So did Drew. Wesley just nodded.

Kaden nodded. "Very well then. We leave at noon."

***

Wesley tied off his pack—filled with spare clothes and a few scrolls he found at the library.

Drew grabbed his jeans that hung over a chair and rolled them as tightly as they would go. The coins that he had put in his jean pocket jingled.

Wesley wondered if they would have need of the money. Leaving Drew to finish packing, he walked out on the balcony.

Anna was already there, leaning on the rail.

"Are you excited about getting to see the elves?" he asked his sister.

She flashed him a wide grin and nodded.

He snorted.

She cocked her head. "Aren't you?"

"Yeah," he shrugged. He stared out ahead.

Anna watched him and said softly, "Just because we haven't found them yet doesn't mean they're not here."

His eyebrows knit, although he never turned his gaze.

"Are you afraid that we won't find them?"

Wesley's mouth opened to speak, but he didn't say anything. He looked at his sister. "We'll find them." Somehow, he had to at least look like he had some faith.

Anna nodded. "I asked God to help us find them if they are here."

Wesley wasn't sure how to answer. He hadn't done a lot of praying lately. God seemed to be the one at fault in all of this.

A horn blew in the distance, saving him.

Wesley flashed a look at Anna. "The horn announcing that they're about to leave. Are you all packed?"

She nodded.

"We'll meet you outside our rooms." Wesley went back into the bedroom and saw Drew pushing something into his bag.

"You hear the horn?"

Drew nodded with a grunt and tugged on the drawstrings of his bag. It barely closed.

"Good grief, Drew! What do you have in there? We were supposed to pack light."

Drew shrugged. "I got some food from the kitchen. Never know how much they'll provide, so you have to be prepared."

Wesley's eyes smiled, though it didn't reach his mouth.

21
TAKING LEAVE

Sun glared off the white steps of the Citadel as the Wesley, Anna, and Drew bounded down the broad stones into the courtyard where the company was waiting. Three horses stood saddled and ready, waiting for their riders.

Anna hurried over to Aleron, the horse she'd been training with, and stroked his mane lovingly. She strapped her bag to his saddle and returned her attention to the rest of the party.

Adius approached the boys with two swords. "These are real, un-blunted blades. And they are yours. May you bear them well."

They took them reverently and admired their new weapons.

"You must be careful with them," cautioned Adius.

They nodded. Drew looked up. "Thank you!"

Adius smiled. "It was time for you to get real weapons. Besides, you may need them on the journey."

Wesley cocked his head, but his unspoken question remained unanswered.

Charmaine stood and watched, along with Sir Rowen, Sir Orson, and his family. Anna's mentor walked over to her and extended a bow.

Anna looked up at Charmaine. "I thought it was just for practice—I didn't know that I'd get to keep it."

"It is yours to keep. You cannot be unarmed when leaving Aloehan. Remember what I have taught you."

Anna accepted the bow, along with the full quiver. "I will do my best. Thank you—for all of your lessons. You really are amazing."

Charmaine smiled politely with a hint of affection in her eyes. She bowed her head and said, "And you are a fine student. You will do well on the journey and I believe you will find the city of the elves to be a marvelous place. Keep practicing all that I have taught you."

Anna smiled. "I will."

The others bid the company farewell. Austin smiled at Anna. "You are getting to see the elves after all."

She grinned.

Austin shook hands with the boys. To Drew he said, "When you come back prepare to be beaten in our next sparring match."

Drew grinned and nodded. "We'll see." Turning away from the castle and the ones who were staying, Drew flashed a grin at Wesley. Knocking the back of Wesley's shoulder with his palm, he said, "Let's go!"

Wesley looked over his shoulder and saw the Citadel peak above the treetops, ever growing smaller. The forest enclosed upon them as they rode farther away from the palace gates. He returned his gaze ahead where Kaden and Adius rode with the other four knights. Drew rode to his left and Anna was just ahead of him.

His body rose and fell with the gait of his horse, Spiker. It felt awkward. Anna looked like a natural and even Drew seemed to have no trouble balancing. Wesley wished he were walking.

They continued to ride until dusk. When they stopped, Wesley stiffly dismounted. His whole body ached.

Adius approached them, seemingly unfazed by the ride. "We have made good time. We have reached the Serrin Woods."

"How soon till we reach the elves?" asked Drew.

The corners of Adius's mouth lifted. "You have amazing endurance when it comes to training, but your patience for waiting is small indeed!"

Drew grinned and shrugged.

"It is a four and a half day journey," Adius answered.

Drew opened his mouth to protest.

"Stop," said Adius. "Be grateful for the time. We will use it to continue your practices."

Wesley inwardly groaned. The thought of sparring right now made him want to throw up. *"Help me make it through this."*

Then he realized he had just prayed.

Adius drew his sword and waited. Drew unsheathed his with more vigor than necessary.

Wesley gritted his teeth, but voiced no complaint.

He was actually surprised at the energy his muscles responded with. Maybe they knew these were real, unblunted blades. So with every attack Drew made, he blocked and dodged with movements that were slower than normal, but still efficient.

After what felt like an hour, Adius called for them to stop. Wesley was too tired to say anything. Even Drew was out of words.

Delmore had made a small campfire and offered them dinner. Wesley and Drew plopped down by Anna. She was conversing easily with Sir Kaden.

Wesley respected the knight, but had yet to have a one-on-one conversation with him. He wondered how carrying on a conversation came so easily to his sister. She seemed like she was able to connect with anyone she met. Wesley had even thought Charmaine seemed a bit standoffish and felt bad when Anna was assigned to her. But he hadn't heard Anna complain yet.

Right now, however, he didn't mind not having anything to say. He was grateful to sit on steady ground. He tried not to think about the motion of the bouncing horse.

Kaden congratulated the boys on their training and then moved to talk to the other knights.

Anna looked at Wesley and Drew brightly. "Sir Kaden is engaged!"

Drew raised his eyebrows and smiled. "Who's the girl?"

"Her name is Elaswén. She's one of the healers at Revowen...she's an elf!" she whispered.

The information surprised Wesley. He wondered if marriages between humans and elves were common. "Do...do the elves here live forever?"

"I asked that and he said they don't. But they do live longer than humans." Then, as if reading his next question, she added, "It isn't common for humans and elves to marry, so they have had a longer engagement than normal. But," she chattered on, "when I was walking through the Citadel, I found a hallway of portraits. There was a painting of a couple. He was a human and she sort of looked like an elf...at least what I think an elf would look like." She cocked her head at Drew. "Actually, the man looked a little bit like you."

"Why, was he handsome?"

"Despite any resemblance, he actually was," Anna quipped.

"What do you mean despite any resemblance?" Drew feigned offense.

Wesley finished eating, and let Drew and Anna continue talking. He went to his saddlebag to retrieve something to read for the evening. He had taken several books and scrolls from the library to occupy himself in his free time. He was about to pick one up, when another one caught his eye. It was a Bible. He had shoved it in his bag thinking he might have time to read it, but with little regard. It had been a long time since he had last opened one.

Slowly, he lifted it from his bag and carried it back to a tree that was close enough to the campfire to provide light, but distant enough to keep him from having to talk to anyone.

He opened it to the Psalms, but didn't read. He stared at the warm glow of the fire. *"I still believe in You."*

He sighed. *"I just don't understand this—When we entered this world, I thought You might be leading us to Mom and Dad. But we've been here for months and haven't seen one sign of them."*

His mind wondered to years passed. He remembered a time when his parents were having financial problems while they were in Africa.

They needed more money for the month, but had no idea where it would come from. They were sitting at the kitchen table.

His dad sat with his elbow on the table and his forehead resting on his hand. "I don't know how this is going to work out," he said wearily. He slid his hand down his face and clasped it over his other hand, resting his chin on his knuckles. He grunted and gave a small smile. "The Lord sure didn't give us minds to understand His ways, did He?"

"No," his mom answered. She placed a dish of yellow pasta on the table. "Just the ability to trust Him when we don't."

The fire crackled, sending sparks into the air. Wesley swallowed and blinked back tears.

"The ability to trust," he pondered quietly, feeling like he had nearly lost that. *"Help me trust."*

22
FIGHT

The next morning, Kaden roused them early. They ate breakfast, packed camp, and were on their way.

They fell into the routine of doing this every morning, riding at a comfortable pace and stopping periodically to water their horses or break bread. By the third day of the journey, Wesley, Anna, and Drew had gotten to know the other knights a little better.

Delmore, the oldest knight among the company, was undeniably friendly. He was a decent cook and could usually be found whistling a jaunty tune.

Cleven was quiet—quieter than Wesley, Drew teased. Whenever the company stopped, he always had his nose in a book.

Castonir was younger than Adius and kept company mostly with Adius and Kaden. When he spoke to the kids, he was polite but brief.

Wesley, Drew, and Anna grew most acquainted with Narin, who was the same age as Adius, but as Kaden commented, looked and acted like he was sixteen. He rode with the teens most of the time, enjoying their company probably more than he would have his fellow knights.

"How soon will we get there?" Drew asked Narin as they rode.

"If I could convince these scalawags to ride any faster we could be there tomorrow," Narin replied good-naturedly.

Adius glanced over his shoulder at them. "If we rode any harder, Narin would not be able to keep up."

Anna giggled.

Narin's mouth opened. "Uh! See here, I could beat you in a race any day."

Adius shrugged and a smile played on his lips. "Perhaps—if you did not insist on riding that old horse of yours."

"Mesbith is a good horse," Narin defended. He said aside to the others, "He just says these things to make himself feel better—his horse is not as loyal as my old Mesbith."

"I heard that," said Adius from ahead.

"Right," Narin cleared his throat.

Anna and Drew chuckled.

Narin spoke louder, "As I was saying, Drew, we are probably a day and a half away from Revowen."

Drew nodded. "Great—I'm really getting sore from all this riding."

"Me too," added Wesley. He had to make a conscious effort not to wear a permanent grimace.

Narin chortled. "You will know when we get close. The tree bark in Revowen and its surroundings is not brown but white and silver. Even silver leaves are blended with the green treetops."

"Have you ever been to Revowen?" asked Anna.

"Yes ma'am. It is quite a sight." He gave a short laugh. "Very different from Aloehan. I prefer my hometown, really—the wagons and shopkeepers and children. Revowen is so...so quiet. There are trickling streams and gentle singing. Everyone speaks in hushed tones."

"Which is probably why you dislike it," said Adius.

"No," said Narin, "That I do not mind. The worst part is when they speak in their own tongue!"

"Most people enjoy hearing the elvish language...it being such a rare treat," Adius commented.

Narin frowned. "I always get the feeling they are talking about me behind my back."

Adius gave a short nod. "They are probably discussing your poor table manners."

Narin perked up. "Oh! Now the food in Revowen—that is something to talk about! There is wonderful bread—"

"Shh!"

"Shush me all you like, but I shall talk as I please." Narin winked at the teens. "Now—back to what I was saying…"

"Shh!" it came again, but this time more fiercely.

Wesley looked up to see Castonir holding a finger to his lips. Everyone fell silent, and the whole company came to a stop.

Castonir's eyes darted. "I hear something."

Kaden nodded. He laid a hand on the hilt of his sword.

Without turning his head, Adius shifted his eyes to trees around them. "I hear it too."

Wesley looked into the distant trees. A shuffling sound. A twig snapped. He caught a glimpse of movement behind the bushes. *What the?*

Adius smelled the air. "Skyrogs," he muttered.

"Draw your weapons," Kaden ordered.

Wesley saw Anna reach for her bow, but a sound in the branches above them drew her attention. Something in the trees moved, sending an acorn dropping. The forest tops were too dense. Wesley couldn't see anything.

Then she screamed.

A beast lunged down at her. She jerked to the side in the saddle, barely missing being hit by the creature that tumbled to the ground. Castonir shot it with an arrow.

More skyrogs approached them from the surrounding bushes and trees. Kaden jumped off his horse to battle the beasts head-on. The other knights did the same.

Wesley and Drew remained in their saddles, frozen at the sight. The skyrogs fought with their claws, teeth and tails, which had spikes protruding from them.

There was an overwhelming number of them.

Kaden, Adius, Narin, and Castonir deftly sliced and hacked at them, felling them one at a time.

Delmore swung a huge sword in long, slow strokes.

Cleven spun two daggers like batons, chopping at the beasts' limbs.

Adius's urgent voice broke through Wesley's thoughts.

"Boys, get off your horses!" their mentor shouted at them.

Drew jerked from his daze and swiftly dismounted. He dodged a swinging tail and ran to join Adius fighting three of the brutes.

Wesley hesitated. Blood spurted from the animals sliced by the knights. The sickening sound of the skyrogs' gurgles and growls mixed with the tearing of flesh stunned him.

He glanced over at Anna who was still mounted on Aleron and fumbling with her bow. The urgency of the moment struck him when he saw his sister.

He jumped from his horse and swung at whatever beast came near him. He tried to compose himself, recalling every stroke that Adius had taught him, but it was so much more confusing fighting the vicious creatures than another human.

He felt his sword penetrate flesh and grimaced. Pulling his sword away, he watched the skyrog fall to the ground. There was no time to dwell on it though, for another one charged him with extended claws.

It barred its teeth, revealing a sharp line under its tusks. When it was close enough to strike, it swung its tail at Wesley's head.

He batted it away and aimed for its neck.

He glanced up and saw Anna scrambling to lace her bow. The arrow in place, she aimed for a skyrog. She was about to release it, but Cleven moved into her line of fire.

Dismounting, she assumed her ready position again and let the string go this time. It nicked the arm of a skyrog. She cringed and looked at her left forearm.

Wesley fought another beast, trying to keep an eye on his sister. His heart leapt. A skyrog pounced on her, knocking her to the ground.

She squirmed out from under its body but it crawled after her. Opening its mouth, it bent down toward Anna. A hand grabbed Anna's arm and yanked her away from the beast's strike. Castonir stabbed the skyrog.

"Thank you," she breathed.

He nodded and continued fighting.

Wesley glanced over and saw Drew swinging recklessly at any skyrog in his perimeter. There was a skyrog approaching him from behind that Wesley knew he didn't see.

Adius was there. He felled the beast in one swift stroke.

Drew nodded his thanks.

"Try to be more careful next time," Adius reproved. Without another word, he turned and continued the battle.

Drew nodded and kept fighting. One swung his tail around Drew's ankles, bringing him to the ground. He yelled and franticly scooted himself backwards, but the skyrog didn't let go. He darted his head around, looking for something he could use. A vine dangled from the trees. He grabbed it and hoisted himself upward. With one hand he held on, with the other he swung his sword at the skyrog holding onto his leg.

Wesley thrust a cut at the skyrog he was fighting and ran to help Drew.

One of Anna's arrows killed one of the skyrogs pawing at Drew, and Wesley hacked at the other.

Angered, the beast released its grip on Drew and turned toward Wesley. It was one of the taller ones, standing over three feet, and also stronger. It swiped at Wesley with its paws, forcing Wesley to back up.

Drew dropped from the vines and attacked the beast from behind. His sword pierced its back.

It fell to the ground, dead. Once he killed the animal, Drew released his sword and stumbled to the ground, clutching his wounded leg.

"You all right?" Wesley ran over and crouched next to him.

Drew grunted but nodded. "Yeah, I'll be fine."

Wesley examined Drew's wound, which seemed to suggest otherwise. He frowned.

He stood and looked around and saw Kaden finishing off the last two.

Wesley helped Drew to his feet and led him back to the where the other knights were gathering.

Delmore panted heavily as he rested his sword on his shoulder. "Whew! I had forgotten how tiring fighting such little beasties could be!"

"Is anyone hurt?" Kaden asked. He saw blood dripping from Cleven's mouth. "Cleven?"

Cleven silently nodded and brushed away the blood.

Kaden saw Drew's bloodied pant-leg. He examined his wound.

Despite his grimace when Kaden touched his leg, Drew reassured them he was fine.

Kaden nodded. "Yes, you will be fine. It will be sore, but thankfully the skyrogs' spikes are not poisonous. Your leg should heal quickly." He turned to Anna. "Are you well?"

Anna nodded. Wesley knew she'd scraped her forearm with her bow, but he admired her for not making mention of it.

Kaden smiled and shook his head. "You are a brave girl. A fine shieldmaiden of Aloehan." He began to wipe his sword, but noticed Narin clutching his shoulder. "Narin," he spoke sternly, "if you are wounded, tell us."

Narin brushed his question aside. "I am well."

Castonir pulled on the seam of Narin's shirt, ripping it to reveal a deep gash.

Wesley's stomach recoiled at the sight.

"Well?" Castonir raised his eyebrows.

Narin winced.

"Narin," Kaden breathed a rebuke as he inspected the knight's wound. "How did you get this?"

"One of the brutes clawed me…and then bit me."

"I can look for crarryweed," Anna offered. Wesley remembered her talking about a plant Charmaine had shown her. It had healing properties.

"No crarryweed grows in this part of the forest," Adius answered quietly.

"Delmore," Kaden barked, "help me with this. Castonir and Cleven, gather the bodies and burn them, Adius…stay with the young ones."

"We can help," Drew protested.

Kaden looked at him. "You are hurt. You will abide by my orders." Looking at Wesley he said, "If you wish, you may help Castonir and Cleven."

Although he didn't wish, he moved to help them. He wasn't so sure he liked this new world.

"But we won." He inhaled, told his body to be calm. *"Just keep taking it one day at a time. One day at a time."*

23
THE ELVIN KING

Two days after the skirmish with the skyrogs, they began to see white bark on the trees, a sign that they were near the elvin city.

Drew's leg and Anna's arm had scabbed over. The others bore only minor scrapes and bruises, save for Narin. After two days, the wound on his shoulder still had not closed, forcing him to constantly keep it bandaged. Several times a day, Delmore poured salve on it to ward off any infection. It did not seem to be getting any worse, but it didn't show signs of improving either.

"It will be good when we reach the elves," Adius commented to the teens as they rode. "They will be able to tend to Narin's shoulder."

Wesley wondered what power the elves possessed that Delmore did not.

He glanced at Adius, "Do you know their language?"

Adius smiled ruefully. "Nay. There are few humans that do. Not even all the elves do...so rare has their tongue become. When humans entered Camnoel, their language eventually became that spoken by the races. So if you hear it, listen well, for the sound does not fall on many ears."

Wesley hoped that he would be able to hear it. Having lived in Africa and Europe, he had heard a variety of languages, and he wondered if elvish would be similar to any.

No sooner had the thought crossed his mind when Kaden's quiet voice commanded their attention, "We are here."

He looked forward. In the distance, an incline in the forest rose from the ground. Tree-covered hills stretched in either direction of the forest. Directly ahead, stone walls blended into the hills. A high archway was chiseled out of the ivy-covered rock. Cream-colored stones formed a path that began at the gateway and extended beyond it.

Two elves, clad in forest-green, stood at either side of the entrance. They stared silently at the oncoming company.

Wesley glanced at his sister. She was beaming.

They came to a stop and Kaden dismounted. With a fist to his heart, he bowed low before the elf guards. "Hail, elves of the forest."

The elf with the silver hair spoke, "Welcome, knight of the Citadel."

Kaden nodded. "Thank you."

The brown-haired elf spoke, "We have been expecting you, Sir Kaden. Elderair is waiting for you. Please follow me."

Kaden looked over his shoulder and nodded to the others. "It is safe to approach." He remounted his horse and followed the second elf through the archway into the Elvin City.

Wesley stared, wide-eyed. When they passed through the gateway, they entered a balcony overlooking a ravine. In the distance, he could see palace-like buildings constructed on a hill. He could hear the faint sound of waterfalls.

The stone path led to a ramp down into the valley, where the path continued. A hush fell over the company as they rode.

The forest creatures were less skittish here. Birds chirped all around and deer grazed a few feet away from the trail. Streams trickled on either side.

As they neared the city, the gush of waterfalls grew louder and more elves appeared in sight. They passed an elf woman who was washing clothes in a stream. Elf children played along the banks, laughing and splashing one another.

Wesley looked on in amazement. The woman straightened and silently stared at them. Her beautiful face was expressionless, neither friendly nor hostile. Curly dark locks hung down her back and her mint green eyes were penetrating as she watched them. Wesley wasn't sure he had seen anyone more regal looking.

The children looked like the children in Aloehan except for their pointy ears, fair skin, and deep, mature eyes.

The elf leading them came to a stop. "Leave your horses here. We must go up the stairs to the palace."

Wesley looked up to see a winding staircase that ducked behind a waterfall.

Drew glanced at him and flashed his excited smile.

The wooden steps yielded to a rope bridge that passed behind the loud falls. It then led to a pathway through a cave lit by glowing rocks. The cave opened to a broad, arched stone bridge.

Wesley gazed out over the bridge. The view overlooking the elvin city was mesmerizing. Rich colors appealed to his eyes. The roofs of the homes were finely carved and colored in warm hues. Brooks and bridges dotted at every other place he looked. Vines and moss with colorful flowers climbed the walls and birds and butterflies fluttered among the tree branches.

"Welcome to Revowen, home of the Ellwood Elves," their guide spoke. He led them across the bridge onto another platform like the first one. This one had doorways on either side leading into halls of the palace. It overlooked a maze of gardens and waterfalls.

"Please wait here," the elf instructed. "I will inform King Elderair that you are here." He disappeared through one of the arched doorways.

They waited only a moment before the elf returned, followed by two other elves. The first was an aged male elf, which Wesley could only tell by his silver hair and the creases that flanked his eyes. He had no beard. He was dressed in royal colors of blue, purple, and crimson and wore a gold band on his brow.

He was followed by an elf maiden with reddish blond hair that hung in long curls down her back. She wore a floor-length gown of mint green and a band like the man's crown. Both were fair-skinned, with pointed ears. She was beautiful.

Kaden bowed before the elf king and in turn took the lady's hand, kissing it. They smiled briefly at one another before Kaden addressed the man.

"King Elderair, Princess Elaswén, these are the knights of the Citadel," he said gesturing to the company of warriors who bowed respectfully. "And these are knights and shieldmaiden in training," he motioned to Drew, Wesley, and Anna. They followed suit and bowed and curtsied as Austin had shown them.

So the woman was Kaden's fiancé.

"Welcome to Revowen," Elderair bid kindly. He faced the whole company and spoke, "I hope that your brief stay here will prove restful and helpful to your future quest. On behalf of all the woodland elves, I give you our thanks for your contribution to the cause of rescuing these captive members." He turned to Kaden, "Which are the ones who will compose the rescue quest?"

"The Citadel has selected five men, a small but capable company to penetrate the enemy's stronghold." Kaden looked at his men, as he called their names. "Sir Adius, Sir Castonir, Sir Delmore, Sir Cleven, and Sir Narin."

Elderair rubbed his chin as he surveyed the company.

"These are not the ones who will rescue the Forsvárerne," he said slowly but surely.

Everyone but his daughter looked at him with confusion.

Wesley felt his pulse pick up as the elf king looked at him, slowly moving his gaze to Drew, and then to Anna.

"These are the ones."

There was a general gasp.

Kaden turned to Elderair and said quietly, "Your Highness…when we brought these three here, we intended that they further their training under your warriors…not go on a quest themselves."

A small chuckle escaped Elderair, who was not at all put off. "Things are not always as we intend them, are they?"

Kaden did not return the smile.

Elderair straightened. "It is of no matter now. Come, I am sure you are weary from your travels, and I can see that some of you are wounded. You are our guests and shall be treated accordingly. Weldin," he spoke to the elf that had escorted them here, "Lead them to the Guest House."

Weldin bowed. "Yes, my lord." He turned to the travelers. "Please follow me."

24
THE QUEST

While the rest of the company followed Weldin to enjoy the Elvin hospitality, Kaden lingered on the balcony, leaning on its edge. He gazed out over the city of beauty with weary eyes that hinted at the weight he carried.

"You once said that Revowen was a place where you enjoyed to be...a place where you could forget your worries."

Kaden turned and saw Elaswén standing behind him. He straightened, walked over to his fiancée, and enclosed her in an embrace.

"I have missed you," he whispered.

"And I you," she returned. She pulled back to look into his eyes. "But tell me, what weighs on your mind? Is it Father's proposal?"

The knight gave a deep sigh and responded. "I respect your father greatly; he is one of the wisest men I know...But," his face contorted at the thought of his words, "this suggestion...I cannot accept."

"Why not?" she asked gently.

He shook his head. "Wesley, Drew, Anna—they are mere youths. They are not ready to go into Ratacin's lairs."

"You fear for their safety, then?"

"Yes!" He lowered his voice to a near whisper. "Elaswén, I wrote to you when we first met them. You do know who I think they may be, do you not?"

Her eyes fell to the ground and she nodded. Returning her gaze to meet his she spoke, "Yes. I thought so too, as soon as I saw them."

"Then you know why I cannot in good faith allow them to be exposed to such danger. What if he caught them?" Kaden shifted his weight. "I believe he knows about their presence."

She looked sharply at him. "How? Was it he who summoned them?"

He shook his head. "No, but we have had a traitor at the Citadel. One of our own knights."

Her eyes filled with pain. "This is dire." Her chest rose and fell with pained breaths. "But perhaps Ratacin does not know."

"If he does not, it is only a matter of time until he does. And regardless, they have fought in only one battle, a skirmish, and that against skyrogs." He leaned on the rail, gripping it with his hands. "They are not ready to face Ratacin's knights. They would be no match for him."

Elaswén slipped a hand over his. "What if it is the will of the Maker?" she asked quietly. "If it is His will to send them into danger, will He not also provide for them?"

Kaden's eyes fell into a daze. "How can we be certain of His will?"

Elaswén fell silent for a moment and then said, "Let us seek Him on this matter. I know my father will do the same. And we will ask them."

"The children?"

"If they are meant to lead this quest, perhaps they will have direction on the matter."

Kaden sighed again and shook his head. "I hate to ask this of them. They have been through so much already." He met Elaswén's eyes. "Drew has never known his parents. Wesley and Anna have been separated from theirs." A faint smile played on his lips.

"They amaze me though, how they carry themselves. Such fortitude. They have known great pain, Elaswén…but they also know great hope."

Elaswén laid a hand over his chest as she looked up into his eyes. "Which is why they are perfect for the task."

***

When King Elderair had dismissed Weldin, the younger elf led the travelers to another wing of the palace. The Elvish palace was wrought of what looked to Wesley like marble, gems, and ivory. Any stones that were used were white or cream-colored. Doors were scarce, being replaced by either curtains or nothing at all. All of the windows were glassless and both doorways and windows were arched.

Nature seemed to be within the walls of the palace nearly as much as it was outside them. Ivy climbed the walls and plants hung from the ceilings. In some rooms there were no roofs at all, allowing the viewer to look up into a clear sky. Indoor waterfalls provided a gentle hum accented by the chirp of birds that flew through the corridors.

Wesley felt comforted by the place. It was foreign, but somehow, it felt right. He glanced at Anna and saw a contented smile touching her lips.

He looked at one of the walkways they passed. He wished he could get lost wandering through these paths.

Weldin led them to another balcony, where a company of elves was waiting for them. Low tables and cushions filled the floor, and on the tables was a feast.

Drew and Narin slapped high fives. Narin, however, was not allowed to stay when one of the elves realized he was wounded. He was promptly escorted, against his will, to the healing ward where he was to be treated.

Weldin bid the others to sit and eat, to which the weary company gladly obliged. "Take liberty to enjoy the gardens as well."

Wesley wanted to take him up on his offer, but his growling stomach helped him prioritize.

Anna took a seat between Wesley and Drew. Her eyes were on the elves playing wind instruments.

"Wesley," she whispered abruptly. "We should ask the elves if they've seen Mom and Dad."

Wesley put down his bread. "I've been thinking about that too," he replied. "But," he glanced around, "I'm not sure who to ask."

Adius, who was sitting on the other side of Wesley, overheard him. "I will ask them for you."

Wesley looked at him. Adius had been quiet since their meeting with the king. "Thank you," he said gratefully.

He watched as Adius spoke to some of the elves. They conversed in low tones for a moment. A black-haired elf looked over at Wesley and Anna when Adius motioned to them. His eyes were impassive as he spoke to Adius.

Wesley's heart sank. He feared it was not good news. Adius returned to the table and confirmed his fears.

"I am sorry. They have not seen or heard news of your parents."

"Hey," Drew spoke quietly. "It's okay. We'll find them."

Anna was quiet for a moment. "I know."

Wesley didn't have her confidence. Despite the beauty and serenity that surrounded him, his mind was a whirlwind of thoughts. *"Every step we've taken, I've hoped that we would find them...when we came to Camnoel...when we went to Aloehan...and now here...only to be disappointed again."*

He felt heat rise in his neck from the anger that simmered inside him. *"Why? Why would You lead us here only to dash our hopes against the rocks?"*

His anger churned into desperation—a frantic fear. What if they never found them? What if they were never given any answers at all? The thought horrified him. His throat constricted and he lost any desire to eat.

He was unaware of the music and merriment around him. He struggled to keep the tears that stung his eyes from falling down his face. Mumbling to be excused, he stood and looked for the gardens that Weldin had told them about.

He ran until he could no longer hear the music, until he could no longer hear any sound from anybody.

He drew his sword, wishing there was something he could slash. All around him was beauty. He dare not touch these plants. So he sheathed his sword and sheathed his anger. For now.

***

The sun had set and the stars shone unusually bright as Wesley strolled through the Elvin gardens. The sylvan walkway had a calming effect on him that he couldn't ignore even if he wanted to.

He could still hear the hum of the songs that the elves sang in the halls of the palace. He was about to walk back to palace when he saw two silhouettes walking towards him.

"Hey loner," Drew's familiar voice was accompanied by a slap on the arm.

"Hey."

Drew took a seat on one of the benches in the garden. "Wes, we need to talk."

Wesley nodded and sat across from Drew and Anna.

"I want to talk about the king's suggestion," stated Drew.

"What do you think of it?" Anna asked Wesley.

Drew leaned forward, propping his arms on his thighs. "I want to do it."

Wesley watched Drew and nodded carefully. He knew Drew would want to do it as soon as the suggestion had been made. And surprisingly, he did too. "If that's what they decide…then, I'm willing to do it too."

Drew nodded solemnly, but his brown eyes were lit with excitement. He looked at Anna. "Anna?"

Anna studied a design on the mosaic stone path before responding. "The thought of going after people we don't even know, to rescue them from evil men, scares me." She looked up and exchanged looks with Wesley and Drew. "But…ever since we've been here, I believed that we were here for a purpose…I still do. Maybe that purpose is this…to help these people."

A smile tugged at the corners of Drew's mouth. "So...
you're in?"

Anna nodded her head once. "Like Wesley said, if that's
what they decide...then yes."

The grin that Drew had suppressed broke forth. "All right!"
Growing serious he added, "Hey maybe we'll find your parents
on this quest."

Wesley knew Drew was being sincere. But he was almost
past hoping for that. Almost.

25
REVOWEN

In the days that followed, Wesley, Anna, and Drew used their free time to explore Revowen and discover its many wonders. They visited Narin at the healing ward, who more than welcomed their company.

All the while, they waited, knowing that Elderair and Kaden were discussing their decision regarding the rescue quest.

One day, as they were walking through one of the many gardens, chatting, and pointing at the unusual rock formations and colors that occupied this particular garden, they saw the elf princess walking towards them. They fell silent. The boys bowed and Anna curtsied.

Elaswén smiled graciously at them. "You need not bow before me."

When they remained silent, she spoke again. "I am glad that I found you, for I was wondering how you are enjoying your stay. Is Revowen to your pleasing?"

"It's great," Drew replied, his enthusiasm tempered only by his respect.

Wesley and Anna nodded in agreement.

"It's the most beautiful place I've ever seen," said Anna. Then with a loving touch to her satin gown that she had been given, she added, "I'm hoping that I can take this back home with me when we go back to our world."

Elaswén gave an apologetic smile. "I am afraid you will not be able to do that. Only those born in Camnoel may take things back into your world. If you tried to bring something from this land with you through a mirror, it would remain behind once you passed through."

When the elf saw their disappointment, she spoke reassuringly, "Which is why we should make the most of your visit while you are with us." Looking at Anna she said, "Kaden tells me you are interested in learning the healing herbs."

Anna nodded.

"If it pleases you, I will show you some of the healing plants we grow in our gardens."

Anna's face lit up; Wesley knew she had been waiting for this offer since they arrived in Revowen. "I would like that."

Elaswén addressed the boys. "You knights are welcome to join us as well."

Wesley and Drew glanced at each other. Pleasure was written on Drew's face at being addressed as a 'knight' even though they weren't official yet. They accepted the offer and strolled with the girls for while as Elaswén pointed out various leaves that aided different ailments.

Anna was eating this up. Wesley found it interesting too. He had always enjoyed learning, regardless the field of study.

Drew's shuffling feet next to him warned him that his friend did not share their interest.

Elaswén was so warm and friendly that Wesley almost forgot they were walking with an elf, and an elf royalty at that. The other elves they had seen were not unfriendly, but remained detached. They watched the visitors with amusement, but rarely made an effort to speak to them.

Elaswén, however, treated them as friends, with not the slightest hint of condescension. The way she taught things reminded Wesley of his mom.

"Look, Anna," Elaswén touched a leaf on a bush with orange blossoms, "These leaves can be crumbled and put in tea to alleviate sore throats."

When Anna didn't respond, Elaswén, repeated, "Anna?"

Anna blinked. "Yes?"

Elaswén stared at her for a moment without speaking. "You must miss them very much."

Surprise crossed Anna's face.

Wesley was surprised too. How did she know?

At that moment, Drew, who had surely zoned out of the conversation, nudged Wesley. "Let's go check out the armory."

"Would you care to tell me about them?"

Wesley didn't want to leave. At the same time, he thought maybe this would be good for Anna to talk with Elaswén alone. When was the last time she had been around a mother figure? Though he was enjoying this time, he figured she needed it more.

"Yeah," he answered as he turned to veer off another path with Drew.

**

There you are."

Wesley and Drew stopped as they were leaving the armory. Turning, they saw that Kaden had spoken to them. King Elderair was with him. The boys bowed in respect.

"You've been looking for us?" asked Drew with cocked eyebrows.

"Yes," said Kaden in a measured tone, "We need to speak with you."

"About the suggestion I made," finished King Elderair.

"Really?" Drew asked with an excited smile.

Kaden did not return the smile but replied, "Yes. Drew, come with me. Wesley, you will speak with the king."

Before either of them could speak, Kaden was leading Drew one way and King Elderair was escorting Wesley another.

Wesley wondered at their chosen method, but said nothing.

He followed the king silently through the palace until they reached what he assumed was the monarch's office. He gazed around the room with awe.

Lining the walls were dozens of shelves that were filled with stacks of books, scrolls, and wooden boxes. A large table with two benches next to it was cluttered with more scrolls and maps. Fascinated, Wesley leaned over, examining the map of Camnoel.

"I have little doubt that you have thought about my proposal."

Wesley lifted his head at the king's remark. He had almost forgotten that there was someone else in the room with him. He bowed his head in a nod. "Yes, sir."

King Elderair sat on one of the benches and motioned for Wesley to do the same.

"And do you want to do it? Do you want to embark on a quest to rescue the Forsvárerne?"

Sitting across from the elf, Wesley nodded. "If you decide that you want us to go, then… yes, I want to do it."

The elf king stared at him with penetrating eyes. Wesley returned his firm gaze.

"And what do you wish to gain from this quest, were you to go?" asked Elderair.

Wesley answered with an honesty that surprised him. "I want to find my parents."

King Elderair sighed, as if he expected that answer, yet was disappointed with it. He spoke softly, "That cannot be all you want, Wesley. Do you not care for the Forsvárerne members who are imprisoned? —the very purpose for the quest?"

When Wesley didn't respond, the king said steadily, "Your parents, if they are alive, are not the only ones in need. There are many who need rescuing."

"Do you think they're here?" Wesley asked. He knew it was bold. He knew this was an elvin king. But at the moment, he just wanted someone to level with him plain and simple. He needed answers.

"In Camnoel?"

Wesley nodded.

The king sighed. "Based on the information Kaden has given me...the fact that your parents disappeared without explanation or trace...yes, I am inclined to believe they are. But where, exactly, I cannot know. This is a world Wesley. It is no small place."

"Sir," Wesley began, "I'm not even from this world. When we came here I had one goal: to find my parents. Though a lot of other things have happened along the way, that's still what I want. I have no duty to these people." He lowered his voice and looked down. "I didn't ask for any of this."

"Wesley, Kaden has told me much about you and your friends...You are a follower of Christ, are you not?"

Wesley looked up, surprised at the question. He hadn't very well been acting like one. He'd barely spoken to God and if he had to pick a chief emotion towards Him right now, what would it be? Anger? Distrust? Frustration? And he certainly hadn't talked with Kaden about his faith.

Anna must have.

But the thought of *not* following God had never crossed his mind, so when he spoke, he answered solidly, "Yes."

The king looked at him without blinking. "Then you have a duty to them."

26
CONSOLATION

The following week, the elves held a banquet one night in honor of the three members who had been chosen for the rescue quest.

At the outside banquet, Wesley, Anna, and Drew sat with one another discussing the recent events. They all felt the same way: although they couldn't believe the council had consented to this arrangement, they felt that it was right.

Wesley had the most difficultly accepting it. Although he too felt that this was the right decision, he was distracted by what the king had told him.

He needed to think. He needed to be alone. He quietly left the party, walking a ways to a secluded spot. He leaned on a bridge that overlooked the bubbling pool of a waterfall.

"I don't understand," he prayed aloud. "I thought that You brought us here to find Mom and Dad...but You seem to be leading us away from them." *"If they're even here,"* he added gloomily in his thoughts.

He sighed. His prayers felt clumsy and awkward, but he pressed on. "Please...God...give me some direction." He stared out onto the water where his reflection rippled back at him. A prick of guilt touched his heart. He voiced his words softly, but with complete sincerity, "I know I haven't treated You the best lately, but please, I'm asking You now...help me."

For a long time, Wesley just stared at the water.

"May I join you?"

Wesley looked in the direction of the voice. It was Princess Elaswén. He straightened. "Of course...your highness," he added, remembering the term of respect.

"Why do you not join the others?"

Wesley shrugged. "I needed to get away...to think."

"You carry many troubles," she commented quietly.

Wesley eyed her with surprise. "How can you tell?"

She smiled softly. "Your face betrays what is in your heart."

Wesley looked away, embarrassed, hoping to guard any more expressions that would 'betray' him. He leaned on the rail and stared at the waterfall swelling in front of them.

"There is no need to feel shame," she spoke softly. "You have a good reason to be weary. Upon the loss of your parents, the weight of leadership fell to you—even in your youth. Yet you have born in like a man. You have done *well*, Wesley." She looked at him, and her shinning eyes radiated her confidence in him.

He wondered how she could feel more confidence in him than he felt in himself.

"I know you are weary," she continued, "and shall likely grow wearier still." Her brow knit in compassion. "I fear things will get worse for you before they get better. But do not loose heart, though the night is dark. The dawn will come. The Maker has not laid upon you a burden greater than you can bear, though at times it may seem to consume you."

She paused for a moment, studying him. "You seem lonely," she commented. She waited, but he chose not to respond, so she continued, "Your sister confides her anguish in you, but you confide in no one."

Wesley turned towards her. How could she know so much about him?

A gentle smile formed on her lips. "Wesley, do not be mistaken. The Maker wants you to trust and confide in Him, and in the friends He has given you. You are not alone on this journey."

She returned her gaze to the waterfall and was silent for a moment. When she looked back at him, she spoke a warning, "Your mind is not on your quest. Focus on what is at hand. The rest will come to you."

Wesley hesitated, and then stuttered slightly. "Can I ask you something?"

She nodded.

"Have you ever lost someone who was close to you?"

Her eyes gleamed in slight surprise at the question. "I have," she answered quietly. "A very dear sister and her husband…They were killed." Then she added softly, "And a brother."

Wesley then understood how she could sense his grief. He felt bad for her. "I'm sorry."

She nodded, accepting his apology. "It is true I have known great sorrow. But I have also known great joy. When my sister died, I thought that I would never be happy again…But over time, the Maker healed my wounds."

She looked at him steadily. "Wesley. Do not think He will not restore your joy as well."

Wesley swallowed hard, moisture stinging his eyes. "Thank you."

She smiled at him. "There is nothing I can give you that the Maker has not already provided for you. But my prayers go with you." She tilted her head gently to the side. "May the desires of your heart be fulfilled."

She reached out a hand and laid it on his head and uttered words in her native tongue, the sound melodic and comforting.

Translating the words for him, she spoke, "Blessed are you, son of the High King. Remember whom you serve: He who is faithful to keep you. He will be with you wherever you go."

When she withdrew her hand, a joyful smile lit her face.

Wesley couldn't manage words, so he simply nodded his gratitude.

Elaswén smiled graciously. "Do you wish to stay here a while?"

He nodded. He watched her walk away, and then he turned back to the waterfall. Its gushing was never-ending. Wesley lost himself in it.

"I was told I would find you here."

Wesley looked up, wondering how long he had been standing here in his thoughts. He glanced quickly upward and saw the moon high in the sky. He had been here the better part of an hour. Wesley switched his attention to the knight in front of him.

"Sir Kaden. Is something wrong?"

"No," Kaden replied slowly, taking a space next to Wesley, leaning on the rail, "unless there is something that you wish to talk about."

Wesley looked at the knight.

"Elaswén told me you were here," he explained. "She said she spoke to you. She said that you were troubled," he added softly.

Wesley gave a small shrug. "I'm not sure what to think."

Kaden waited for him to go on.

Wesley bit the inside of his mouth. He always had trouble articulating his thoughts, and he especially felt self-conscious when talking about serious things like his own emotions. It was easier just to handle them himself.

Yet Kaden's intention to seek him out gave him reassurance and fostered the thought inside him that was telling him to share what was on his mind.

"It's just," Wesley started, "it's just that I thought I would find my parents here." His fingers rubbed at the stone rail. "I don't know why God would bring us here and then not let us find them." Wesley glanced at Kaden from the corner of his eye, wondering if the knight would understand.

Kaden was silent for a moment, absorbing Wesley's words thoughtfully. "Wesley, I will not pretend to understand the ways of the Maker. They are far beyond mine. But I do believe He has a purpose in all that He does...even in your coming to Camnoel." He paused. "Do you believe that?"

Wesley pushed away from the rail and looked at Kaden. For a long moment, he couldn't voice an answer. "I want to."

Kaden didn't seem bothered by Wesley's lack of assurance. "That is a good start." Kaden faced Wesley, his hand resting on the hilt of his sword. "Know that I will always do what I can to help you. If it comes to battle, you will have my sword, and in all of life you will have my prayers."

Wesley stared back at him, and he knew that Sir Kaden meant those words with all of his heart. Wesley's throat tightened and he felt tears that he had kept at bay for so long flow over.

Kaden reached out his hand for Wesley to shake, but then thought better of it, and wrapped him in an embrace.

27

FORSAKING SECURITY

The day after the banquet, King Elderair called a meeting with Wesley, Anna, and Drew, along with Kaden, Elaswén, Adius, and some elvin elders.

Once everyone was seated in the council room, a circular room with a domed trellis for a ceiling, King Elderair addressed the youngest three.

"Although we do not have as much time as I would like, I do not wish to send you off unprepared and ignorant of your task. Let me inform you exactly what the Forsvárerne is, and how it came to be formed."

Wesley was thankful. He had been hoping for some direction in their quest, some inclination of purpose. He leaned forward and tuned his ears to what was about to be said. He wanted to absorb every word.

The elf king straightened in his seat and began. "It all started with a man named Rigórik. He is a halfling; his mother was an elf and his father a dwarf. His upbringing was in Kalegon among the dwarves, but he had the benefit of learning the elvin history from his mother. Growing up, his closest friend was his dwarf cousin, Ramee. Though as the two young men grew older, they chose separate roads.

"Rigórik became a blacksmith in the dwarves' mines of Kalegon. Ramee decided to travel the world.

"In the course of his travels, the cousins kept contact through letters. Rigórik was concerned, then, when Ramee wrote telling him that he had joined an elf named Ratacin. He enthusiastically told his cousin that Ratacin was an independent leader who meant to better society and that he was fortunate to be a part of his work.

"During this period, Ratacin had gathered support from other elves. He wandered for years and made a home for himself beyond the desert, between the mountains of Hadis Shale. With his followers of elves, and a few men and dwarves, he built a fortress and the city that became Racin Dor.

"He sought out more support, and he found Ramee. He also began the enslavement of other races, namely vuls. Ramee, like many others, thought that Ratacin was showing kindness by involving these creatures in his work.

"Ramee wrote to Rigórik of all of the positive things that Ratacin had promised to do. But Rigórik was not so easily convinced. While the deed of Ratacin's betrayal had gone unnoticed by most of the world, and forgotten by many, the elves remembered. Rigórik's mother told him of the foul deed. Rigórik warmed Ramee, but his words were unheeded. Ramee did not want to believe Rigórik's admonitions, but after two years of serving under Ratacin, he wrote to Rigórik of his regret."

King Elderair paused and drew a piece of paper from inside his tunic. "I have with me a copy of his letter." Unfolding the paper, the king began to read:

To my cousin Rigórik,

I write to you hastily for fear of what I am writing. My cousin, you were right about Ratacin. Everything you tried to warn me about but I refused to listen to is happening. I cannot go into detail, but only warn you: beware! His strength is ever increasing and I am sure that he plans to take over all of Camnoel. The world in all its peacefulness will be taken by surprise. This is no small threat. The world as we know it is about to change.

Alas, it is too late for me; my feet are too far buried in this muck to be withdrawn. But you cousin, I warn, you, wise one, who was not taken by his lies. I envy you. I assure you it will be better to die by Ratacin's sword then to aid in his strike. My heart suffers at the thought that I have had part in his deeds. But what can be done? I wait for my doom.

Your faithful cousin,
Ramee

King Elderair refolded the paper and tucked it into his pocket. He looked at his audience and resumed, "Rigórik was troubled by his cousin's words. Thus he took action by forming a group of individuals who were committed to opposing Ratacin.

"He named this band the Forsvárerne, thinking it to be the last hope for Camnoel. The Forsvárerne operated rescue quests for captive prisoners. They tried to uncover whatever information they could of Ratacin's plans. Ramee periodically sent information to his cousin, and Rigórik passed it along to the Forsvárerne. The Forsvárerne has made allies with Aloehan and Revowen.

"Several months ago, Rigórik called a Forsvárerne meeting in Erion. He had just received new information from Ramee about a fort that Ratacin had built within the past year. Ramee had also sent him a roughly drawn blueprint of the fort.

"Rigórik believed that the safest place for these blueprints was here in Revowen. So from the meeting in Erion, he dispatched four members, Hwen, Hadrian, Glenge, and Ralphan. During their journey here they were intercepted by vuls and captured. Only Ralphan escaped. He was grievously wounded when he reached us. He died two days after his arrival."

King Elderair again reached into his tunic and pulled out more papers. "These are the plans to Kurgon Fort. Our elves have redrawn them from the sketches Ralphan brought." The king stood and walked over to Wesley. "You will need these on your quest. I have also included maps of the land."

Wesley dipped his head in a nod.

Drew drummed his fingers on his chair. "King Elderair, how do we know for sure that they're being kept at Kurgon Fort?"

King Elderair kept his gaze fixed on Drew for a moment before responding. "We do not know—for sure—that is. It is a risk we are willing to take...if you three are."

***

The next day, Wesley, Anna, and Drew stood with the others from the Citadel, along with King Elderair and Elaswén by the southern gate of Revowen. With bundles tied to their backs, the three stood prepared to leave on their quest.

"Drew, Wesley, Anna," King Elderair spoke solemnly as he looked into each one's eyes, "you go on this quest to rescue three members of the Forsvárerne, our faithful alliance: elf maiden of Miershire, Lady Hwen, dwarf lord of Kalegon, Sir Glenge, and warrior of Clavilier, Sir Hadrian.

"Their fate lies in your hands. On behalf of every land that opposes Ratacin, we send you out. Remember, this quest is secret; tell no one but those you feel certain are friends...and only of those whom you must. You will know those faithful to our cause by this symbol."

With his staff, King Elderair drew a marking in the dirt. It was picture of a sun rising over two squiggly lines representing a sea. Wesley recognized it as the emblem on Aloehan's flag.

"Use this symbol to seek out allies, but be careful where you draw it; not everyone views it favorably."

He paused to look upon them. "May the Maker watch over you and keep you safe. You go with the blessing of Revowen."

Elaswén spoke, saying goodbye to each of them and giving them encouragement. Each of the Citadel knights shook their hands.

"I shall miss your company," Narin said with a smile.

"We'll miss you too," Drew replied and clapped his shoulder. Narin hollered in pain. "Not my bad shoulder!"

Drew choked back a laugh. "Sorry."

Adius stood before the three with his arms crossed. "Promise me when you come back that you will finish your training."

Wesley and Drew nodded. "We promise."

"Remember what I've taught you." Then he nodded. "You will do fine." He looked at Anna. "And you will do fine as well with these two looking after you."

She smiled with a glance at the two boys. "I know."

Adius turned back to his apprentices and clapped their hands and embraced them.

Kaden stepped forward. "Know that you go with the blessing of Aloehan as well." He took a deep breath before continuing. "I shall pray for you every day."

One by one he laid a hand on their shoulders and spoke to them. To Anna he said, "It has been a joy getting to know you, Anna. Elaswén feels so also."

"Thank you, Sir Kaden. And I like your bride-to-be very much."

A smile flickered across his face. "Keep being a light to all around you. Whether it be as a shieldmaiden or healer, you will be excellent at whatever you choose."

He turned to Wesley. "You will make an invaluable knight of the Citadel one day, Wesley, if you so choose. Stay diligent. Stay focused."

Wesley nodded.

Kaden looked at Drew. "You also, Drew, will be invaluable to Aloehan. Your courage will be vital to this quest." Lowering his voice, Kaden spoke, "Lead them well."

Drew nodded. "I will."

King Elderair spoke a prayer of blessing over them.

When he finished, Drew spoke, "Thank you." He stuck his thumbs behind the straps of his backpack and nodded. "We'll see you in a little while. And we'll have company." He turned and headed through the gate into the woods.

Wesley and Anna lingered for a moment, looking back at their friends. A tear trickled down Anna's face. "Goodbye," she said.

Wesley echoed her farewell and they too turned and followed Drew.

***

Wesley looked at the map in his hand for the fifteenth time. It outlined the course they were to take to Dradoc, the nearest city to Revowen. Once there, they were to look for the shop with a sign of a quill. There they would find an ally by the name of Mr. Lampwick, a penman who lived within the city boarders.

"Would you put that away, Wes?" Drew said. "We know where we're going."

"This map has more than just where we're going. It shows all of Camnoel. I'm studying it."

Wesley saw Drew shrug, but didn't mind. He continued to examine the parchment in his hands. *"I want to be familiar with the land,"* he told himself, *"Just in case I need it."* After all, he did plan to search for his parents after they completed this quest, and he had no idea where he would need to look. *"So I want to be prepared."*

He inhaled the earthy forest air and silently added a prayer to his thoughts. *"I want to trust You…with everything…with our future, and the fate of Mom and Dad. Everything is in Your hands…right?"*

After they had walked all day, stopping only for brief intervals, they made camp at night. Drew plopped down on the ground, and slid out of the straps of his backpack.

"I am really missing Gallagher right now!" he said in referral to his horse.

Anna sat down next to him. "I miss Aleron."

Wesley glanced at them, as he searched for some food in his bag. "I'm sure not missing Spiker."

Drew laughed out loud at the thought of Wesley's horse. Known for his independent nature, Spiker often galloped and bucked when Wesley specifically told him not to.

Wesley shrugged. "I like walking better, that's all."

Drew nodded with a grin. "Right."

Once they had eaten dinner, Drew and Wesley sparred several matches and Anna practiced her archery. Then they gathered around the campfire.

Wesley sat with his back against a tree, staring into the dancing flames. "Do you think we'll be able to do this?"

Drew and Anna looked at him.

"Do what?" asked Drew.

Without removing his gaze from the fire, Wesley answered, "This quest." Then he looked up. "Do you think we'll be able to rescue these people?"

Drew shifted against the log he was leaning on. "Yeah."

Wesley knew his answer was not one of feigned confidence to make them feel better. Drew honestly believed they could do it.

"I hope so," Wesley replied earnestly. "These people's lives are depending on us. It's a big responsibility."

Drew picked up a twig and broke it in his fingers. "It is a big responsibility." He tossed the twig into the embers. "But I don't think Sir Kaden would have let us go if he didn't think we could do it."

28
DRADOC

The next several days, the Wesley, Anna, and Drew followed the stream southwest towards Dradoc, the landmark city between Revowen and Kurgon Fort.

Wesley blinked awake and eased his body into a sitting position. Sleeping on the ground made him sore. He wondered if he kept this up long enough, would his body would eventually get used to it.

Anna and Drew had already made a fire.

Anna grinned at him. "Happy birthday!"

He looked at her strangely.

She giggled. Drew smiled as he rolled up his mat.

"It's my birthday?" asked Wesley. He had lost sense of time since entering Camnoel. And if it was his birthday, that meant they had been gone months. He hoped Mr. Smith had figured out what had happened.

Anna nodded and smiled.

After they ate, Anna handed Wesley and object folded in cloth.

"Presents?" Wesley shook his head. "Anna, you're too much."

"No she's not," Drew defended. "She's just being a good sister."

"I know." Wesley observed his younger sister. "Thanks, Anna."

He unfolded the cloth and pulled out a candle that was shaped like a sword. The hilt was a shiny candle stand, and the wick protruded from the tip of the sword.

"We got it in Aloehan the day we went into town," explained Anna.

Then Drew reached into his pouch, pulled out something, and handed it to Wesley. "Happy Birthday."

Wesley looked at what Drew put in his hand. It was a shiny brown cross on a strand of sterling silver. He looked up at Drew, curiosity written on his face.

"One of the elves at the silversmith gave it to me. He said it would be good for trading in Dradoc." Drew shrugged. "I thought it looked cool."

Wesley stared at Drew. "You should keep it."

Drew shrugged again. "It'll mean more to you than it would to me."

Wesley glanced at him. Although he hadn't been Christ's most loyal follower lately, Wesley still wished Drew believed in Him. Drew was the best friend he'd ever had, but he had never shown any interest in Wesley or Anna's faith. It was one of the few things they didn't talk about.

Wesley stood. "Well, thanks for the party, but we'd better be on our way."

They traveled for days before they saw fuzzy outlines of buildings on the horizon.

"Dradoc," said Wesley. Two days ago, they had left the confines of the Ellwood Forest and trekked grassy hills. Now the dark shapes of the city grew crisper as they walked closer. In the light of the setting sun, they saw the wooden wall that surrounded the town.

When they came to the open gates, the gatekeeper, seated on a landing on top of the wall, looked upon them with a cagey stare. Drew made eye contact, nodded, and then looked straight ahead.

Wesley looked at the man out of the corner of his eye. He was still watching them. Although the gatekeeper didn't wear armor, he made Wesley uneasy.

Dressed in black and brown, his scraggly beard blended into the dirt that was smudged on his face. Wesley stepped closer to Anna as his hand moved to the hilt of his own sword.

When the three entered the town, they were surprised to see it still very active. Aloehan's shops closed before sunset, but this town was still bustling with activity even though it was almost dark. Torched lanterns lit the town, casting the dirty streets in an orange light.

Everything in the town was made of wood. The buildings were lined with wooden walkways and there was little vegetation lining the dusty roads.

"Where's this guy we're looking for?" asked Drew.

"Sir Kaden said his house was at the northwest side of town," Wesley replied as he looked around, searching for some sign of direction.

The town seemed too large to simply roam around until they found Mr. Lampwick. Knowing that they had entered from the Eastern Gate, Wesley led them directly ahead.

They asked for directions several times, and weaved in and out of buildings and back roads. As they walked farther back, it grew quieter. Near the front of the town, they had passed loud wagons, storeowners, and people leaving taverns having had too much to drink.

They also saw men dressed in dark armor, which made Wesley extremely wary. *"Those aren't knights from the Citadel,"* he thought to himself. Then he remembered the knights they had seen in the tavern in Vladoc. Ratacin's men. A shiver ran down Wesley's spine.

On the northwest side, however, there were very few people on the streets. The homes and shops were built closer together, not allowing room for wagons to pass. The sparse lighting emanated from streetlamps and windows of homes, not open shops and inns. The sun had completely set by the time they reached the north wall.

"Look," Anna pointed. "It's a sign with a quill."

"Good," Wesley said with a hint of relief. He had an uneasy feeling about this town and felt that the sooner they find this ally, the better.

As they stood in front of Mr. Lampwick's house, Wesley studied it. It was built into the wall of the city and connected with other shops on either side. It was one of the few homes that had plants growing in front of it. A lamp hung over the doorway, illuminating the carved sign that depicted a feathered quill sticking out of an ink jar.

Drew gave a hard rap on the door.

Wesley looked either way before drawing in the dirt with his foot.

The door opened, spilling golden light onto the dark street and three travelers. An elderly man appeared. Something was perched on his shoulder. He looked curiously upon the three strangers at his doorway, and then noticed the drawing on the ground. It was a rising sun over two squiggly lines.

A light of recognition flickered in his eyes.

"Come in, come in!" He beckoned.

He held the door open until each was safely inside. Wesley brushed away the drawing before following Drew and Anna into the house.

The home was lit with the warm glow of a crackling fire. A large table and chair were at one end of the room, covered with parchment paper and inkbottles. The other end served as a kitchen and den. A large cushioned chair by the fire was accompanied with a stand piled high with books. At the back of the room was a doorway that Wesley guessed led to a bedroom.

Wesley looked around and inhaled the safety of this shelter amidst a foreign place.

Then he surveyed the older man before them.

He was a small, bony man, clad in a loose white tunic tucked into brown britches. He wore a leather belt at his waist and soft leather shoes. A brown cloak was fastened across his chest with a wooden broach. His thin white hair circled his head, framing his leathered face, but leaving the top bald. Copper-rimmed spectacles rested at the edge of his broad nose.

Drew was the first to speak, "Mr. Lampwick?"

The man smiled and his blue eyes sparkled. "Yes, I am Lampwick, and this is Shadow," he said gesturing to the lump of fur on his shoulder.

"You have a pet squirrel?" Anna asked with delight.

"A most entertaining companion," assured Mr. Lampwick.

Anna grinned.

"Now," said Mr. Lampwick, "You obviously know my name, but I have yet to learn yours." He moved to pour each of them a cup of tea. Wesley couldn't help but think of Mr. Smith.

They each introduced themselves and Drew explained their purpose for coming.

"Indeed," the old man murmured when they had finished. He sat for a moment, cupping his mug of tea, before speaking. "I knew that the Citadel or the elves would send help soon. They sent me word of that. But I did not know who that company would be." He smiled at them. "I am sure they have chosen the perfect people for the task," He nodded his head to affirm his words.

Wesley wondered for a moment if he was being serious. "You mean you're not surprised that we're so young?"

"It is not what I expected, I admit. But I trust those at the Citadel and the Council of King Elderair to make wise choices. Sir Wesley," he leaned a little closer, "the longer I live, the more I see that things are rarely as I expect them. And that is not always a bad thing.

"Anyways, I mean to accept whomever they send my way and help the cause of the Citadel in whatever way I can."

"We appreciate you taking us into your home," said Anna.

"You are most welcome, my dear."

"We only plan to stay a night," said Wesley. "We'll be on our way in the morning."

"Of course. I am sure your task requires urgency. But know that you are always welcome here." He was then interrupted by Shadow's chirping at his ear, trying to drink from his mug. Mr. Lampwick pulled him away and put the animal on the floor.

He lifted his head with a smile. "Now one thing that can always be expected is that Shadow will try to steal my food!"

"How far are we are from Kurgon Fort?" asked Drew.

"Three days on horseback taking the main roads," replied Mr. Lampwick. "But I presume you are traveling on foot?"

Drew nodded.

"Then it will probably take you at least six days. Maybe more if you keep to the back roads." He set his cup of tea on a table and stood.

He handed Shadow, who had jumped back onto his lap, to Anna. "Would you mind holding him, dear?"

Anna grinned. "Not at all!" She carefully reached for the furry animal.

"Right now I think we should have some dinner." The old man scurried around the small kitchen, preparing their meal. As he hooked a pot over the fire, he asked them questions. "May I ask if you have a plan to rescue these people?"

Drew shrugged. "No," he replied honestly. "We figure we just try to go in, get them, and come out alive."

The corner of Mr. Lampwick's mouth twitched, and he turned to look at them. "That is a good plan. It is always desirable to come out alive."

Wesley stared at him, wondering if he was making fun of them.

Drew obviously was wondering the same thing, because he replied rather stiffly, "We're still working on the details."

Mr. Lampwick said quietly, "Take no offence, Sir Drew; I meant no harm. I am sure you will know the details of your plan the very moment you need them, no sooner, no later."

Drew nodded acceptingly.

Mr. Lampwick stirred the stew that simmered over the fire. It smelled like beef and vegetables. "Now if I may offer you some advice regarding your stay in Dradoc, I will certainly do that."

"We'll accept any advice we can get," said Wesley.

"Be very cautious when you are in the city. You may have already noticed guards patrolling the streets."

Wesley straightened. "Who are they?" Though he already had a hunch, he wanted confirmation.

Mr. Lampwick's face darkened. "They are knights from Racin Dor…Ratacin's men. Stay away from them."

So Wesley had been right.

"What are they doing in this city?" asked Drew.

"Ratacin has sent his men into every city that will not resist him. He is setting up posts in all of the major trading towns."

"Why?" Anna questioned as she moved Shadow from one hand to another.

Mr. Lampwick looked at her and hesitated. "Why do you think, child?" Then looking at the boys, he said, "He wishes to take over the whole realm. He is recruiting men from all over to follow him. He has already gotten vuls to do his ill bidding. In the weaker towns, he has made slaves of those who will not bend to his will. I am afraid some of his slave trade takes place even in this town. Some of the locals have thrown in their lot with him as a way of making a profit. They round up people who owe them money and sell them to Ratacin's knights."

Anna's face contorted. "Are you safe here?"

He smiled gently. "In places of darkness, someone needs to shine light. I live here as a penman yes, but my true purpose lies in helping people like you. My home is a safe place for those who oppose Ratacin."

"But," sputtered Anna, "will they not hurt you?"

"Right now, they are so busy with their own affairs, they hardly know of my existence." He smiled.

Wesley glanced at Anna. She nodded at Mr. Lampwick's response, but frowned. He knew that Mr. Lampwick's news upset her.

Trying to change the subject he asked, "Mr. Lampwick, what is a penman?"

Mr. Lampwick seemed surprised at the sudden change, but obliged by answering. "Why, it is nothing more than someone who is paid to pen documents for others because they have not the ability or the handwriting to do it themselves."

Wesley continued to ask Mr. Lampwick about his work, and made small talk to avoid any more heavy conversations for the night. He soon found himself enjoying the conversation. The more he learned of Camnoel's culture, the more he wanted to know.

When they finished dinner, Mr. Lampwick showed them where they would sleep. He removed a rug that covered part of the living room floor to reveal a trapdoor in the floorboards. He lifted the square hatch and went first down the ladder into the secret room.

Drew was first to follow him. "Do you use this room a lot?"

"I use it whenever people like you need a place to stay—that can range from several times a month to months with having no guests."

Anna and Wesley followed Drew down the ladder and looked around the earthen room. Several cots were spread about the small quarters, along with cabinets lined with dried food and casks of water.

Mr. Lampwick propped his hands on his hips. "It is not much, but it serves its purpose."

"It'll be perfect," said Wesley, "better than sleeping outside."

Drew nodded at Wesley and grinned.

Mr. Lampwick smiled. "If there is anything you need, be sure to let me know."

"Thank you," said Anna. "If you don't mind, I'd like to stay upstairs and sit by the fire for a while."

"Of course," smiled Mr. Lampwick.

Anna followed him back up the ladder.

Wesley hesitated and then followed her.

She had claimed a seat in front of the fire while Mr. Lampwick retired to his bedroom. Shadow was curled on a blanket in front of the dying embers.

"Hey."

She looked up.

Wesley took a seat adjacent from her. "You okay?"

She waited a moment before answering. "I think so." She was quiet. Then she whispered, "It's horrible, Wesley...what Ratacin does. When I think of the people that have suffered at his hand..." she couldn't finish. A tear slid down her face. "And what scares me is..." she shook her head, "what if he has Mom and Dad?"

Wesley felt his shoulders tighten, but he kept his breathing steady. He didn't speak for a moment. "We just have to take things one day at a time, Anna."

He knew it wasn't the comfort she was looking for. But it was all he had to offer.

29
DIVISIONS

At the crack of dawn, Mr. Lampwick awoke his three guests and fed them a hearty breakfast. By the time the sun had risen, they were packed and ready to go into town.

As they readied to say goodbye, Mr. Lampwick stood before them, smiling sadly. "I shall miss you three."

Shadow chirped from his perch on Mr. Lampwick's shoulder as if to note his agreement.

"But I know you will do fine," he continued. He winked. "I shall expect to see you again, but next time with three others."

"We'll try to come back this way," said Wesley, "but I don't know if it will be safe to travel through Dradoc with three of Ratacin's prisoners."

"Of course," Mr. Lampwick consented. "But you do know to not go by the way of Erin Dule."

Drew cocked his head. "That's what Sir Kaden told us, but he never said why. What's wrong with that road?"

"You should avoid that path unless it is your last resort. It is treacherous, filled with blue flames."

"Blue flames?" asked Wesley.

"Freezing fire. If you fall into a flame, it will freeze you, often resulting in death."

Drew tipped his chin. "Good to know."

Mr. Lampwick chuckled. "You better be on your way."

"Goodbye, Mr. Lampwick," said Anna. "Goodbye, Shadow."

They retraced their steps back into the center of town, where dozens of shops surrounded an open square.

As they neared the town's square, Anna peered closer to the cluster of people gathered there. "What are they doing?" she asked as she came to a stop.

A crowd of knights with wagons and horses were gathered near a line of raggedly dressed people.

The people were tied in ropes.

One of the knights spoke with a man dressed in town's clothes. The knight handed the man a leather pouch that jingled as is was transacted.

"Wesley," Anna muttered hoarsely. "What are they doing?"

Wesley stared painfully at the scene before him, but guided Anna by the arm. "Come on. Let's go inside."

Wesley quickly exchanged some money with the shopkeeper for a few sacks of dried fruit and meat and some loaves of bread.

When they exited the shop, Wesley and Drew tried to head in the opposite direction of the crowd, but Anna stood planted, her eyes glued to the scene.

Most of the people bound were men, some young, some in their prime. Wesley saw one boy among them. Looking no older than twelve, he stood quietly, his hands and feet bound. His once red hair was smudged with dirt and his eyes darted around fearfully.

Wesley knew Anna noticed him too.

The prisoners' ankle ropes were connected to one another, so when one man moved, the boy was caught off guard and stumbled.

"Get up!" a knight shouted at him, thrashing a whip at the boy's legs.

Anna gasped.

Wesley's heartbeat quickened. He glanced nervously around. Other townspeople had gathered to watch and didn't seem to mind the acts of cruelty being displayed before them.

The knight continued to whip the boy, screaming at him.

The boy cried out in pain.

"Wesley, do something," urged Anna. She looked franticly at him.

Wesley's heart pinched. "Anna, there's nothing we can do."

Anna spun to Drew. "Drew," she whispered. "Please."

Drew moved a hand to his hilt.

"No, Drew," Wesley commanded. "There's nothing we can do. There's too many of them." He cast a glance at the dark-armored knights and estimated there were at least ten of them, and probably more roaming the rest of the city.

The boy's cries commanded Wesley's attention. He writhed under the whip of the knight. The boy looked up, and for a brief moment, their eyes met. Another cry tore from his throat as the guard kicked his side.

"Stop!" Anna cried. She ran towards the knight, pushing through people to get there.

"Anna, no!" Wesley shouted, sprinting after her, cursing her compassion.

Anna continued weaving through the people. The knight raised his arm to deliver another blow. Anna grabbed it midair. "Stop!"

The man turned indignantly to see who dared to defy him. "Out of my way!" he yelled with a backhand to her face that knocked her to the ground.

Drew yanked his sword from its sheath and kicked the man in the back.

Wesley's heart sunk.

Knowing that conflict was inevitable now, Wesley drew his own sword. The first soldier angrily climbed to his feet and drew his sword, plunging into a fight with Drew.

Most of the townspeople who had gathered around the auction, backed away onto the boardwalks along the shops. A few drunken onlookers entered the brawl.

The other soldiers quickly joined in the skirmish. Wesley warded two off with a string of attacks. He tried to find Anna.

She had crawled over to the boy and was sawing at his bonds. The ropes fell away and the boy stared at her for a moment.

He scrambled to his feet and ducked away from the crowd of people.

She quickly worked to cut the ropes of a few more prisoners. Some of the men who had been freed joined the fight with Wesley and Drew.

One soldier noticed some men escaping. "The prisoners!" he shouted. "They're getting away!"

Other knights scrambled to secure the remaining ones in bonds and dragged them to their wagons.

Wesley batted furiously at the attacks aimed at him. He jerked his head around, trying to confirm Anna's position.

His heart dropped. Two soldiers were headed straight for her.

A sword cut in front of Wesley, but he thrust it away. He spun his head again in Anna's direction, and tried to make his way over to her but was intercepted by a soldier at every turn.

He slashed at a guard's sword arm, causing the man drop his weapon in screaming pain.

Then he saw her. His stomach constricted. A soldier grabbed Anna from behind and dragged her towards a wagon.

"Anna!" Wesley screamed.

She turned at the sound of his voice. "Wesley!" She shrieked. She reached for him, kicking her legs in protest to the man's grip.

Her eyes were filled with fear as she kept her head turned so she could see him. "Wesley, help!"

Wesley ran, but two soldiers blocked his way. He swung his sword between theirs, hewing at one man's shoulder, and the other man's side. More knights were beyond those, separating him from Anna.

The remaining soldiers mounted their horses and wagon seats, making for the city gate. When the last soldier in their way had ridden off, he saw Anna for a brief glimpse.

The soldier stuffed her in the cart and slammed the door to the wooden wagon. He mounted his own horse and followed the other knights. The wagon driver snapped the reigns, sending the horses stirring the dust as they galloped through the city gates.

Anna's faced pressed against the iron bars, her knuckles clenching them in fear. "Wesley!"

Wesley and Drew sprinted after them until they reached the gate. As soon as the wagon passed, the gatekeeper shut wooden doors.

Wesley pounded on the doors. "Let us out!"

The gatekeeper spat in the dirt from his perch above them. "Can't. Officer's orders to shut the gate after the last wagon. If I was you, I'd find shelter while I was still alive. There's more of them, you know." He spat again.

Drew swore loudly at him. "If you don't open this—!"

"You'll do what?" the man snapped. "There be no way for you to get up here, except by that door in the wall to what I alone got the key! So get!"

Drew yanked on the door, but it was locked. He uttered a string of curses at the man and turned his simmering gaze away from him.

A few wounded bodies littered the dusty ground.

Wesley cut into a back street between two buildings. He leaned against the side of a building and sunk into a slouch. Drew knelt beside him. Both were panting.

Wesley gripped his stomach as he felt a heave rising in his throat. Hot tears stung his eyes. He leaned over and wretched.

"That was my dream," he said hoarsely.

Drew looked up at him, blood running down the side of his face where he had been hit.

"The dream I had about Anna being in trouble…" he shook his head. "We couldn't get to her."

As Drew listened, his jaw tightened. His lip quivered.

Wesley grabbed a fistful of dirt and gave a loud, frustrated cry. Slamming his fist to the ground, releasing the dirt, he let his tears spill over. His shoulders shook as he bent his head over his arms.

After a long moment, he said, "I have to go after her."

Drew looked up.

"I don't know how, but I have to."

Drew nodded. "I know." He paused. "What about the Forsvárerne?"

Wesley locked eyes with him. "My first duty is to my family."

Drew nodded again. "Me too."

Wesley swallowed and fresh tears poured forth. He nodded.

Drew stood and extended his hand, helping Wesley to his feet. He wrapped Wesley in a firm hug. "We'll get her back. I swear it."

PART 2

30
THE TRACKER

Anna clung to her knees as the wagon jerked her body over the rocky roads outside of Dradoc. The cart that caged her was dark, completely boarded up except for a few shafts of light that escaped through the iron bar window on the door.

She was alone in the wooden cart.

Her body quivered as sobs rose in her throat. When the cart lurched over a rock, she reached out a hand to steady herself. The wooden boards left a splinter in her palm.

All she wanted was to be held by someone she loved. She longed for her father's warm embrace or her mother's loving touch. She wanted Wesley's shoulder to cry on, or Drew's strong grip to comfort her.

Instead, she was separated from everyone she held dear. She had no idea where her parents were, and now Wesley and Drew were trapped inside Dradoc, unable to reach her.

As soon as the soldier had shoved her into the wagon and closed the door, she had grasped the iron bars, her face pressed against the window. She saw Wesley and Drew running after the wagon, but then the gates shut, blocking them...leaving Anna utterly alone.

The thought terrified her and more tears flooded. Her chest heaved as she cried. Thoughts of what the guards—especially those who would frequent a town like Dradoc—would do to her made her shudder with fear.

"Jesus," she wept. "Help me." She held her shoulders in her hands. "Father, I can't do this. Please don't let them…" her breath came in short gasps. "Oh, help me, God." She fell onto her side, her whole body shaking with sobs. "Please…please."

Anna awoke as the wagon reeled to a stop. She opened her eyes and saw that it was night. She pushed herself into a sitting position and gave a quiet moan. Her body ached from sleeping on the wooden boards. *"I wonder what time it is."*

She had lost her watch shortly after Wesley's birthday party. Was it just after sunset, or had they been riding much longer than that?

She heard a rustling of movement outside the wagon. People were walking around. Footsteps neared her wagon, and her heartbeat quickened. Fear slithered tendrils around her middle.

"Breathe." She inhaled. *"Give me courage."*

She gathered herself into a ball into the far corner of the wagon. A shadow passed in front of the night sky that peered through her small window. A knight threw something between the bars, startling her. Then the shadow disappeared.

Cautiously, she crawled to the door and looked at what lay on the floor. A lump of hard bread. Something close to relief touched her.

Hesitantly, she picked up the food and dusted it off. Her stomach growled with hunger, but she had trouble forcing herself to eat the provided food. She bit down on the bread. It crunched between her teeth. Anna picked up her satchel that she had been wearing on her back.

Inside, she had packed food and a change of clothes for their journey. She also had her cask of water with her. She was about to eat the meat instead of the stale bread, but thought better of it.

"I may need that for later." She forced herself to eat the food provided, and took two swallows of water to go with it. *"Africans walk miles to get fresh water every day. I can make this cask last."*

When she finished her meal, she leaned against the wagon wall. They had started riding again.

Her eyes were puffy from all of her crying. When she thought about her situation, she wanted to cry some more. Her head hurt. She sniffled, trying to stop her tears.

Taking deep breaths, she told herself. *"I need to think. I need to be calm."*

She sat quietly for a few moments. Scenes from earlier that day flashed through her mind. She saw the prisoners, who had been sold as slaves, standing in line. She saw the boy with the smudged red hair. She remembered his expression as he was whipped, and then the gratitude in his eyes when she cut his bonds.

Anna swallowed, thinking about it. "I exchanged my freedom for his."

Suddenly, she was angry. Regret hissed in her ear.

"I hate being here! I hate this wagon! I hate—" She cried harder as she realized the thoughts going through her head.

"I'm sorry," she whispered. "I'm sorry." She wiped her sleeve across her face and stared despondently into the blackness. "But why did the price of his freedom have to be so great?"

Then, quietly, the words came to her, *"The price of your freedom was great."*

Anna looked up. Tears flowed. Not from self-pity, but from empathy. She saw Him. And grateful awe filled her.

She squared her shoulders. *"You have granted that we suffer with You."* Biting her lip, she added, *"Just please help me bear it."*

***

Once Wesley and Drew had decided what they wanted to do, they agreed to go to Mr. Lampwick for advice on how to do it.

When they explained to Mr. Lampwick what had happened, he was distraught.

The old man sank into a chair by the fireplace and rubbed his wrinkled brow. "This is grievous." He looked up and met the boys' gaze. "I am so sorry. I should have seen you to the gate. I should have…" his voice trailed off to unintelligible words.

Wesley swallowed the lump in his throat, unable to speak. He had difficulty recounting the horrendous events. Now, seeing Mr. Lampwick's tears, made him want to cry all over again. He resisted the urge, steeling himself instead.

"We're going after her," Drew said, his voice hard and flat. "Do you have any idea where they would have gone with a group of prisoners?"

"Most likely the very place you intend to go: Kurgon Fort." He sighed. "But we have no way of knowing for sure."

"And if they don't go there?" asked Drew. "How can we track them?" He glanced at Wesley and back at Mr. Lampwick. "Neither of us knows the land very well."

Mr. Lampwick leaned back in his chair and rubbed his chin. "There might be someone who could help you with that."

He paused, deep in thought.

"Mr. Lampwick, we don't have much time," Wesley said.

"His name is Faulburn. He lives on the west side of town. He is a tracker by trade."

Drew tipped his head. "What do you mean by 'tracker'?"

"He tracks animals mostly, but I am sure he could track a band of Racin Dor knights with wagons and horses."

"You think he'll help us?" Drew asked.

Mr. Lampwick pursed his lips. "He is no friend of Racin Dor, that much I know. But whether he will agree to help you, I cannot say. At nightfall, go to his house and speak to him; you two should not be on the streets during the day. If he agrees to help you, the three of you come back here and leave the city through my house. My bedroom window opens directly through the city wall. You should not leave by the gate. There may be people who recognize you from this morning."

Drew wet his lips and looked at Wesley.

Wesley nodded.

"For now," said Mr. Lampwick, "You should sleep. You could be traveling all night long."

Wesley knew he wouldn't be able to sleep.

He met Mr. Lampwick's eyes. "Do you trust this Faulburn?"

Mr. Lampwick hesitated. "I do not know him well, but I believe him to be honorable. He will not betray you to the enemy. He paused. "I believe it is your best interest to seek his help…it may be your only hope of rescuing Anna."

***

When Mr. Lampwick woke Wesley and Drew, it was dark outside. He gave them directions to Faulburn's house and sent them on their way.

They took the back roads.

A cat darted out in front of them, making Wesley jump.

"Here it is," said Drew after several minutes of walking. One of the homes had a blank sign in front of it. Mr. Lampwick had informed them that this was Faulburn's home.

Wesley didn't like the look of it. The shutters on the windows were cracked and collecting cobwebs. The floorboards on the porch were in disrepair.

Drew stepped onto the porch and knocked on the door. There was no answer. He moved to the window and peered in.

Wesley followed him. Nothing inside could be seen in the darkness.

Wesley's shoulders tensed. There was a noise behind them. He glanced at Drew who returned his cautious look. He had heard it too.

Wesley turned around and froze. A sword tip held his chin. Wesley's eyes followed the length of the blade until he was looking into the face of its carrier.

The night cast shadows on dark eyes and dark hair. He was dressed in black.

"Who are you?" the man demanded in a low voice.

Drew moved a hand to his hilt.

"Do not so much as move one muscle or your friend will be dead," the man ordered without even looking at Drew.

Drew lowered his hand but lifted his chin.

Wesley put his hands up in surrender. "I'm Wesley. This is Drew...Are you Faulburn?"

"How do you know that name?"

"By Mr. Lampwick, who sent us to you."

"And why would he do that?" The man kept his sword steady at Wesley's neck.

"Because we need your help," Wesley met the man's eyes. "Because we need the help of a tracker....for an urgent task."

The man took a step back and lowered his sword. "We will speak inside."

Faulburn was first to go in his house and waited for the boys to follow him. They entered tentatively.

He locked the door behind them and lit a tall candle. From the one candle, he lit more until the small room flickered with dim light.

Wesley looked around. Animal skins hung on the walls and tables. On one wall hung different metal contraptions and numerous weapons. Instantly, Wesley realized that if they could trust this man, he could be an invaluable help to them.

If they could trust him, however, was an entirely different matter.

Faulburn turned to them and stood with his arms crossed over his chest. In the better light they could see that he was no older than twenty-five, if that. His eyes were dark and watched them closely. Wesley was sure that not much escaped this man's attention.

"So what is this task that Mr. Lampwick thinks I can be of aid to you?" Faulburn's eyes narrowed. "And what makes you think that I will want to do it?"

"My sister was taken by knights from Racin Dor. A band of about thirty of them, with wagons of prisoners, left the city before noon...possibly headed for Kurgon Fort...it's a secret base of Ratacin's, several days journey from here...They took her with them. We're going after her."

Faulburn lifted his chin. "Then you are the ones who confronted the Ratacin's knights today. You made quite an upset in the town. People are talking about two young men who challenged the knights. The guards are looking for you."

"We were protecting Anna," Drew defended.

"But not protecting her enough."

The remark stung, and neither boy made a reply.

"Tell me," said Faulburn, "how do two…" he eyed them, "boys…get caught in a fight with Ratacin's trained knights and lose their sister in the process?"

Drew glanced at Wesley, bristling by the look of his twitching jaw. He recounted the story for him.

Hearing the events retold made Wesley's stomach revolt.

Faulburn listened quietly, and remarked when Drew had finished, "It was rather daring of you to take on all of those knights by yourselves." He eyed them challengingly.

Drew's jaw squared.

"It is a wonder you were not killed."

Wesley looked up and met the man's gaze.

Faulburn stared at them and spoke quietly, "I think there is more to this story than you are telling me."

Wesley didn't respond.

"That you were able to hold your own against Ratacin's men says something of your ability to fight," Faulburn answered. "You have been trained. My question is by whom?"

"By knights of Aloehan," Drew clipped. "We know how to fight."

Wesley studied Faulburn to gauge his reaction. Whatever the man was thinking, he didn't show it. His face was impassive.

"And now you seek my skills of tracking to hunt this band of knights who has your sister," he said flatly.

"Yes," said Wesley. "Will you help us?"

Faulburn looked at Wesley and was quiet for a moment.

"Aye," he said finally. "I will help you."

Relief flooded Wesley. They had just gotten an ally. At least he hoped so.

31
IN PURSUIT

After several hours of monotonous riding, Anna felt the wagon roll to a stop. She guessed that it was before midnight. Movement outside the wagon and dimly flickering lights told her that the knights were setting up camp here.

She tried to open the door, but it was firmly locked. Sitting back down with a sigh, she tried to fluff her bag into a pillow and make herself comfortable.

It was little use.

She stood up to pace. "I should keep my mobility. Keep up my strength."

As Anna tread the narrow confines of the wagon, she voiced prayers, first for herself, then for her parents, then for Wesley and Drew.

Raucous laughter sounded from somewhere outside.

She stiffened.

Swallowing, she kept pacing. Slowly, Anna recalled scripture passages that she had memorized as a child. She catalogued Bible stories, remembering characters that faced giants, approached kings unbidden, and faced fiery furnaces. *"Please…let me have their courage."*

***

Wesley looked up at the stars in the night sky forming their own unique constellations.

The only sound to be heard was his breathing and the soft footsteps of Drew, Faulburn, and himself.

He and Drew had watched as Faulburn quickly packed supplies from his home for their journey.

He had sheathed several knives to his belt, alongside the sword and dagger that already hung at his waist. He packed a bow and a quiver full of arrows.

He had tossed knives to Wesley and Drew and shown them how to conceal them under their clothes.

Then, the three young men had tread swiftly to Mr. Lampwick's house and escaped the city through his window.

"I will keep you in my prayers," Mr. Lampwick had told them. He had looked directly at Wesley and said, "Do not give up hope."

Wesley now stared straight ahead as the three figures walked in the darkness outside the city walls. They traveled by the light of the stars and moon on the dusty terrain.

Faulburn led them to the road that skirted the north side of Dradoc. "This fort you speak of—Kurgon Fort—I have seen it before on one of my hunting trips, though I did not know its name until now. If the knights were headed there, they would have taken this road."

When they reached the road, Faulburn searched the ground for wagon tracks. He knelt down, brushing the dirt with his hand. "They came this way...not ten hours ago."

"Then all we have to do is follow this road, right?" Drew said.

Faulburn stood. "We will make for Kurgon Fort. If we are fortunate, we will catch them before they reach the stronghold. But we will not take the main road. It is too well traveled and there could be those who would recognize you. By now there is a warrant for your arrest as the ones who committed treason against his lord's men."

"Treason?" Drew scoffed.

"Dradoc was officially aligned with Ratacin two days ago. A deed challenging Ratacin's authority is considered a crime."

Wesley frowned, still considering their predicament of which path to take. "The back roads will take longer. We should get to the fort as quickly as possible."

Faulburn was not going to be argued with. "We keep to the woods."

Wesley wasn't convinced and stood planted where he was. "No."

"C'mon, Wes," Drew urged, "We better get going."

"You don't understand how important this is!" Wesley blurted.

Faulburn turned and stared at him. "I know the gravity of the task," he spoke lowly, "but I also know things about Ratacin's knights that you don't. We will travel by way of the Grayback Mountains."

Drew gave Wesley a concerned look. "Come on, Wes. It'll be all right...I care about her too," he added quietly.

"Not like I do," Wesley spoke firmly. "She's my sister. You have no idea what it's like to lose your family."

"Oh right. Because I've always had a big happy family to live with. Wes, remember I don't have my parents either." Drew was getting annoyed. "I understand."

"No you don't!" Wesley raised his voice. "You never knew your parents. Don't tell me you understand."

Drew stared at Wesley, his brows knit tightly together. "You think I don't care about Anna?" he challenged. "You think I don't care about your parents? Because I'm the jerk that swore to you I'd help you find your parents and I swore to you I'll help you get Anna back!" He stepped closer. "Don't tell me I don't understand." With a disgusted look, he spun on his heel and started walking away.

"If it weren't for you, Anna would still be with us."

Drew stopped. He turned around slowly. "What did you say?"

"You heard me," Wesley muttered. "If you hadn't challenged that knight, she never would have been captured. Stupid, reckless—"

"What?" Drew walked back to Wesley.

Wesley stared at him. "We could have stopped her. Talked to them. But you had to go and attack him."

"At least Anna had some guts to do something. You weren't gonna do a thing." He shoved Wesley, causing him to stumble backwards.

"Guts? So when those knights do what they want with her, you're gonna say it's okay because she had guts?"

"They're not going to because we're going to get her back!"

"What if we don't?" Wesley yelled back. "Not everything turns out the way we want!"

"No," Drew answered lowly. He stepped closer and stared him in the eye. "We don't give up." Defiance burned in his gaze. "No." He turned away.

Wesley stared after him, his jaw tight. What if Drew was wrong? What if they were too late?

Faulburn stood looking on, arms crossed over his chest. "Are you two finished?"

He stared at each boy with hard eyes.

Neither one answered.

"We have wasted enough time. Let us be on our way." He turned and led them away from the main road.

Drew and Wesley did not protest but followed him silently.

The moon waned in the sky as the three travelers came to a stop. Faulburn had led the boys through the greater part of the night, trekking over rocky terrain. Now it was a few hours before dawn.

Most of the night, they climbed over or around boulders. Now they stood at the foothills of towering mountains. The short shrubbery that had accompanied their path yielded to taller trees that grew at the base of the mountain range, providing better shelter.

They found a nook in the rocks that formed a natural shelter. Faulburn threw down his pack. "We sleep here."

"I'll be back," Wesley mumbled.

Drew glanced up but didn't say anything.

Wesley wandered away from the campsite. He walked farther than what Faulburn probably would have wanted, but at the moment, he didn't care. He was suffocating from the tension of their company, or the bottled up thoughts in his head.

Angry, incoherent thoughts whirlpooled through his mind as he ran through the woods, brushing aside branches and tripping over fallen logs.

He came to a small clearing and ripped a twig off a branch, snapping it in his palm and squeezing it until it drew blood.

He breathed hard, more from anger than exertion.

"How could You do this?" Wesley shouted at the sky. "Why?" he dropped the twig, picked up a stone and threw it at a tree. It startled a bird that fluttered away.

"Was it not enough to take my parents?" he screamed. "You had to take my sister too? What kind of sick cosmic plan is this? Who *are* You?"

His lip trembled. His voice broke as he whispered, "I hate You."

Wesley was shoved to his knees as the earth vaulted beneath him. He looked for something to grab onto, barely having the coherence to wonder what was causing this earthquake.

A roar of thunder roared overhead. The sky was stormy, and a wind currant ripped through his clothes. It intensified and through he tried to move, he was pinned in place.

The wall that he had built with so many stones of resentment crumbled like brittle clay. He trembled at the Presence.

"Will you question Me?" the voice came to his spirit.

Wesley looked for words to answer and found none.

"Who are you to demand from Me?"

All he could do was stare at the earth as pieces of dirt and pebbles whipped around him in the windstorm.

"Would you command the universe?"

Utter fear gripped him. It overwhelmed him.

The paralyzing wind broke, and he crumbled, bringing his hands up to his tears.

"I can't do this," Wesley wept. All his strength, all his effort, all his anger failed him.

"Please help me." More sobs. "I give in. I can't fight You."

The chill became warmth around him and strong arms surrounded him, lifting him to his feet.

Wesley turned around but saw no one. He looked up and saw the first light of dawn piercing through the trees, shinning directly on his face with more warmth and comfort than he would have thought possible.

"Trust Me."

Wesley cried, still feeling the ache of loss. "You've taken everything from me."

"Not everything."

Wesley knew what He meant. He had taken everything. Everything but Himself. And it was right where He wanted Wesley. If the thought had come to him before the storm, Wesley would have resented Him even more, but now he could feel only gratitude.

And then he knew, he *knew*, He was doing this for his good.

The warmth got warmer, like a father's proud smile.

Wesley searched for the fear and anger that he had carried inside him and was surprised they were nowhere to be found.

"Trust Me."

Wesley inhaled a long, full breath. Then, not with resignation, but with peace and resolve, said, "You win."

When Wesley walked back to the cave, Drew was already asleep. Faulburn was shifting on the cave floor. Neither one of them seemed to have noticed the earthquake.

Wesley didn't mention it. He curled up and let rest's fingers close his weary eyelids.

***

Wesley woke to the bright light of mid-day. He squinted and turned over, facing the back of the rock crevice. He turned over again and saw that Drew was still asleep. Wesley sat up and surveyed the area.

Faulburn was gone.

Wesley noticed Faulburn's bag was still leaned against the side of the rock and felt a measure of relief.

He rolled up his mat and tied it in place. Footsteps were in the entranceway.

A figure formed a silhouette against the daylight. Faulburn stepped closer and dropped something on the ground.

Wesley looked up at him.

"Breakfast."

Wesley glanced at the dead rabbit on the stone floor.

Faulburn woke Drew and sent him to collect firewood to cook the meat. Faulburn drew a knife and started skinning the dead animal.

Drew wordlessly left the cave. Wesley's forehead creased when he thought of their argument. He was still mad at Drew. He was mad at their situation. *"We have to get to Anna as soon as possible."*

He recalled the words he had spat at his best friend. He had blatantly accused him of Anna's capture. He knew it wasn't fair. Sighing, he stood to follow him.

He spotted Drew in the distance among the trees, piling dry sticks onto his arms. Wesley picked up a stick and added it to Drew's pile.

"I'm sorry about what I said last night."

Drew made no reply, but kept walking.

Wesley kept in step. "I was wrong. I know you care about my parents…and I know you care about Anna."

Drew stopped and looked at him.

Wesley cringed, remembering the other hurtful words he had spoken to his friend. "And it wasn't your fault she was captured. In fact, I probably would have been too, had you not been there…I'm sorry Drew."

Drew looked away. "It's okay," he mumbled.

Glad to be done with his apology, Wesley was about to turn back, when another thought struck him. Grunting, he said, "No…it's not okay. See…I shouldn't have acted like that…That's not how a follower of Christ is supposed to act. You were right; I was panicking…losing hope."

Drew shrugged, still wearing a frown. "It's all right." He kept walking for a moment, but then stopped and turned to face Wesley. "You once told me when I was upset about my parents that for those who love God…"

"all things work together for good, for those who are called according to his purpose," Wesley finished. He marveled that Drew had remembered that.

"Yeah," Drew nodded. "You believe that?"

Wesley stared at Drew for a moment. "Yeah. I do."

Drew squinted. "How can you? I mean, you have no idea where your parents are. And now Anna's been captured. You think that's God working for your good?"

"Drew," Wesley rubbed the back of his neck, "I don't understand it all. But I think that 'good' doesn't always mean easy. But it's good because it's God's will…and He knows what's best." The words felt strange coming out of his mouth.

Drew grunted. "That's a heck of a lot of trust."

"Trust I don't always have," Wesley admitted. He was silent for a moment before adding, "But I think He's helping me."

Drew didn't make much of a response. "We need to get this firewood."

32
QUESTIONS

After Wesley, Drew and Faulburn ate the cooked rabbit, they set out on the trail again with Faulburn in the lead.

Wesley looked up at the tree-covered mountains that ascended far into the sky. They possessed majestic beauty that he knew Anna would have appreciated. Thinking of her caused his stomach to knot in sickness and frustration.

Earlier that morning, as he was packing his things, he had seen the candle that Anna had given him for his birthday in his pack. It was a painful reminder. He took a deep breath and turned his thoughts toward prayer. He prayed silently as they traveled quickly and quietly over the hilly ground.

But something else was eating at Wesley's mind. He kept thinking how unusual it was that Faulburn so swiftly agreed to help them and leave his work. Wesley didn't believe that it was out of sheer kindness. After they had traveled in silence for several hours, Wesley decided to mention it.

"Mr. Lampwick said you hate Ratacin's knights," he commented to Faulburn.

Faulburn glanced at him. "As should anyone who has any sense of justice."

Wesley agreed, but felt like there was more to Faulburn's story. "Have you encountered their injustice?"

Faulburn stopped walking and faced Wesley. Drew watched.

"Why do you need to know?" Faulburn demanded in his quiet, low voice.

"You joined us on our quest," said Wesley, "which involves my sister. I need to know how committed you are to it."

Faulburn stared at him for a moment without speaking. Then, still wearing his blank expression, he replied, "I have."

Wesley wanted specifics, but respected Faulburn's privacy.

Faulburn turned ahead and resumed walking.

"Then we're both wanting the same thing," Drew said.

Faulburn gave him a half glance.

"We both want revenge on Ratacin's knights."

Faulburn dipped his head in a nod. "Agreed."

Wesley frowned. *That's not what we want...is it?"* He questioned himself, and realized that part of him did. *"No,"* he told himself firmly. *"I'm not after revenge. I just want my sister back...and then we can rescue the Forsvárerne."*

Wesley's thoughts were interrupted by Faulburn speaking.

"I have a few questions for you two, as well."

Wesley and Drew listened.

"What would two boys who have received training from the Citadel...but who wear no armor...be doing in a city like Dradoc?"

"We're not knights," Wesley admitted. "Just friends with the people there."

"You still have not answered my question."

Wesley and Drew exchanged glances.

"That's our business," Drew answered.

Faulburn cast a lingering glance at Drew and Wesley, but did not ask any more questions.

***

A soft thud sounded as a knight tossed food through the window bars of Anna's wagon. She turned her head at the sound and ran up to the door, grasping the iron bars.

"Wait!" she cried, trying to beckon the man's attention. Through the bars she saw another wagon behind hers and numerous knights walking around. They had stopped for the midday meal. She could see that trees rather than barren hills now surrounded the road they were on.

The soldier who had fed her turned back to her with an annoyed expression on his face.

"Please…" Anna faltered, "will you tell me where you are taking us?"

"Where we keep our prisoners," he spat. "Kurgon Fort…a lovely place," he said with a smirk. He turned and walked back to where the other soldiers were congregating for their meal.

Anna stared out her window, not releasing her grip on the bars. *"Kurgon Fort,"* she repeated to herself. *"Where the Forsvárerne is."* She inhaled slowly, allowing herself to hope. *"If that's where they're taking me, then Wesley and Drew will be able to find me…and we can save the Forsvárerne."*

Anna reviewed in her mind the people for whom they were to look. An elf maiden by the name of Hwen, a dwarf called Glenge, and a man named Hadrian.

Soon she felt the lurch of the wagon and knew they had resumed their travel. She sat down and leaned against the wagon wall as the cart rolled over the bumpy terrain.

After several hours of riding, Anna noticed the lighting in the wagon grow dimmer. It was dusk. She heard shouting outside the wagon among the soldiers but could not make out their words.

Anna felt a bump in the ride and the sound of the wagon trekking on dirt roads changed to that of a hollow grinding noise. She stood to look out the window.

Although the narrow square only afforded a view from the back of the wagon, she saw that they were crossing a wooden bridge. Murky water flanked both sides of the overpass that spanned away from the dirt road they had been taking.

A grating noise erupted from somewhere ahead of the wagons.

"Keep the gate open!" a voice bellowed. "We've more prisoners for his highness."

Anna's heartbeat quickened.

They had reached Kurgon Fort.

She stared out the window as the wagon carried her into the fort. The clatter of the wagon wheels on wood yielded to the clop of wood on stone. From her small view, she saw huge, iron doors being drawn shut, causing the light to wane until she was enveloped in darkness.

The air was thicker inside the building, and its dampness clung to her skin.

She could distantly hear more armored knights clanking through the fortress and speaking to the soldiers who had just arrived with the wagons.

Anna swallowed. "Lord," she whispered. "Give me the strength to endure whatever lies ahead."

33
THREAT FROM THE SKIES

Wesley brushed the away sweat from his brow with his sleeve. Even though the night air was cool, their continuous movement had created a layer of sweat over his whole body.

Since rising, they had lapsed between a brisk walk and a jog over the mountainside in pursuit of the Racin Dor knights. They stopped only for brief intervals.

"How soon until we can rejoin the main road?" Wesley asked Faulburn.

"Soon."

Wesley desperately hoped that they were not too late. Beside him, he could hear Drew breathing hard as well. He glanced at him and saw beads of sweat running down his face. His friend wore a frown.

"Do you hear that?" he asked.

Faulburn stopped and listened in the darkness. Wesley did the same. The wind howled, causing the trees to ripple above them.

Wesley looked at Faulburn, whose expression had suddenly turned darker. Wesley sensed his concern and then heard the noise as well.

A howl, almost like a screeching, sounded somewhere in the distance.

"What is that?" asked Drew.

"Vuls," Faulburn answered shortly. "Come," he said resuming a quick stride. "Let us be on our way."

"Wait," Drew said, jogging to catch up with him. "Where? Where are the vuls?"

"They fly by night. By their howl they sound yet far off. But they are fast flyers. They will be over us within the hour."

Wesley's pulse quickened. He recalled their meeting with a vul at the Citadel. Although he hadn't seen the creature fly or heard him scream, he saw enough to be wary of it. And Adius had said they were good fighters.

Wesley instinctively moved his hand to the hilt of his sword. He wanted to be ready for an attack.

They continued moving through the woods, weaving in and out of branches and underbrush.

Then they heard it.

A piercing scream stabbed the silent night. The scream was followed by another, and another, and then the sound of beating wings.

Faulburn stilled and lifted his chin. "They are above us."

Drew reached for his sword.

"You cannot fight them with swords," said Faulburn. "Can you use a bow?"

Both boys nodded.

"Draw them, but do not fire unless fired upon." He scanned their surroundings and promptly led them to a better covering of brushwood and crouched under it.

"They'll never see us down here," Drew wagered. "Not in the dark."

"They have an acute sense of smell," the tracker warned.

Wesley cast him an apprehensive glance. He remained quiet and peered through the branches skyward. He could feel his heart beating in his chest. Then his jaw tightened.

Silhouettes of winged creatures appeared in front of the moon. There were at least thirty of them.

A shrill scream pierced the silence.

Wesley winced and covered his ears.

Faulburn's jaw squared, but his face remained expressionless. "They've caught our scent."

The vuls flew in a large circle, hovering the area. Some swooped lower, sniffing the ground below them.

Wesley saw that Faulburn had strung his bow and now aimed at the sky.

"Prepare to fire upon my signal," he ordered.

"But you said not—," Wesley objected.

"If we wait for them to fire on us, it will be too late. They know we are near but they do not know our exact location. Now do as I say."

Wesley and Drew obeyed and waited with their bows taut.

"As soon as we fire, they will know where we are," said Faulburn, "so restring your bow as quickly as you can." He inhaled, "Ready...fire!"

All three men let their arrows soar.

A thud was followed by shrill screams and a crashing sound as two vuls were shot from the sky and tumbled into the forest below.

Wesley and Faulburn had hit their mark.

The other vuls swiveled in the air toward the source of their menace and dove lower. Darts showered from the sky and spiked into the earth around the boys.

Wesley, Drew, and Faulburn continued to fire their arrows as they dodged the oncoming weapons. Just as they were doing so, a rustle in the bushes near them commanded Faulburn's attention.

"They've landed!" he shouted. "Run!"

Wesley hardly had time to look over his shoulder as they darted from their position and ducked by a thorn bush. He saw the form of a six-foot vul treading through the bushes where they had just been.

The creature was bare-chested and displayed rippling, sinewy muscles. Oily dark hair hung from its bony head, and the creature's black eyes locked with Wesley's.

Wesley reached behind him and felt the feather of an arrow. The vul did the same.

They each laced their string and pulled it taut.

The vul released his grip a second before Wesley, sending an arrow soaring toward his shoulder.

Wesley ducked and straightened and released his cord. The arrow met the vul below his head and the creature fell forward, dead.

After firing another arrow, Wesley felt Faulburn shove him with a shout. "Move!" Wesley turned his head and saw an arrow pierce the ground where he had been standing.

He looked at Faulburn and nodded. "Thanks."

The tracker nodded and continued fighting.

Wesley heard Faulburn grunt and saw him wince in pain. He looked to him in question.

"Keep fighting!" Faulburn ordered. He followed his own command, silently and swiftly eliminating creatures from the sky. Soon, the ones that remained saw their loss and batted their wings in retreat.

Drew turned in a pant from a vul he had felled with his sword and saw Faulburn with a hand to his upper arm. "You all right?"

"An arrow grazed my arm, but I am fine. Thankfully, it was not one of their poison-darts." He looked at the boys and nodded with approval. "Well done. You know how to fight."

"You're not so bad yourself," Drew returned. He smiled. He and Wesley both knew it was good they had this man with them. He was a deadly weapon against their enemies.

Wesley looked at Faulburn. "On to the main road?"

Faulburn nodded. "On to the main road."

34
A TASTE OF FORSVÁRERNE

Anna stumbled as a guard shoved her forward. The moment she had been let out of the wagon, a soldier had bound her hands and roughly pushed her towards a passageway.

She observed the scene around her, trying to memorize the details that could prove to be important later. They were inside a dimly lit stone fortress. Torches hung on the walls, providing minimal light. The wagons were unloaded inside a large hall with numerous corridors branching from it.

A guard led Anna down one of these passageways. She glimpsed other prisoners being led by guards and recognized them as some of the ones in Dradoc.

The soldier leading her held her in a firm grip, with one hand on the back of her head and the other on her hands that were tied behind her back.

He stopped, causing her lurch backwards slightly.

He asked a superior soldier where to put her, and the other man grunted, "Ah with the other female. Top tower."

The guard holding Anna jerked her towards a wooden door and forced her to climb several flights of stone stairs. They passed several doors until they reached the top of the staircase where a wooden door stood before them.

The guard kicked it open and pushed her forward. She grunted in pain, and he swore at her. Anna bit down on her lip, trying to keep herself from crying.

In the room were cells with iron-barred doors. Walls made of iron bars or stone separated the cells.

Anna looked at the cells, afraid of what she might see. Everything in her revolted at the thought of being locked away up here. She thought she was going to be sick. *"Oh Lord, help,"* she prayed desperately.

To her surprise, the cells were nearly empty. She could see one figure curled against a wall in one cell, but that was all. There was either no one else in this tower, or they were behind the stone walls in cells farther down the isle.

The guard pushed Anna to the cell next to the one with the person in it. Only a row of iron bars separated the two prison chambers. He untied her ropes and shoved her into it, swinging the gate shut with a loud clang.

Anna stood where she was, casting only her eyes around the room. A tear spilled over, and a sob heaved within her. She nearly let herself cry but remembered the person in the next cell. Slowly, she turned her head.

A small person garbed in earthy colors of green and grey was huddled in the far corner of the cell. It was a woman, but not like any woman Anna had ever seen.

She sat cross-legged and had every appearance of being a young lady except for her hair. It was white, but she wasn't old. Her green almond shaped eyes were nearly hidden by her bangs as she wordlessly watched Anna.

She had a small face and petite features. Then Anna noticed her ears. Peaking slightly from behind her hair, Anna saw the defined point that identified one race, the race of elves.

"Hwen."

Anna's chin trembled on the brink of tears. Overwhelmed by the plight of her own situation and the situation of the woman before her, who had endured months of this treatment, Anna could bear it no longer.

Tears flowed freely as sobs escaped her. She put a hand to her mouth and cried.

The elf stood, her movements fluid and graceful despite her dangerously thin frame. Wordlessly, she extended a hand through the iron bars. Anna took it and stood there holding it for a moment.

When Anna regained her composure, she released the elf's small hand and sniffled. "I'm sorry."

The woman smiled softly. She was shorter than Anna. "You needn't be. The strongholds of Ratacin are places of darkness. They cause heartache for many."

Anna nodded.

"What is your name?"

"Anna," she replied and met the elf's gaze. "And you're Hwen."

***

Wesley watched as Faulburn let the dirt sift through his fingers and fall back in place on the road. The tracker's jaw tightened. Standing, he faced Wesley and Drew.

"They have passed this way. The wagon tracks are in the dirt."

Drew sighed. "So we're too late?"

"The fight with the vuls delayed us," Faulburn responded.

Wesley crossed his arms as a quiet sigh escaped through his nostrils. His eyelids felt heavy, his body ached, and now this. But with resolve, he raised his head. "To Kurgon Fort, then."

Faulburn nodded. "We will make camp here tonight—in the woods. We leave in the morning." He eyed the boys. "Kurgon Fort is well-fortified. Rescuing her will not be an easy task... It will be very difficult."

"Wouldn't matter if it were an impossible task," Drew shrugged. "We'll get it done."

***

The elf's eyes widened at Anna's knowledge of her name. "Have we met?"

"No." Anna glanced around the room. "Is it safe to talk here?"

"Yes," said Hwen. "The only others here are my two companions in the cell yonder," she nodded over her shoulder to the stone wall on the other side of her cell. "And guards come occasionally."

Anna was relieved that there would not be guards often.

"I was sent, along with two others, by a council at Revowen, including King Elderair, Princess Elaswén, and Sir Kaden from Aloehan." Anna saw Hwen's eyes widen.

She continued, "We were in Dradoc on our way here to rescue you, along with your companions, Hadrian and Glenge." Anna lowered her head. "We were separated, and I was captured." Lifting her gaze, she proceeded, "But if I know Wesley and Drew, they're on their way right now to rescue me."

Hwen was quiet for a moment, absorbing all that Anna said. Finally, she asked, "Wesley and Drew are your companions?"

Anna nodded. "Wesley is my brother and Drew is our friend...I'm sorry things didn't turn out how we wanted them too."

Hwen looked at her with a wry smile. "We did not believe anyone was coming to rescue us. We are grateful that you took that risk," she rapped on the stone wall, "aren't we, Glenge?"

Someone cleared his throat. "It is not as if we needed anyone to rescue us!" a deep voice gurgled.

Hwen rolled her eyes. "You will have to excuse Glenge; he eve-drops...and is rude."

The dwarf on the other side of the wall harrumphed.

For the first time in what felt like a long time, Anna smiled.

Hwen smiled also. "You have met Glenge, now meet Hadrian. Hadrian, say hello," Hwen called an order toward the stone wall.

"Hello, my lady," came a lighter-pitched male's voice. "Welcome to our temporary abode."

Hwen sat back down, cross-legged.

Anna did the same. She noted once again how small the elf was. She figured that the woman was already petite, but she wondered if the months in prison had carved her even thinner.

"So Anna," the elf began, "Tell me about things in Revowen. Is all well?"

The two conversed for a while about Revowen and Aloehan. Their conversation was light and pleasurable, sprinkled with comments from the males sitting in the next cell.

"You know, you don't look how I imagined you," Anna confessed.

Hwen smiled. "That is probably because you have only seen the Ellwood elves. Miershire elves are smaller framed—nimbler in climbing and running...perfect for warfare from the treetops," she winked.

Anna cast her a quizzical stare, but Hwen merely smiled.

"Perhaps you will have chance to visit my city."

Anna smiled. "I hope I do."

***

Drew added another stick to the campfire that he and Wesley had just made. Faulburn stood a ways off, skinning his most recent catch.

"When are we gonna tell him, Wes?" Drew asked.

Wesley plopped down beside Drew and clasped his arms around his knees. He shook his head. "I don't know."

"You know he suspects something," Drew commented.

Wesley nodded. "Yeah, I figured that."

"So," Drew prodded, "do you trust him?"

"He saved my life—I don't distrust him." Wesley paused. "Still, King Elderair told us not to tell anyone about our quest...I don't like going against his orders."

"He told us not to tell unless we have to," Drew corrected.

Wesley looked at Drew. "You think we have to?"

Drew shrugged. "We're gonna have to tell him sooner or later."

35
ANSWERS

As they ate their dinner, Wesley wished for the warmth of a campfire, but they couldn't risk the light of a flame.

The air had grown cooler, not only from the cover of night, but the change in season. He had noticed during their long intervals of walking that the trees around them had exchanged their velvety green for warmer shades of gold and orange. Camnoel was in her autumn.

"I wonder what season it is back home," he mused as he absently fingered the cross necklace Drew had given him.

Thoughts of home sent a wave of longing over him. He remembered the days when his parents, Anna, and himself would sit around the table and eat meals together. He wondered if he would ever get to experience that again.

"Kurgon Fort will be difficult to penetrate."

Wesley stirred from his daydreaming to listen to what Faulburn was saying.

"Once we get closer," the trakcer continued, "we will plan our rescue and execute it as quickly as possible. There must be no lingering there once we find your sister." He watched them closely when he said this, as if searching them.

Wesley looked back at Faulburn, but said nothing. Inwardly he felt the tracker's suspicions of them. It was as if he was bating them, challenging them.

Out of the corner of his eye he saw Drew looking at him. Drew's quiet stare asked the question, *"Can we tell him?"* Wesley inhaled quietly and gave a slight nod.

Drew looked at Faulburn. "There's one more thing we need to do at Kurgon Fort."

Faulburn crossed his arms and leaned back against the rock behind him, waiting.

Drew launched into the explanation of their quest and ended by saying, "So now you know."

Faulburn was quiet for a moment. "This will make the rescue more difficult."

Drew nodded.

"Wait," said Wesley. He hesitated, and then asked, "Are you not surprised to learn of our mission?"

Faulburn rubbed his chin. "I had guessed that whatever brought you to Dradoc had something to do with Kurgon Fort."

Drew cocked his head, impressed. "How did you know?"

"You knew the name of a fort that most people do not even know exists. Even I did not know what it was called until you said its name. Then you were unwilling to speak of you business in Dradoc."

"I guess we should be more careful with what we say," said Wesley. "Still, now that you know…are you still willing to help us?"

Faulburn tipped his head. "I will help you…but allow me one thing."

"Name it," said Wesley.

"To accompany you when you return to the Citadel."

Wesley and Drew nodded. Wesley had wondered when Faulburn might leverage his aid. "Deal."

"Well," said Drew, "Now that he does know, we should show him the maps we have."

Faulburn stared at Drew. "You have had maps all this time and have not shown them to me?"

Drew shrugged innocently with a small smile. "You're a tracker."

***

Anna leaned against the stone wall of her cell as she finished the food that had been provided them. Despite herself, she had laughed as Glenge grumbled about the food not being fit for dogs. Although the food was bad and their circumstances unpleasant, the dwarf had a way bringing the others humor by his exaggerated complaining.

"Anna."

She looked up at Hwen. "Yes?"

"How did those at Revowen know where to find us? And how did you know where to look for this fort?"

Anna's countenance darkened. She did not want to be the one to share this news. "I'm sorry." She stopped, a cry catching in her throat.

"Ralphan," Hwen said simply.

Anna nodded. "He made it to Revowen after you three were captured. He accomplished his task and delivered the plans of Kurgon Fort to the council of elves." She hesitated. "But, King Elderair told us that he was badly wounded when he reached the city. Although the elves tried to help him, it…it was too late."

Hwen remained composed. "Thank you, Anna. I know you did not wish to share that news."

Anna's eyes misted. "Hwen…"

Hwen's eyes glistened, but she remained calm. "Ralphan completed his task. He knew the risk he was taking when he chose to go on our mission, as did we all."

She paused and then added, "As did you, your brother, and friend when you chose to come to our rescue."

Tears slid down Anna's cheek, singly dropping to the stone floor. She looked helplessly at the elf across from her, trying to be strong. She imagined Hadrian and Glenge on the other side of that stone wall and their reception of the news.

Muffled sobs from the dwarf pierced her heart.

"We will mourn the loss of our friend," Hwen spoke again. "But we understand the cost of freedom and are willing to pay that price."

Anna swallowed. Her eyes were tired and her cheeks were still wet. "Is it worth it?"

Hwen stared at Anna for a long moment. Anna felt like she was looking into her soul.

"What do you think?"

It hurt to think. Thinking meant remembering her parents and not feeling the comfort of their nearness. Thinking meant reliving the rough handling of the guards, the fear on Wesley and Drew's face. Thinking meant wondering about the uncertain future, about what could happen to her and those she loved.

She hoped Hwen could see her feelings, because right now, she couldn't use words to express them.

Hwen lifted her chin. "I believe it is."

Anna looked at her, amazed at her fortitude.

"Anna."

Anna lifted her head and recognized the voice as Hadrian's. It was huskier than usual. "We see it as worth it, because we do what we do in order to help people…If we do not act now," he was silent for a moment, and Anna waited, "…though some of us may lose our lives…if we do not act now, Ratacin will take over…and many more lives will be lost."

Upon this speech, Hwen nodded.

A resonant, "Aye!" sounded from Glenge.

Anna felt like she didn't have the energy to adopt their position. But where else was there to turn?

She inhaled deeply and nodded. "I know."

***

Sweat rolled down the side of Wesley's face as the ground flew beneath him. He, Drew, and Faulburn had kept a grueling pace since they awoke that morning. They pressed onward toward Kurgon Fort.

He noticed Faulburn slowing his pace and adjusted his to match their guide's. "Why are we stopping?" he queried in an irritated tone.

"We are close," Faulburn replied. Wesley pulled out the maps and the two huddled over the parchment papers.

Drew put his hands on his hips and caught his breath, waiting for them to announce something.

Faulburn looked up from the map. "We need to bear a little more north and we should be there before dusk. We will stop here and break for a meal and then resume," said the tracker.

"We should keep going," Drew insisted.

"I think even a man trained at the Citadel should not strain himself that much," replied Faulburn. He nodded his head. "Come, we will stop briefly. You will need strength for the rest of the journey."

Wesley nodded in agreement. Drew glanced at him with surprise, but Wesley didn't bother explaining. His mind was on the goal.

36
PLANNING

Anna stared at the stone floor in front of her. A ray of sunlight brightened a column of stones in her cell. The small light snuck into the fortress from a little window chiseled high in the wall of her quarters. Anna was grateful for it.

She had found small things to be thankful for during her confinement. The guards had not taken her satchel away from her, so she still carried with her a scroll of the Psalms, which she and her friends took turns reading silently or aloud.

She was thankful for her newly made friends. She and Hwen passed hours through conversation. Although she had yet to see Glenge or Hadrian, she enjoyed talking with them as well.

She had recounted her story of entering Camnoel and her journey of training at the Citadel and traveling to Revowen and then to Dradoc. And though it was painful to tell, she explained her capture at the trading city.

Anna learned bits of their stories as well, including why they had chosen to join the Forsvárerne. Hwen had heard stories of the alliance group while living in Miershire. Intrigued, and longing for adventure, she had left home and joined their ranks. Though her family and friends questioned her decision, they did not impose. She said she missed them though, for various quests for the Forsvárerne had kept her away from home for three years.

Hadrian's father had served with Rigórik in the Forsvárerne, and when he became too ill to participate any longer, Hadrian took his place. Originally a fisherman from Clavilier, he was eager to make a difference in the world and saw the Forsvárerne as his chance.

Glenge had been chosen by the dwarf council at Kalegon to join the Forsvárerne. The underground city wanted to send a representative to the Rigórik's posse and assigned the task to Glenge.

Anna was interested in her friends' stories, but she could not help missing her old friends. She thought of Charmaine and Adius. She wondered how Sir Kaden, Sir Rowen, Narin, Castonir, Cleven, and Delmore were doing. She hoped that Sairla and Austin and Orson were safe. She wondered how Miraya was doing since Drail's betrayal.

Then she thought of her more recent acquaintances in King Elderair, Princess Elaswén, and Mr. Lampwick. Each had served a special role in her life. She hoped to see them all again.

But more than any of these, her mind strayed to thoughts of Wesley and Drew. Her heart ached when she thought of them. *"Father, please keep them safe,"* she pleaded. *"And help them not to worry about me. Help Wesley to trust You. Help him to be a good example to Drew, to be strong for him. Please...let Drew come to love You like Wesley and I do."*

***

The sky had taken on a golden glow in the light of the waning sun. Wesley, Drew, and Faulburn walked slowly to avoid the crunching of leaves.

Wesley stared at the ground as they ascended a hill. He had been quiet most of the day, wrapped in his thoughts. He'd murmured incessant prayers as they drew nearer to their destination, pleading for Anna and for their cause, constantly batting away fears that harassed him.

Even now, his stomach fluttered as he pondered what they were soon to attempt. *"Please let it work,"* he prayed. *"Please let us get through."*

He inhaled the brisk, autumn air. The raw scent of leaves, dirt, and sweat steadied him. Stirring from his thoughts, he noticed that Drew and Faulburn had stopped. They were at the top of the hill, staring ahead.

Wesley saw the object of their attention.

"Kurgon Fort," said Drew.

Wesley drew in a long breath as he surveyed the structure. At the bottom of the hill, nestled in a valley of mountains and bordered by a thick moat, two stone buildings rose from the water. One of the two had a large drawbridge facing east. It was currently raised.

Another drawbridge spanned the distance between the two structures, high above the moat. The buildings were of uneven height, so the bridge slanted downward. Parapets guarded the tops of the buildings and smaller edifices were enclosed on the highest level of the fort. A few armored guards patrolled the roofs, but otherwise there was little activity stirring the place.

"That will be our entrance," Faulburn spoke softly.

Wesley looked to where he pointed. At the base of the fort were several archways chiseled out of the stone, allowing water to enter.

Wesley stared at the entryways and imagined what lay through those arched tunnels. "Are you sure we'll be able to get in?" he asked Faulburn. "Won't those have iron bars inside?"

Faulburn shrugged. "It is our best chance." He turned back toward the forest. "Come. We must plan our move. Wesley, get out your map."

Wesley produced the map of Kurgon Fort and handed it to Faulburn.

The tracker stared intently at the paper.

"There are three prisoner-holding rooms: two in the larger building and one in the smaller. One is on the bottom floor of the first—probably where those archways lead, the second is on the top floor—the floor beneath the roof, that is," he specified. "The other one is in the second building, the smaller one." He looked up at the boys and locked eyes with them. "We have no way of knowing for sure which one Anna is in."

"We'll find her," Drew said shortly.

Faulburn eyed him. "There will be guards."

"We should split up," suggested Drew. "There are three jails and three of us."

Wesley shook his head. "No. We need to stay together. I don't want one of us getting trapped and facing the guards alone."

"Wesley is right," Faulburn asserted. "We must stay together and hope for the best." He crossed his arms. "Once we have her and the Forsvárerne, we will try to lower the drawbridge and escape by it, but if not, we will return by the way we came."

"And if she's in the other tower?" asked Wesley.

Faulburn tilted his head. "We will do what we can." He refolded the map and handed it to Wesley. "I would suggest that we try to get some rest, but I doubt any of us would be able to sleep."

Drew grunted. "You got that right. Not a chance in the world we'd sleep with Anna this close."

Faulburn nodded. "All right then. We will wait for the cover of darkness and then move. In the meanwhile, let us look for some logs."

***

Anna looked up at the grating sound of the prison room door being opened. A guard entered followed by another man dressed in black. Anna glanced at Hwen apprehensively, wondering the meaning of this visit. It never took two guards to deliver food.

Hwen gave a reassuring nod.

Anna turned her gaze back to their visitors. Then she gave a faint gasp. The man in black turned his head to her, their eyes meeting.

Anna's stomach tightened. *"Drail."*

Drail's eyes widened. "Anna. How are you?"

Anna could not bring herself to say anything.

Drail took a tentative step closer to her cell. "This is uncomfortable. I am sure your detainment has been a mistake. I shall arrange for your release as soon as possible."

Upon her unbroken silence, Drail stated, "You are surprised to see me here. Knight of Aloehan in the courts of Ratacin."

Anna felt her throat go dry. Finally, she managed to speak, "I know about your decision to join Ratacin…as well as Miraya's to stay behind."

Anna shuddered as she watched Drail's piercing eyes go cold. She had to will herself not to look away.

The corner of his mouth lifted. "Does Miraya regret her decision?"

"Miraya did what she thought was best."

"Mm," he grunted, condescension dripping from his voice. "I think I have chosen what is best. I am already second-in-command."

"Some would disagree with you."

"Including you? How devastating," he said dryly. Lightening his tone, he asked, "Where are Wesley and Drew? How did you manage to get captured without them?"

The remark stung. Anna had no leverage, so she answered honestly, "I don't know."

He eyed her for a long moment. She wanted to look down. Instead, she blurted, "Drail, how could you? You helped us! You—"

"I had a better offer." Changing the subject, he waved his hand toward the other cells. "Do you know who these people are?"

Anna said nothing.

"Traitors," he answered shortly. "They wreak havoc by creating opposition to one who would better the world."

"Does bettering the world include conducting slave trade and imprisoning the innocent?"

Drail stepped closer to her cell, so that his nose nearly stuck through the bars. "You know nothing of such things…or of his lordship Ratacin."

Tears forming in her eyes, she asked, "Do you?"

Drail stepped back, lifted his chin and let his eyes work their stare. Without removing his gaze, he spoke to the guard who had stood silently behind him. "Mark the Forsvárerne down for the midnight questioning."

"Yes, my lord. But...what of her?" he asked in referral to Anna.

Anna stared at him, willing him to change his mind.

His stare was blank. "Leave her."

***

Moments later, after Drail and the guard had left, Anna sat with her hand through the iron bars between Hwen's and her cell, clinging to the elf.

Her hand was trembling.

The elf held tightly to Anna's hand. "It will be all right, Anna."

"What did he mean by the 'midnight questioning'?"

"Most likely nothing of significance."

From the other side of the wall, Glenge harrumphed. "Do not lie to the girl. When they say 'questioning' they mean questioning by means of torture."

Anna's eyes widened.

Hwen frowned.

"Hwen!"

Hwen held her hand firmly. "I told you, Anna, everything will be all right. The Maker will give us strength to endure whatever lies ahead. I do not fear them."

Anna's brow scrunched. "Have they already hurt you?"

Hwen looked down. "We have given no information."

Anna bit her lip.

Hwen looked up and met her gaze. "Do not fear, Anna. The Maker will sustain us."

"What do you think he'll do with me?"

"Did he know that you three came from the other world?"

"Yes. He's the one who found us."

"Ratacin shows great interest in the prospect of anyone from your world, but exactly why, I cannot say."

Anna drew in a quivery breath. "I hope Wesley and Drew are safe."

Hwen gave Anna's hand a squeeze. "Let us pray for them. You too, Hadrian and Glenge. I feel they will need our prayers now more than ever."

***

Thunder rumbled distantly, and the air smelled like rain as Wesley, Drew, and Faulburn stared at Kurgon Fort from the cover of the woods. The sky was dark, and torches flickered at the top of the fortress, but otherwise there was little light, which was exactly what they needed for their plan to work.

As Wesley considered what they were about to attempt, a thought struck him. "This isn't going to be the time for revenge. We need to get in and out of there as quickly as possible."

Faulburn kept his stare ahead of him. "I know."

"And you're still all in?" asked Wesley.

Faulburn turned to look at him. "I have not come this far to forsake you now. My revenge will come in due time."

Wesley inhaled and gave a slight nod.

"Let's go," said Drew. The shortness in his voice betrayed his impatience. He was restless to perform their task.

Faulburn nodded.

"Wait," said Wesley.

Both turned to look at him.

"There's one thing we should do first."

They waited.

"Can we pray?"

***

Father," Anna prayed, her hand still holding Hwen's, "please be with Wesley and Drew. Guide them. Go before them and protect them from harm. Jesus, I know that You care about them…more than I do. They are in Your hands. We trust You."

37
EXECUTION

Wesley pushed away from the bank into the murky water surrounding the fort. With his left arm holding a log, he used his right arm to paddle. Drew held onto the log behind him and Faulburn was to his right with a separate branch.

The dark water flowed quietly as they inched through the moat. Wesley resisted the urge to kick his legs and go faster. He reminded himself that Anna's fate depended on the secrecy of their mission.

He prayed every minute.

Faulburn reached the arched opening first. Wesley and Drew followed, expecting the tunnel to lead to further darkness. But as they passed under the archway, the water grew lighter.

Faulburn glanced back at them and nodded. Wesley looked ahead and saw what had pleased Faulburn.

Steps.

The archway led to a small stone landing and a narrow stairway.

Faulburn released his log, and hoisted himself onto the stone platform. He pulled his log out of the water onto the stone. Wesley and Drew did the same.

Before continuing up the stairs, each man drew his sword.

The light brightened as they scaled the short staircase. It opened into a prison room with torches on the walls.

Wesley scanned the iron cells. He saw only men.

Breaking into a quick pace, he darted about the prison, glancing into every cell. The ragged prisoners eyed him warily.

"Where's Anna?" he demanded.

Drew did the same. Aiming his sword at a man behind bars, he questioned, "Where's Anna?"

The man shrugged. "Don't know who you're talking about."

Wesley felt panic rising.

"Hey!" a coarse voice shouted.

Wesley turned and saw a guard pointing at them.

"What are you doing?" he demanded.

Before the knight could draw his sword, Drew and Faulburn were upon him, each with a blade to his neck.

The man slowly raised his hands.

Wesley approached him and stood directly in front of him. "Tell me where you are keeping the Forsvárerne."

The man stared blankly at him.

"A female elf, a man, and a dwarf," Wesley clarified sternly. "And a girl."

"I don't know," he spat. A bead of sweat trickled into his beard.

Drew pushed the edge of his sword deeper against the man's neck. He spoke in a fiercely low voice, "I swear if you don't tell us, I'll run this blade right through you."

More sweat ran down the guard's face. "Top floor...of this tower. Up the stairs," he motioned with his eyes behind him, "across the lobby, and up the other stairs."

Wesley nodded. "Good."

"You will never make it," the guard spoke shakily. "They will spot you before you are half way."

"Are you the ward for this jail?" Wesley asked.

"Yes."

"Give me the keys."

Keeping one hand raised, the guard lowered a hand to his belt, unhooked a key ring, and handed it to Wesley.

"Thanks," said Drew as he hit the man on the head with the pommel of his sword.

Moments later, they were on the stairs with Drew wearing the knight's armor.

When they reached a platform, they stood at one of many entryways into a large, open room. To their right was a massive wooden door: the drawbridge.

"He said across the lobby," whispered Wesley.

"I know, I know," said Drew.

He brusquely pushed Wesley and Faulburn forward, as they pretended their hands were bound.

At the other side, there were two doorways next to each other. One was closed, and one led to a hallway. Drew chose the hallway.

"Good," Wesley thought when he saw stairs.

As soon as they reached the stairs, all three of them broke into a sprint. There were twists and turns and several doors and openings at the various landings, but they kept looking for the next flight of stairs, until they reached the top.

A single wooden door stood before them and one more flight of stairs led to the tower roof. Wesley fiddled with the keys on the ring until he found the right one. His fingers fumbled.

"Come on," he muttered frantically.

Finally it gave.

He shoved against the door, stumbling into the room, and then stopped.

The cells were empty on the left. Shaking himself, he ran deeper into the room and saw the cells on the right.

He stopped, a lump catching in his throat.

***

Anna's head jerked up at the sound of someone pushing against the door. Her heart pounded. Then her eyes widened and her fear melted into joyful surprise. Leaping to her feet, she ran to the edge of cell. "Wesley!"

Wesley stuck his hand through the bars and gave her hand a tight squeeze. "Have they hurt you?"

Anna shook her head. "No."

A look of relief washed across Wesley's face. "We're going to get you out," he assured her.

An armored body appeared next to him.

"Drew!" Anna exclaimed. She clasped his hand as well.

He smiled. "Hey Anna."

A man in black appeared next to them.

Anna tossed a questioning look at her brother.

"He's a friend," Wesley answered shortly as he worked the lock on her cell.

"Oh, Wesley!" Anna remembered as she bent to pick up her satchel. She looked to Hwen, who was already standing her in own cell. "This is Hwen, from the Forsvárerne, and Hadrian and Glenge are in the cell next to us."

Wesley nodded at the elf and swung Anna's door open. Anna sprang forward and wrapped her arms around her brother, burying her face in his chest.

"We have to hurry."

She let him go and nodded.

Drew caught her in an embrace. "Are you all right?"

She nodded. "How did you—?"

"No time to explain," said Drew.

Hwen joined them as Wesley unlocked the males' cell door. The man in black kept an eye on the door.

Anna turned and saw Hadrian and Glenge step out of their cells.

"Much obliged to you," said Hadrian.

"Yes," the dwarf said reluctantly, "Although we would have found a way out."

Anna grinned. "It's nice to finally meet you," she said. She was about to shake their hands, but Wesley urged her forward.

"We have to go," he said.

They quickly filed out the door and descended the steps.

A door opened, and Wesley yanked Anna back into a corner with the others. She held her breath as a knight took the stairs to the lobby.

After several tense moments, the man with Wesley and Drew nodded them forward. They reached the bottom where the short hallway led to the great lobby.

Anna was at the front of the line and peered beyond the wall. She recognized the place as where the wagons were first brought. There were no wagons now and only a few guards at the other end of the dimly lit hall. Then she looked more closely. Some knights, seventy feet away, had just come out of one of the side rooms, escorting a female prisoner.

Anna's heart lurched. "Mom!"

The blond-headed prisoner, hands bound, looked up at the sound of the voice. Anna gasped. It *was* her mother! Anna started to break towards her, but Drew grabbed her arm.

Her mom stared across the dim room. Her mouth moved, forming the word, *Anna.*

The knights turned their heads at the sudden outburst. Drail, who stood among them, darted his head also. Instantly he saw Anna and Drew.

"Guards!" he shouted. "After them! Prisoner escape!"

Drew yanked Anna back into the hallway, shoving the others back toward the stairs. "Run!"

Anna hesitated, moving toward the opposite direction, toward her mother. "Mom…"

Drew clutched her arm and dragged her the other way, sprinting up the stone steps.

Not far behind them, they heard the clanking of soldiers.

"Hurry!" shouted Drew.

"Confounded girl!" Glenge puffed. "Gave away our hiding spot!"

Anna panted as she ran, stumbling numbly forward. Drew ran with a hand on her arm, pulling her forward.

As they rounded a spiral curve, a knight was gaining on them.

The guard brandished a sword, cursing angrily. Using the advantage of his height, Drew kicked the man and slashed at his shoulder, sending him tumbling down the stairs, causing a stumbling block to the guards that followed.

The man in black led them past the door to their cell and up the flight of stairs that led to the top. Pelting rain accosted them as they reached the roof of Kurgon Fort.

The man let everyone pass him, commanding Drew and Wesley to take care of the guards that roamed the perimeter and were now headed towards them.

**

Wesley charged at one of the tower guards, sword drawn. The cold rain made the metallic blows shock his hands.

He glanced back and saw Faulburn engaging a cloaked man. Wesley was calculating another means of escape. They'd obviously alerted the whole fort to their presence.

This was not going as planned.

He heard a growl and saw the dwarf bring a knight to the ground in a body-slamming tackle. Hadrian claimed the fallen knight's sword and helped Wesley and Drew fell the others.

Faulburn and the cloaked man's blades met with a steel ring. The cloaked man drew back and savagely leapt forward, causing Faulburn to back-step.

Wesley's heart sank as a fresh throng of soldiers stampeded up the stairway.

Faulburn looked past him.

"The bridge!" the tracker ordered "Cross the bridge."

Drew understood first and herded the others toward the drawbridge that sloped downward toward the other tower.

The cloaked man seized the moment of Faulburn's inattention and slashed his sword across Faulburn's left upper arm. The tracker let out a yell and brought down his sword with such force that it knocked his opponent's weapon from his hand.

Wesley glanced back at the others. They were on the bridge. He waved at Faulburn. "Come on!"

Faulburn joined him. The bridge was slippery from the rain and was perched high above the moat below.

"Raise the bridge!" a knight sounded.

Wesley felt a lurch as the wooden planks began to pull back, rising to an even angle, and then slowly tilting upward.

He stood at the edge and waved his arms to catch his balance. He turned his head to Faulburn. "We have to jump!" he shouted over the sound of pounding rain.

The tracker nodded.

Wesley looked back at the tower below them, moving ever farther away. Sensing the presence of the elf next to him, he took a deep breath.

The elf nodded her agreement to his plan.

Wesley and Hwen leapt off the rising bridge and crashed onto the stone tower below. Regaining their feet, they readied themselves to help the others. Anna, Drew, and Hadrian dove off and landed next to them.

Wesley looked up, afraid that Faulburn and Glenge weren't going to make it. The bridge was inclined at a steep angle now.

With a shout, the dwarf and tracker plunged over the rim toward the tower. Hadrian caught Faulburn as they stumbled to the floor.

Glenge was just short of the floor and smacked against the wall, desperately hanging onto the edge. He grunted as his weight threatened to pull him into the dark moat.

Wesley and Drew reached for his arms and were joined by Hadrian and Faulburn.

They pulled him to safety.

The cloaked man ordered for the lowering of the bridge again. When it didn't move fast enough, he commanded bows to be brought out.

Wesley searched for a way of escape.

He saw Hwen take a flight of stairs that descended into the tower, but she came sprinting back out a moment later.

"More knights!"

Wesley darted his head between the lowering bridge with a host of knights ready to march across it and the stairway where the thundering noise of armored guards sounded.

"We have to jump," he said.

The others looked at him.

He ran to the ledge of the tower opposite the bridge. Standing on the wall he yelled, "It's the only way."

A flying arrow seconded his statement.

"Blasted knights! Stop shooting at us!" shouted Glenge.

Faulburn nodded. "Go."

Anna was at his side. He looked at her and nodded.

With a brief look into the moat far below, they jumped.

Wesley gasped for air as he resurfaced. Arrows fired into the water next to him. He kept swimming.

He reached the shore and helped Anna out.

"They've reached the shore!" one of the knights shouted.

"Into the woods!" ordered Faulburn.

They ran up a hill, weaving among the trees. Wesley came to a stop at the top of a steep slope and the others piled behind him.

"Glenge, slow down!" Hadrian called.

Too late.

Wesley pummeled forward along with all the others.

He shut his eyes tightly against the rocks that flew in his face as he rolled down the hill. His body came to a slow stop as he reached the bottom of the slope. Shaking himself off, he stood and looked around and noticed the others were doing the same. They were soaking wet and covered with dirt and grime from the fall, but everyone wore a look of relief.

Faulburn wiped his blade. "Well, they will not be following us down here."

"Why not?" Wesley puffed.

"They would not dare enter where we just have," replied the tracker.

Wesley cocked his head.

"Erin Dule," he answered.

Wesley let out a breath. People had told him the place was treacherous, but for now he was simply glad to have escaped with his sister and the Forsvárerne. It felt too good to be true.

He scanned the crowd and saw Anna, trembling with cold, but free. His gaze drifted over the three newcomers: the elf, Hwen, the man, Hadrian, and the dwarf, Glenge. *We did our task.*

Anna caught his eye. She shuffled over and hugged him again. Wesley held onto her.

Her face buried in his shoulder, her shoulders shaking. Wesley didn't cry. He was simply relieved.

"Wesley," she said, lifting her head. "I saw Mom."

Wesley had heard his sister yell out and part of his heart had lurched with it. But being hidden in the hallway, he had seen nothing.

"They're alive?" he spoke aloud, just wanting to hear the words.

Anna nodded. "They're alive."

He glanced up as Hadrian approached them.

"Anna, if your mother and father are being held captive there, I promise you we will do our best to free them."

Drew came around and put an arm around Anna's other shoulder. "That's right." He looked around at the people. "Wanna turn around now and get them?"

Wesley's own reaction surprised him. This whole time, he had wanted to find his parents, but right now he was just thankful his sister was safe; he didn't want to risk endangering her to attempt another rescue mission.

"Kurgon Fort will be on high alert," said Hadrian. "It will be best to wait, and return another time. But the time *will* come."

Anna gave him a watery smile.

Wesley shook his head. His sister was so sensitive. How in the world did she make it through this imprisonment?

The dwarf waddled over to Anna. "Yes, lass, only to return the favor…we will see what we can do to spring your parents free."

Anna nodded her thanks. Then the petite elf embraced Anna.

Wesley noticed how different this elf looked from the Revowen elves.

Holding Anna at arms length, Hwen looked into her eyes and said, "He heard our prayers."

Anna nodded. She bit her lip. "He did."

Suddenly, Wesley knew how she made it through.

His gaze swept away from them and caught Drew staring at Anna and Hwen. Wesley knew Drew didn't believe in God like he and Anna did, but he thought he saw a spark in his eyes. Had Drew also realized that God had heard their prayers?

Whether he did or not, Wesley knew what needed to be done. He knelt on the soggy earth floor as the rain continued to splatter them. He closed his eyes and his lips moved in silent thanksgiving. When he opened them, he saw that Anna and Hwen were with him.

38
ERIN DULE

Wesley pulled his cloak more tightly around him to block out
the gusting wind. Ever since they had started traveling that
morning, the wind had not ceased to rage. Two nights before,
the travelers slept on the margin of Erin Dule, under the
protection of the sheltering forest. Yesterday morning, they had
set foot upon the perilous land. There would be no going
around it. With Kurgon Fort behind them and sharp mountains
on their left, their only option was to go forward.

Erin Dule spread ahead of them as far as they could see. The
vast expanse was a barren wasteland. No trees provided
protection from the merciless draft. The only vegetation that
grew was a short, stocky plant that was able to survive the
tundra. A few rock formations peppered the area, which would
afford some shelter.

But the most mysterious and threatening facet of the desert
was the blue flames that littered the land. All over, the miniature
fires boiled out of the cracks in the surface.

Wesley remembered Mr. Lampwick's warning about this
place, particularly the blue flames. He said that they were
'freezing fire', and could freeze a person, rather than burn them.

The company traveled slowly, against the current of the
wind, cautiously avoiding the fires.

Wesley's face stung by now and his whole body shivered with cold. He had not packed nearly enough warm clothes.

There was little conversation amongst the companions as they trudged forward. None of them had ever crossed this region, so they could only hope they were heading in the right direction. At night they followed the course of the stars, bearing northeast toward Ellwood Forest.

Wesley took a seat next to his sister as their questing party sat around a campfire. They had set up camp next to a large rock opening that supplied some reprieve from the wind.

Hadrian cooked a stew over the fire from some game that Faulburn had caught, and a few dried vegetables from Wesley's pack.

The aroma of the simmering soup and crackling of the fire was a comfort. Although it was only their second day after departing from Kurgon Fort, the trek had been strenuous. They had stopped frequently because Anna and the Forsvárerne members were weak.

Wesley felt no need to complain though. In fact, he felt more content now than he had in a very long time.

"I'm sorry for not trusting You," he thought. *"You have proven Yourself trustworthy."*

Wesley glanced around the campfire. Faulburn quietly sharpened one of his knives. A bandage was wrapped around his upper arm where he had been cut in his fight with a knight. Hwen and Hadrian were discussing when they would be able to return to other Forsvárerne members while Hadrian watched the stew. Glenge puffed on a pipe.

Drew threw down his bundle and stretched his arms before coming and joining Wesley and Anna. Anna watched the campfire. Her cheeks were paler than usual.

Hadrian ladled stew, using the bowls and cups that Drew, Wesley, and Anna, had packed with them.

Wesley, Drew, and Anna fell into conversation while the older ones spoke in another circle.

"Why would Mom be in Kurgon Fort?" Wesley asked aloud.

"And Dad too," Anna added, "At least…hopefully he was with her…I didn't see him."

"The important thing is that now we know where they are," said Drew. "So we can get them back."

Wesley stared absently, still haunted by questions. "Why would Ratacin want Mom and Dad?"

"Who knows what that elf wants," Drew mumbled.

Anna straightened. "Did you see him at Kurgon Fort?"

"Ratacin?" asked Drew.

"Drail."

Wesley's eyes widened. "The man who was fighting Faulburn."

Anna nodded.

"So he's working for Ratacin," Wesley murmured.

Anna told how he came to her cell and spoke to her.

"Did he hurt you?"

"No."

Wesley frowned. Why would Drail have betrayed them? He had protected them and brought them safely to Aloehan. What shifted his allegiance?

"If I ever come near him again with a sword in hand..." Drew shook his head.

"He said that he was second-in-command," said Anna. "He must have joined as soon as he left Aloehan."

"He'll be first in command soon," Drew wagered. "Whoever was first-in-command at Kurgon Fort will get the blame for your escape."

Anna's eyes widened. "He'll search for us."

"Let him come."

Wesley didn't share Drew's cockiness.

Drew shook his shoulders. "Soon we'll be back at Revowen, planning our next rescue mission."

Wesley hoped that was the case, but wondered whether or not Sir Kaden would allow them to go on the next rescue mission. Sure, they had accomplished this mission, but barely. And now that Drail knew them and would be wanting revenge, would it be safe for them to return?

Please let Sir Kaden understand how important it is that we get our parents back.

But Wesley knew that the guard of the Citadel had more to think about than just the well being of one family. He was concerned for the fate of all of Camnoel.

He recalled the words of King Elderair when the elf lord was interviewing Wesley for the quest:

"Your parents, if they are alive, are not the only ones in need. There are many who need rescuing."

Wesley had argued that since he wasn't even from Camnoel, he had no duty to its people. King Elderair had rebutted that since Wesley was a follower of Christ, he did indeed have a duty to them. Wesley glanced across the campfire at the older members of their company. The Forsvárerne members were in an earnest conversation with Faulburn over the security of various cities.

Wesley understood King Elderair's statement a little better.

39
BLUE FLAMES

We had better hope that it does not pour down snow on us,"
Glenge grumbled as the company marched northeastward the
next morning. "Although with our luck, it probably will," he
added in a low mutter.

A peal of laughter rang out from Hwen. "With our luck,
Glenge, it is a wonder that we do not have blue skies and
sunshine. We were sprung from jail and are on our way to
safety. I would say our fortunes have been quite fair."

"Yes, but I would credit that to Providence, not fate, my elf
friend," said Hadrian.

Hwen dipped her head and smiled. "Well met."

A small smiled tugged at Wesley's mouth. They were
pleasant people to be around. And even though they were still
physically recovering from their imprisonment, their spirits were
undaunted. It gave him hope that maybe his parents could come
out of Ratacin's grip unscathed.

As they continued north, the ground became rockier and
more unleveled. The blue flames were abundant and closer
together.

"Watch your footing," Faulburn called as he led the line with
Wesley.

Wesley was cautious, but with all they had faced already, he hardly worried about the blue flames. Better theses than knights shooting arrows at them.

Still, the white pebbles were slippery, and he could feel the cold that the blue flames projected.

There was a scream.

Wesley jolted and turned around. "Anna!"

She was lying in a flame, her body shocked to unconsciousness.

"Anna!" Drew reached her first.

He pulled her body out of the flame and leaned over her.

Wesley rushed to her side. She was cold stiff.

"Anna!" he barked, grabbing her face. "Anna, wake up."

Her eyes fluttered open and weakly met Wesley's. They fell closed again.

Drew sat down and pulled her onto his lap, rubbing her arms. "We gotta warm her up."

The others circled around them.

"Great gander," said Glenge. "She's dead!"

Wesley's heart thudded.

"No she's not!" said Drew.

Hwen knelt down beside her. "Drew is right. She is not dead, but she is suffering from severe freezing. We must keep her warm. Glenge, start a fire. Hadrian, gather all of the extra blankets that we have." Hwen stood and looked at Wesley and Faulburn. "We must look for white bark on the stems of the underbrush. The branches, when cracked open, have a juice that may be helpful to her."

"You're an elf!" Drew exclaimed. "Why can't you heal her?"

Hwen met Drew's fiery eyes, "I am not a healing elf, Drew. But we will do all that we can. Keep holding her. She will need your body heat."

Drew opened his cloak and held her close, defiant lines on his face.

Wesley stared, swallowing. He pulled himself away and blinked, trying to remember what Hwen told him.

He could hear Drew's panicked whispers. "Come on, Anna. You gotta wake up."

"Yes," Wesley's thoughts echoed. *"Please wake up. God wake her up."*

He took a deep breath to settle himself as he continued to move quickly. He crouched low to examine the bark of a shrub. No white bark. He ran to the next bush. *"I know You're in control. You helped us get Anna out of Kurgon Fort...You can heal her now. Please God..."* Taking another deep breath, Wesley bit the inside of his mouth.

His heart pounded. He didn't know if it was from fear or knowing what he needed to do. In his heart, he knew what he had to choose. *"Surrender."*

"Okay," he spoke quietly. "I trust You with her life." Had he taken the time to think about it, Wesley would have been surprised at his own calmness. Instead, he continued to pray, sometimes in his thoughts, sometimes in whispered mutterings, all the while searching for the white bark. Then, the words came to him that Elaswén had spoken to him on the bridge, *"I fear things will get worse for you before they get better. But do not lose heart, though the night is dark. The dawn will come."*

Wesley nodded to himself. He would not lose heart. Casting a brief glance to the overcast sky, he said in his thoughts, *"The dawn will come."*

A call from Hwen sounded that she had found a white-coated shrub. Wesley scrambled over to her and drew his sword from his scabbard. Cutting off several limbs of the thick stock, he held them out to her.

"Take them to Anna. Pour the liquid in her mouth. I will look for more."

Wesley obeyed and ran as fast as he could, avoiding more flames.

He took one look at Drew's wrinkled face and read his concern. He looked down at the body in his arms and was scared for a moment he was too late.

Wasting no time, he drew his knife and sliced open the branches. A purple liquid spilled over. He put it to Anna's lips and poured. Most ran out the side of her mouth, but some pooled inside. Then, a faint movement in Anna's throat indicated that she had swallowed.

Drew looked up at him. "We have to get her to the elves."

Wesley continued to pour the liquid. "We need more juice. Hwen said this would help."

Moments later, Hwen and Faulburn returned with more branches.

"She will need to drink this three times a day," said Hwen.

"How long does the freezing last?" asked Drew.

Hwen stared at him for a moment. Before she could answer, Glenge did. "Lad, it does not last long…the victim dies within a few days."

Drew's grip tightened around Anna and his jaw squared. "No," he said lowly. "No."

"We must keep moving," Faulburn's deep voice commanded. "If we can reach Revowen, the elves will help her."

Drew stood, still holding her. "Let's go."

***

They kept a brisk pace with the hopes of sighting Ellwood Forest. With none of them having been in Erin Dule before, they could only guess how close they were. They took turns carrying Anna, but more often than not, it was Glenge who bore her still form. As a dwarf, he had a greater capacity for carrying loads than the rest of them, and declared it was his duty to perform such a service.

Whenever they stopped, Hwen gave Anna more of the purple juice. At times Anna showed signs of stirring, moving listlessly in her sleep, but she never woke.

The day after Anna had been burned the company sat around a campfire for their supper. No one had much of an appetite, and conversation was scarce.

Hadrian sat next to Wesley and tried to offer some encouragement. "Your sister showed great fortitude when she was in that prison cell. She is a strong girl."

Wesley had been monotonously watching the fire. "I know," he answered distantly. Then, pulling himself out of his daze, he straightened and looked at Hadrian. "She is strong. She'll make it through this."

Drew looked across the fire at Wesley, meeting his gaze as if searching for hope.

"You've been calm," he said to Wesley as they were rolling out their mats that night.

"She's gonna be okay," Wesley answered.

Drew's eyes looked scared. "She has to be okay." Drew cursed. "Wes, she has to," he couldn't finish. Tears came to his eyes.

Wesley stood to meet his friend. He hugged him, and Drew held on tight.

***

Wesley awoke to the wind hissing at his face. He pulled the edge of his cloak higher around his cheek, but opened his eyes. Faulburn, Hwen, and Hadrian were already moving about. Wesley rubbed the sleep from his eyes and quickly got moving.

As soon as he rolled his own pack, he checked on Anna. Asleep and bundled in blankets, she lay close to the fire. Her complexion was still dangerously pale. Wesley looked up and caught Hwen watching him.

"How is she?" he asked her.

The petite elf walked over and crouched next to Anna. She put a white hand to Anna's face as Wesley waited for her reply. She looked up at him. "Pray for her, Wesley."

Wesley inhaled and nodded. Her answer wasn't what he wanted to hear. "Can we get moving?"

"We will," Hwen answered. She nodded over to where Glenge and Drew still slept. "We were trying to let them catch up on their rest. Glenge needs to regain his strength. And I fear your friend is going to make himself sick with worry. But," she inhaled, "we should be moving. You should wake them so we may eat and be on our way."

Within the half hour, the company was on the road again. They trudged silently. Mid morning it began to snow. Bearing the cold downpour with grim determination, the travelers moved forward.

Glenge buried Anna's face in his beard as he held her close to his chest and plunged his boots into the ever deepening snow.

"Look!" Wesley could barely hear Faulburn's voice over the blistering wind.

Wesley and Drew looked to where the tracker pointed. Wesley deciphered a dim shadowy outline on the horizon.

"Ellwood Forest," the tracker announced.

A surge of hope swept through Wesley. Soon they would be out of this barren, coldland and on their way to the city of the elves.

They reached the forest a little after midday. The company had skipped lunch, hoping to cover more ground. They stopped only to give Anna the juice and collect more white-coated branches.

As soon as they stepped into the confines of the forest, the temperature changed drastically. As they continued to walk, Wesley could feel his body thawing.

"Look!" said Drew. He was staring at Anna's face, which was now draped over Glenge's shoulder. "She's got some of her color back."

"So she does," said Hwen excitedly. "We must keep moving…and move fast."

40
MEMORIES AND MEETINGS

Kaden leaned on the rail of one of the many stone bridges in Revowen. He stared absently into the water that pooled tranquilly beneath him. A small stream trickled over mossy rocks, feeding the pool, which delivered into another stream that meandered deeper into the elvin city.

All around him the trees breathed warm hues. Rich shades of gold, red, and orange decorated the white-barks. Scattered leaves blew in the breeze and kissed the gentle water, riding its current.

It was a scene of beauty that enveloped him, yet the he could not shake the troubles that weighed on his mind. His thoughts drifted to a memory from several weeks ago, in the halls of King Elderair's palace. He had visited the Mirror Room and stood before the mysterious glass, hoping for a glimpse of the children.

The elegant glass with a pearly frame was propped on a table, leaning against the wall. A velvety blue blanket was spread underneath it.

Kaden gazed into the mirror, but saw only his reflection, staring tauntingly back at him. Soft footsteps at the door finally drew his gaze.

Elaswén, clothed in a gown of velvet cranberry, stood in the doorway. Her reddish blond hair fell in long curls around her shoulders.

"Have you or your father seen a vision of them in the mirror?" Kaden asked his fiancée.

"No."

Kaden pressed his lips together.

"The mirrors show things as they will," Elaswén reminded. "Just because we have not seen a vision of them does not mean they are not succeeding."

"It would mean something if it showed them alive."

Elaswén looked at him with searching eyes. "Have you given up hope for them?"

"I am not willing to resign to that yet." He sighed deeply. "You know what troubles me so," he spoke it as a statement not a question. "Every life is precious; I realize that every time I commission a quest or lead men into battle. When a soldier falls, the loss is felt deeply. But the lives of these three children hold my attention with painful acuteness," Kaden paused while Elaswén waited.

"I believe their lives will impact the fate of all of Camnoel. I cannot bear to see that destiny stolen from them," he looked her in the eye, "and should something happen to them, I could not bear the guilt of knowing that I had a part in sending them to their doom."

She met his gaze and held his eyes. "As strong as you are, the fate of Drew, Wesley, and Anna does not lie in your hands. When we sent them on this quest, we knew we were releasing them from our power and committing them to the Maker's."

Kaden rested a hand on the wall. "My head knows that, but my heart still yearns for their safety. I know the tasks that lay before them possess danger, but I do not wish them to encounter that danger prematurely… surely you understand that."

Elaswén joined him. "Whenever I think of my sister and her husband, I want more than ever to see the children safe." She dipped her head for a moment, and then looked at him. She lifted a hand to turn his face toward hers. "And I have hope that we will."

Kaden kissed the top of her head. "So do I."

Kaden straightened upon the memory. "I do have hope," he muttered to himself. "Oh, Maker…I do have hope that You will bring them back safely."

He watched another golden leaf disband from a branch and float delicately onto the water's surface.

"Sir Kaden."

In the distance, a young elf male stood on the path. "You asked us to inform you if we sighted any visitors. Our watchmen spotted a company in the woods beyond the city."

Kaden's heartbeat quickened. "Thank you!" he yelled as he sprinted toward the Western Gate.

He passed dignified elves who glanced at him with amused expressions, and ran agilely through the wooded paths of Revowen until he reached the Western Gate. He came to an abrupt stop. A jubilant smile spread across his face as he caught sight of a familiar face. "Wesley!"

The teenage boy looked up in recognition. Kaden saw him mouth his name. The knight ran towards him.

The entire group was breathing heavily, as if they had just run several miles.

Kaden extended a hand to Wesley, but the boy caught the man in a hug. Surprised, Kaden returned the firm embrace. "It does me good to see you."

Wesley pulled back and nodded. "It's good to be back."

Kaden saw his eyes. "Is all well?"

"Sir Kaden!"

The knight turned around and saw Drew. They shook hands and clapped each other on the back.

After the greeting, Kaden saw Drew's concerned gaze as well. Drew wore a frown and looked at Wesley. "Did you tell him?"

"Tell me what?" asked Kaden.

"Anna's sick," Wesley answered.

Kaden turned his gaze and saw four new additions to the company: two men, an elf woman, and a dwarf. Three of them he guessed were the Forsvárerne. They had succeeded, Kaden realized with wonder.

Who the other man was he did not know. Then he saw the dwarf holding a limp body. It was Anna.

Kaden's eyes darted worriedly from Anna's still form to Wesley and Drew.

"She fell into a blue flame in Erin Dule," Wesley explained.

Hwen was already speaking rapidly with one of the elves that had escorted them. The male elf nodded. He turned to Glenge and took Anna from his arms and moved quickly along the path back to the city.

"He is taking her to the healing ward," Hwen told the others.

Kaden nodded. He let his eyes take in the Forsvárerne. Not hiding his marvel, he said, "You completed your task."

"Of course we did," Drew replied matter-of-factly.

Kaden smiled.

Kaden glanced at the other man. He had not said a word and was dressed in dark clothing.

"This is Faulburn," Wesley introduced. "He helped us break into Kurgon Fort. We couldn't have done it without him."

Kaden bowed his head. "An honor."

The tracker nodded humbly. "The honor is mine."

Kaden turned again to Wesley and Drew. "I will tell Elaswén about Anna right away. In the meanwhile, the rest of you should refresh yourselves. You look exhausted."

Drew put his hands on his hips, his breath still heavy. "We ran the last leg of the trip to get her here in time."

Kaden nodded. "Well done." He looked up at the other elf who had been standing guard. "Will you see that they are taken care of?"

The elf nodded.

Kaden caught Wesley and Drew's eyes before they left to follow the elf back to the city. "We will do our best for Anna."

41
WAITING

An hour later, after Wesley, Drew and Faulburn had been treated to elvin hospitality, given new clothes, and fed a warm meal, they gathered in a lobby outside the healing ward. It was an outdoor, circular room with plush furniture.

Vinery in rich shades of gold, red, green, and orange climbed along the cream-colored stone walls. Although Camnoel was in her autumn, and everyone was dressed in long sleeves, Wesley couldn't help but notice the improvement of weather over that of Erin Dule. Drew had commented that it felt like summer.

The elves had taken the Forsvárerne into the healing ward to tend to them as well. After being tended, they were to meet with King Elderair.

Wesley looked up and saw Kaden glancing between him and Drew. "The king wants to speak with you, but will wait until Anna is able to join you. I spoke to Elaswén and she is attending to Anna personally...your sister is in good hands."

Wesley nodded his thanks.

Kaden sat down beside him, his large frame filling up the chair. "There is much I want to speak with you about," He said rapidly, and then added, "but we shall wait until Anna's recovery...I do not believe it will be long."

Upon the interlude of silence, Faulburn addressed Kaden. "You are a knight of Aloehan?"

"I am."

"I would like a word with you," said the tracker.

Kaden consented and gestured to a path they could take as they talked.

When they left, only Wesley and Drew remained in the waiting chamber.

Wesley sat quietly as the sun waned in the sky. He felt some assurance in the thought of Elaswén tending to Anna. He trusted her. And even more than he trusted her, he trusted God. *Thank You, for letting us reach Revowen. Please help the elves heal Anna now."*

Drew stood and paced restlessly around the small circular chamber. His agitation was written on his face as he strode back and forth.

Wesley watched him for several moments. "Drew, she's going to be okay."

Drew stopped his pacing and looked hard at Wesley. "You think that elves will be able to heal her?"

Wesley shrugged. "If not the elves, then Someone will."

Drew squinted at Wesley. "Someone..." then his forehead creased as he grasped his friend's meaning, "you mean...God?"

Wesley gave a subtle nod.

"How can you be so sure?"

Wesley thought for a moment. "I believe Jesus cares about Anna...and He's going to do whatever is best for her...whatever that looks like." He paused for a moment. "It's like God's asking us, 'Do you trust Me?' And we have to choose to...with His help." Wesley paused, "Maybe Jesus is trying to get your attention, Drew. He wants you to find Him."

Drew stared at Wesley.

Wesley shrugged. "He's already found you."

***

That night, Wesley lay in the lush elvin bed, exhausted. The soft sheets cocooned his body, and he could feel sleep claiming him.

Drew was in the bed across the room, turning and sighing restlessly. Wesley wanted to tell him to be quiet, but decided against it. Finally, he heard Drew get out of bed and go out their bedroom door.

He fell asleep without hearing Drew return.

***

Wake up, Drew," Wesley pushed his friend's shoulder. The morning sun sent shafts of light through the lattice ceiling.

Drew turned over groggily and opened his eyes. "Huh?"

"Huh?" Wesley echoed and slapped him on the shoulder. "Good, you're up. Hadrian just came by and said that our group is going to have breakfast together. Hurry up."

Drew yawned and blinked sleepily.

"You're like waking a hibernating bear," Wesley said as he fastened a crimson tunic over a white shirt. "Didn't sleep well?"

"Yeah," Drew answered absently, as he sat on the edge of his bed. "I slept fine, just not much."

Wesley dipped his hand in the washbowl on the nightstand and flicked Drew with water.

That shook Drew from his daze. He stood and stretched, and then made a move to douse Wesley. Wesley sidestepped it and grinned.

"Up late?" he asked Drew.

"Yeah." Drew replied casually.

"Where'd you go last night?"

Drew shrugged. "Just out."

Wesley grinned. "Did you find a cute elvish teenage girl?"

Drew laughed in spite of himself. "No. Gosh, you're chipper."

"Did you go see Anna?"

"No, just...took a walk."

Wesley looked at him long. It wasn't like Drew to be vague. He didn't push him, though, his growling stomach reminding him of their destination.

"Ah, herald the sleep kings!" Glenge bellowed as they entered the dining hall.

The boys received a warmer welcome from the others as they took a seat at the table. An array of fruit, wafers, bread, quail, pigeon, and other unidentifiable foods covered the low sitting table.

Everyone at the table was dressed in fresh garments that had been provided by the elves. Their faces were clean, and their hair was combed, a contrast to how Wesley had first seen the Forsvárerne members.

Hwen wore an earthy green gown and a barrette of leaves was pinned in her whitish-blond hair. Hadrian sported a royal blue tunic over a white shirt with a high necked collar. His beard was trimmed and his hair neat. Glenge appeared stiff in a golden, button up shirt with a high collar. His curly red mane and beard looked cleaner, but still unruly. Although Faulburn had also been give new clothes, he still chose to wear them in dark, layered hues.

"Are you glad to be back here?" asked Hwen. Her eyes displayed her liveliness at the joy of being in city of her own race.

"Yeah," said Wesley. "You three are looking better."

"Yeah," agreed Drew.

Wesley dipped his head, embarrassed, "I mean…not that you didn't…"

"That is all right," Hwen came to their rescue. "We feel better, I assure you. But it will take some time to recover our strength."

Wesley nodded. "Thanks…for all you did for Anna."

"I believe we are the ones who should be thanking you," said Hadrian.

"What news from King Elderair?" asked Drew.

"He spoke for a very long while yesterday, and you would probably be bored if we recounted everything," said Hadrian.

"So you're going to spare us?" asked Drew.

Hadrian smiled. "Not at all."

Hwen intervened. "Our meeting with King Elderair was meaningful to us, Wesley and Drew.

He spoke of many things pertaining to our quest, information we learned while in Kurgon Fort, future plans...and of our fallen comrade, Ralphan. We were shown his burial ground where we paid our respects."

There was silence at the table for a moment. Then Wesley asked Faulburn, "Did you talk to Sir Kaden?"

The tracker set down a goblet. "We spoke about me helping the cause of the Citadel and the elves," he answered.

Wesley wanted to ask for details, but did not press the matter. The only other information he learned from Faulburn was that the tracker had been attended to by the elves for the slash on his arm he received from Drail. Then the conversation fell to other topics regarding the elves.

"One day," Glenge said to Wesley and Drew, "you must visit my home. The dwarven cities..." he said, bobbing his head, "now that will give you something to talk about!"

Drew smiled. "You wanna brag about your home, too, Hadrian?"

"If you ever get the chance to see Clavilier, you can decide for yourselves if it is worth bragging on. I am fond of my city, but I will own that it hardly compares to the city of the Fair Folk."

"There you are."

Wesley turned his head to see Sir Kaden enter.

"I had to ask around to find out which dinning hall you were in," said the knight. "I was told to come and wait with you all."

"Told by who?" asked Drew.

"By someone who is soon coming," he answered elusively.

Wesley took a good look at the man who had been one of their first contacts in this world. The broad-shouldered knight looked as muscular as ever, dressed in unarmored garb of a blue shirt and black tunic. Wesley thought that the lines on his face were deeper than he remembered, and his beard a little more filled out.

Wesley wondered if Sir Kaden could detect any change in him.

"I have *changed a lot since I first came here,"* Wesley mused. But before he could delve into that thought, a warm and pleasant voice pierced the room.

"Greetings, friends."

Wesley looked up and saw Elaswén standing in the arched doorway.

Everyone seated at the table rose respectfully.

The sun on her back, Elaswén's slender figure stood tall and elegant. Wesley thought she looked very unchanged, still strikingly beautiful. She was garbed in white, and her strawberry blond hair was clasped partly behind her head, with her pointy ears peeking delicately out between strands of her hair.

He hoped that she had come with news of Anna.

For a moment, Elaswén did not speak. She stood there taking in the sight. Wesley thought he saw tears in her eyes and wondered at her show of emotion. From what he had perceived, the elves often guarded their emotions, but the elf princess did not seem to feel that obligation.

Wesley wondered what had provoked such a response in her. He hoped that it didn't have to do with Anna.

She graciously spoke to the Forsvárerne and Faulburn when Kaden introduced them. When she came to Drew, she placed both her hands on either side of his head and kissed his brow. Doing the same to Wesley, she said softly to them, "It does my heart much good to see you both safe here."

When they had seated themselves again, Elaswén spoke so all could hear, "I have good news." A joyful smile touched her lips.

Wesley and Drew both straightened, alerted to the fact of what her tidings might be.

"You may see Anna now."

42
REUNION

It was a tie between Wesley and Drew who jumped out of his seat first. They had to purposefully slow their steps so that Elaswén could guide them to the healing ward.

As the elf princess led the seven of them, she carried the conversation. "We have attended Anna faithfully since you brought her here. She must have been burned very badly, for the frost poison was deep. But she is better now. She awoke for the first time just before dawn and has been sleeping sporadically since."

"Is she awake now?" asked Drew.

"Yes. But she is tired; the frost fever has left her weak."

Wesley looked up. "Will she regain her strength?"

"Yes, Wesley."

Elaswén led them onto an elevated veranda that was lined with colored doors. Wesley was surprised. Most of the rooms in Revowen did not have doors. Perhaps only the healing ward did.

Elaswén stopped when she reached a golden door. Gently pushing it open, she spoke softly. A moment later, Elaswén reappeared and smiled. "You may enter."

Wesley and Drew were the first to enter, both walking slowly.

Wesley paused in his steps when he saw his younger sister. In the center of the room, she was lying on a large round bed. Her dirty blond hair framed her face on the pillow, and the color had returned to her cheeks. Her eyes were open, and when she saw them, a weak smile lit her face. Wesley smiled...and felt a weight drop from his shoulders.

She spoke their names happily, but Wesley could hear the tiredness in her voice.

When he approached the bed, she lifted a hand to him and he took it for a moment.

"Hey. You scared us pretty bad."

"I'm sorry." She looked past Wesley and held out her hand also to Drew, who took it in both of his. "You okay?" he asked.

"Yes. I'm excited to get out of this bed though." Then she noticed the others trickling in through the door. Her mouth parted in a humble smile. "Hwen, Hadrian, Glenge, Faulburn...Sir Kaden!"

They surrounded her bed, each offering kind words. Hwen bent down and kissed Anna's cheek. Hadrian smiled warmly, and Anna extended her hand to Glenge.

"I was told that you carried me much of the time while I was unconscious."

The dwarf shuffled his feet. "Ah...well... I suppose."

Anna smiled gently. "Thank you."

Glenge swallowed, cleared his throat, and gave a single nod. To everyone's surprise, he was misty-eyed.

Drew laughed. "Are you crying, Glenge?"

The dwarf harrumphed. "Of course not! This elvin air makes my eyes water."

When the chuckles subsided, Anna acknowledged Faulburn and Sir Kaden.

"It's so good to see you again!" she said to the knight.

A smiled deepened the crow's feet around his blue eyes. "The same to you."

***

The following morning, Anna was dismissed from the healing ward and allowed a room in one of the main guest halls.

After they all slept in, Wesley and Drew met up with Anna.

"Ready to see Revowen again?" she asked.

"Absolutely," said Drew.

Anna smiled. Her eyes ran over the boys, and she grinned. "You're taller."

Wesley and Drew nodded at each other.

"And bigger," she added, clearly enjoying their pride.

Drew backhanded Wesley on the chest. "Didn't I tell you?"

Wesley shrugged and smiled.

For several moments, they walked in silence. They had been through so much, it was almost hard to know what to talk about.

The pearly stone path they followed led them down curving steps, past waterfalls and the cathedral-like buildings of the elves. The paths were covered in the fallen leaves of autumn hues.

"While the elves were tending to me for frost poison, they also healed my scar," said Anna. She showed them her forearm where she had received a scar from shooting a bow the day they fought the skyrogs. Now it was completely gone. "I'm sure they could do the same for your leg Drew."

"No way," said Drew. "I'm keeping every scar I get."

Anna didn't say anything but an amused smile tugged at her lips.

"Scars are cool," Drew defended.

"Yeah," added Wesley, "Faulburn's going to have a good one on his arm."

Drew nodded his agreement. "That was a pretty sweet cut."

Anna cocked one eyebrow. "Really."

"Yep" Drew grinned. "They look cool. And they're manly."

"They show that you're adventurous," said Wesley. "They prove you've fought for something."

Drew nodded. "Mm hm, they show that you're courageous."

"But if you have too many, they show that you're reckless," Wesley added.

"Well," Anna teased, "I never would have known. Thank you for educating me so fully."

Drew grinned. "You're welcome."

When the sun was directly above them, they headed toward the palace, to a particular stone bridge by the cascades, where Kaden had asked to meet them. The cascades were a series of three waterfalls, one feeding the other two.

When they reached the arched bridge, Kaden was waiting for them. The bridge extended to a balcony protruding from the palace with seats to watch the falls, and to archways beyond the balcony leading into the palace that towered into the sky.

When he heard their footsteps, Kaden turned toward them and a smile touched his eyes.

"It is good to see the three of you together again."

"It's good to be together again," Drew replied.

"I said that there were many things I wanted to talk to you about, and there are," Kaden began. "But first, there is someone who would like to see you, although I insisted upon her waiting until you were better," he said, glancing at Anna.

Anna cocked her head. "Who is it?"

"Me," said a voice, as a young woman started up the path toward them.

Anna burst into a smile. "Charmaine!"

The swordmaiden allowed a smile. Tall and proud as ever, she approached them elegantly and seemed taken back when Anna embraced her. She nodded to Wesley and Drew.

"How come you're in Revowen?" asked Anna.

"I came to see your return," she answered. "And to visit the city of the elves."

"Did you travel here alone?"

"I am quite capable of taking care of myself, Anna, as I hope I have taught you to do so."

Anna smiled apologetically.

"Oh, Anna's capable of it all right," said Drew. "You've gotta hear about the adventures she had."

"And she will," interrupted Kaden, "but for now, I must beg an audience of you three alone." He then nodded to Charmaine.

Charmaine was about to take her leave, but stopped at the sound of approaching footsteps.

Wesley glanced over his shoulder and saw Faulburn walking toward them. He slowed his steps when he reached their circle on the bridge.

Kaden crossed his arms. "It seems arranging a private meeting is more complicated than I thought."

Faulburn slowed when he saw all of them. "Forgive me. I meant to speak with you, Sir Kaden, but I have come at a bad time. I will take my leave." He bowed his head to go, but Anna stopped him.

"Wait."

The tracker looked up.

"Have you met Charmaine?" Upon his blank stare, Anna continued. "Charmaine, this is Faulburn. He helped Wesley and Drew rescue me while I was at Kurgon Fort." Anna turned to the tracker, "Faulburn, this is Lady Charmaine, daughter of the steward of Aloehan. She taught me everything I know," Anna added with a smile.

Faulburn bowed his head and took Charmaine's hand in a sign of respect. "My lady."

Charmaine acknowledged him with a nod, her eyes taking in his mysterious demeanor.

Wesley noticed Faulburn's hand twitch.

"Sir Faulburn, I shall speak with you soon," said Kaden.

Faulburn looked at Sir Kaden and dipped his head. "Thank you." Straightening, he glanced at Charmaine again.

"Sir Faulburn," she murmured.

"My lady."

He turned and left.

Wesley stole a glance at Charmaine. She watched Faulburn as he left. Wesley glanced at Anna's smug expression and smiled to himself. Leave it to his sister to set up an unlikely pair. He didn't think Faulburn seemed like that type, but perhaps he was wrong.

Kaden motioned to the balcony where the bridge led. Extending a hand, he invited, "Shall we talk?"

Charmaine excused herself, but Wesley noticed she didn't walk in the same direction as the tracker. *"It was probably nothing."*

43
EXPLANATIONS

Sir Kaden seated himself with a sigh on a bench across from Wesley, Anna, and Drew. He fingered the ivy that grew on the arm of the stone bench for a moment before speaking.

Finally he looked up at them, appearing to study them.

Wesley wondered if he was noting any changes that he beheld in them, and if so, he wondered what changes Sir Kaden saw.

Finally Kaden spoke, "There are many things that I wish to say to you…and to hear from you…I hope that you are not in a hurry."

A small laugh escaped Drew. "From the journey we just got back from, we won't mind resting."

Kaden nodded. "Would you tell me your story?"

For the next hour, Drew, Anna, and Wesley took turns recounting the details of their trip, starting with the departure of Revowen, recalling their experiences in Dradoc, meeting Mr. Lampwick, Anna's capture, the boys soliciting the help of Faulburn, their tracking, and their battle with the vuls. Anna shared her experiences of traveling to Kurgon Fort and those once she got there. Then, with added emphasis, she told of her encounter with Drail.

"I knew that he had left the Citadel, but that didn't lessen my surprise at seeing him."

Drew nodded. "He was also the one to lead the chase as we were escaping the fort. And he gave that cut to Faulburn on his arm."

Wesley frowned. The treachery of that man made him sick.

Kaden sighed. "Drail's choice is regrettable. It was exactly what Sir Orson was afraid of. He never liked his daughter's suitor, and now his cautions have been justified."

"When Drail found us and took us to Vladoc," said Wesley, "I think he had made friends with some of Ratacin's knights. He was already warmed up to them when he met them in Dradoc."

"I think it is worse than that," Kaden said softly. "Sir Orson thinks that he accepted even before he had told Miraya about it. Although we can only guess what happened next, we have a probably guess, especially now with the information you just told me; when he eventually went to Dradoc, he must have been deported to Kurgon Fort.

"While working there, he may have heard that Ratacin takes a great interest in people from your world, and thus shared his knowledge that three youths from your world were walking around Camnoel. If he has not disclosed his knowledge yet, we can be sure that he will. You three are no longer hidden."

"Why?" asked Wesley. "I mean, why is Ratacin so interested?"

"Yes," added Anna, "Hwen also mentioned that." She paused. "It's more than simple curiosity, isn't it?" she said it like a statement.

Kaden pressed his lips together for a moment before answering, "Yes, Anna. It is more than curiosity. However, it is not my place to answer that question. But do not worry; I will explain more in due time. Please, for now, continue your story."

Wesley watched Kaden, a weight creeping back into his heart. What was it he couldn't talk about? It occurred to him that their journey wasn't coming to a close...it was merely beginning.

He half-listened as Drew and Anna recounted the rescue mission, their close escape from the fort, and trek across Erin Dule.

Anna had nearly blurted that she had seen her mom, but Wesley shook his head. "Wait, Anna. We'll tell him later."

Kaden did not press the matter, so they continued with their story. When they had finished, the knight nodded. "Thank you for telling me. You three have certainly had a remarkable past several months. I would say it was quite an adventure."

"And one that I thank you, most deeply, for taking."

They looked to see who had spoken.

King Elderair entered the balcony through the arched doorway from the palace.

They all stood in respect.

He smiled warmly. "Welcome, children, to my home once again." The lines around his eyes crinkled as he grew serious. "I speak on behalf of all my people when I say that I am grateful for the deed you have done." He spoke slowly, pronouncing each word carefully, "It is a good thing that you have done."

"Well," said Drew, "You're the one who chose to send us."

King Elderair's chest rose with an intake of air. "Yes...there is something I need to tell you about that. The reason I suggested that you three be the ones to perform this quest, is not solely because I *felt* that you three ought to be the ones. Two days before your arrival at Revowen, I saw a vision in the mirror. The vision was not clear, but I saw three youths in a fortress, that is Kurgon Fort. When you came here with Sir Kaden, I felt quite strongly that you needed to be the ones to go to Kurgon Fort."

Drew cocked his head. "Why didn't you tell us of your vision before we decided to go?"

"I did not want to influence your decision. I wanted to see if you truly cared for the task...if you were willing to complete it."

"And we were," Drew finished.

"Yes," said King Elderair, "you were. And now, our cause is helped for we have regained three crucial members. We are indebted to you." King Elderair continued. "Tonight, a banquet shall be held in celebration for your deed and the return of the Forsvárerne members. It is but a small token of our gratitude, but we hope that you will accept it."

"We will," Drew replied, "Thank you."

"Wait," Wesley said, his insides churning. Something wasn't right. "You saw a vision of us in the mirror. Does Ratacin have a mirror?"

"He does," the elf answered.

"Can elves manipulate what the mirrors show?"

King Elderair frowned. "Some have this ability, it is true."

"Would it be possible for Ratacin to have created that vision you saw? I mean, if Drail had told him about us, do you think he could have cast that scenario?"

King Elderair's face blanched.

"He was baiting you," Kaden whispered.

"But it didn't work," Drew said. "Maybe he was. But his plan failed."

"You meant evil against me..." King Elderair quoted.

"But God meant it for good," Kaden finished. The two men exchanged a look.

King Elderair asked Kaden. "Have you told them?"

"No, sire," the knight replied quietly. "I have not." Kaden looked to Wesley, Anna, and Drew. "I believe there was something you three wanted to share with me."

He paused, "Would you be willing to share that now? For there is something I must tell you as well, but I would wait until we have discussed every other thing you wished."

Anna looked to Wesley. He nodded.

"While we were escaping Kurgon Fort," she hesitated. Her brow creased. "I saw my mom."

Kaden's eyes lightened. "You did?"

Anna nodded and recounted the story.

When she had finished, Kaden spoke slowly, "Are you certain it was your mother?"

"Yes," Anna replied firmly. "And I think that my dad was probably nearby and just hadn't come out of the room yet."

King Elderair nodded. "This is good news indeed."

Kaden crossed his arms and stroked his bearded chin absentmindedly. His hand stilled while he asked, "And you are sure that she was a prisoner?"

Wesley's head jerked up from where he had been staring at the stone floor. "She wasn't working with them if that's what you're asking," his voice held an offended tone.

Kaden dipped his head. "Forgive me."

Anna spoke quietly. "Her hands were bound. She was their prisoner."

"And now that we know where their parents are," said Drew, "We're going to go back and get them. As soon as possible."

Kaden nodded slowly. He sat back down on the stone bench. Wesley watched him and waited for his answer.

The knight finally looked up at them. "I am very happy that you have located your parents' whereabouts...truly I am. I have prayed on your behalf for that very thing." He paused, "You will not like this, but I speak it in your best interest. I caution you to not return to Kurgon Fort immediately."

"Why not?" Drew asked.

"My answer to that question is tied to what I wanted to tell you...at least part of it." Kaden inhaled and began, "There are things that you three need to know, but they are things that would best be told by someone else."

"Which is why," said King Elderair, "Sir Kaden, as an authority from Aloehan, and myself, as King of Revowen, are sending you back to you own world."

"What?" Drew blurted.

Anna tilted her head.

Wesley remained still.

Kaden proceeded. "We want your caretaker, Josiah Smith to be the one to speak to you. When he does, you will know why."

They were silent for a moment, and then Drew spoke. "Is that your final decision?"

"It is," King Elderair replied quietly.

Wesley looked at Kaden. The knight's eyes were sad at their disappointment, but he was also firm in his decision.

Drew wasn't satisfied yet. "Why can't you tell us whatever the news is?"

"It is not our place," answered Kaden.

Drew let out a breath and nodded. "Then let us go back to our world as soon as possible so we can come back and get on with the rescue."

"You may leave in the morning," said Kaden.

Drew gave a quick nod and stood. "King Elderair, Sir Kaden," he acknowledged and began to leave. Anna followed him. When they were on the bridge, Drew stopped and looked back at Wesley.

A silent understanding passed between them. Drew turned and resumed his course. Anna hesitated, still watching her brother, but relented and followed Drew.

"What is it, Wesley?" the elvin king's quiet voice pierced the heavy silence.

Wesley had been staring at the toe of his boot, but looked up to meet the monarch's gaze. "Sir, I mean you no disrespect... and I don't want to question your judgment. Up till now, you and Sir Kaden have guided us well, and I appreciate all that you have done for us," he looked at both men, directing his comments to Kaden as much as to the king. "But...we've also done things for you. We enlisted on a mission that had nothing to do with us. We put ourselves in danger for your cause. We've done everything you asked of us...even though we didn't understand it."

Wesley paused, "I'm asking this of you...that you won't send us back." Wesley's brow creased as he felt the weight of his own words. "Surely you understand how important this is to us..." he nearly choked on his next words, "we *have* to get our parents back."

Both men were quiet for a moment after Wesley's request. Then the elf king spoke. "Sir Wesley," he began. Wesley tilted his head. The king had never used that honorific with him before.

King Elderair continued, "We do thank you for your submission. After all, you have no written obligation to us...As you have said; you are not from our world.

And what I mentioned to you before about your duty as a follower of Christ, well…even that was a matter of your choice. You could have said no to the rescue mission we gave you. I hope that we are able to convey our appreciation to you for saying yes. And I am asking you to do the same now. We will force nothing on you. Once again, the choice is yours."

Wesley stared at him for a long moment, not feeling any more settled inside. He wished that the king had given him a verdict one way or the other, but instead the responsibility had fallen upon him…once again. He thought he understood now why the king had called him 'sir'. It was because he was treating Wesley like he was a mature man able to make wise decisions, as knights were supposed to. Wesley wondered if he really possessed that maturity. *"Probably not,"* he thought…which is why he should heed those who did.

"I'll abide by your cautions," he spoke.

Both King Elderair and Sir Kaden seemed genuinely appreciative of his response.

"Thank you, Wesley," said Sir Kaden.

***

Wesley entered their room as Drew was buttoning up a dress shirt.

Wesley tipped his head at the formal clothes that Drew had changed into.

"Apparently the banquet tonight is a fancy get-up," Drew explained. "The elves brought some for you too," he nodded to Wesley's bed.

Wesley's eyes scanned the clothing that was laid neatly on his bed.

"So what did they say?" Drew asked.

Wesley looked up. "Huh?"

"You asked them if we could stay, right?"

"How did you know?" asked Wesley.

Drew grunted with a smile. "I know you. So…what did they say?"

"They said no," he responded quietly. He relayed his previous conversation.

Drew tugged on his stiff sleeve. "Well…I guess they have their reasons."

"Yeah," answered Wesley as he shrugged out of his shirt, changing into the clothes given to him, "I guess so. I'm anxious to hear what it is that Mr. Smith has to tell us."

"Hey, me too. But don't worry; when we come back, we'll get your parents."

44
A GIFT OF HONOR

The sound of lilting music wafted through the air as Wesley, Anna, and Drew approached the courtyard where the banquet was being held. Lanterns with soft glows were hanging from the trees and posted around the perimeter of the courtyard. Low-sitting tables were scattered around, each heavily adorned with food. The elves floated around the scene, some leaning against trees, other sitting with wind instruments, and still others standing and talking among themselves.

Wesley was surprised at how warm it was inside the circle of the banquet. There had been a chill in the air as they walked from their rooms to here, but now he felt no cold. He wondered if that was the work of the elves. His eyes scanned their surroundings and observed them.

Their skin was light and their ears pointy, although some had sharper points than others, he noted. Generally, their hair was long and silky, although he noticed that some had very short hair.

"There they are."

Wesley stirred from his reverie when he heard Drew speak. He pointed to a table where the Forsvárerne members and Faulburn were sitting. The three made their way over to them and joined them.

Although the banquet was being held in their honor, they still hardly knew anyone and wanted to be with friends.

"Greetings!" Hwen spoke warmly.

The kids greeted them and sat down. Anna took a seat across from her elf friend and Drew and Wesley sat on her other side.

Hwen gave Anna's hand a friendly squeeze. "How did your meeting with Sir Kaden go?" She began to pass Anna dishes of food.

Anna's countenance fell slightly. "He and King Elderair are sending us back. Tomorrow morning."

"Back," asked Hwen, "to your own world?"

Anna nodded.

"They are?" asked Hadrian, who was sitting next to Hwen. "Whatever for?"

"Great gander!" exclaimed Glenge from Hadrian's other side. "They cannot do that! Why, can they not see that you three are capable warriors?" He began to mutter to himself.

Anna turned her head, surprised that they had all been listening to her conversation.

"Be quiet," Hwen chastened her two comrades. "Let her speak." She returned her attention to Anna. "Please, go on."

"They want us to speak to our caretaker, a man named Josiah Smith. They said he has something important to tell us."

Faulburn looked up from where he sat next to Hwen. "Will you return?"

Drew answered for her. "As soon as we can."

"I am sorry to see you go so soon." Hwen looked at Anna. "I had hoped to enjoy some time with you in the city."

Anna smiled.

"They have their reasons," Wesley spoke.

"Oh course," Hadrian supported. "King Elderair and Sir Kaden would never do anything idly. If they say it is important, then it must be."

The conversation fell to other topics, and the company chatted for several moments.

Anna asked Hadrian if he had finished making his flute from Erin Dule.

The man tilted his head, surprised that she remembered. "Why, yes, I have. Though…I have not had an occasion to play it."

Anna smiled. "Would you play it now?"

His eyes widened. "Why, Anna…the elves," he said as if that explained everything.

"He thinks his playing be not as fine as theirs," explained Glenge. "Quite a bit of balderdash, really. Their music is nothing special," he grumbled.

"I would very much like to hear you play," Anna offered Hadrian.

Hadrian smiled. "I suppose a short tune would not hurt." He pulled his fife out of his vest pocket and put it to his lips. He blew a soft, testing note, and then began to play a quick, moving tune.

Anna grinned. It was soft and happy, not haunting or majestic like the music of the elves, but pleasant nonetheless. Then more music filled the air, in an altogether different tune. The elves had resumed their songs.

Hadrian withdrew his fife from his mouth and looked at the others at the table with wide eyes. They all broke into laughter.

"Apparently they did not like it," Hadrian whispered.

"Well I did," Anna whispered back, reassuringly.

"Mind if I join you?" asked a familiar voice.

They looked up to see Sir Kaden standing there. He took a seat next to Wesley.

"Do those at Aloehan know that we have returned?" Wesley asked him.

"Yes. We sent a message."

"Through mirrors?" asked Wesley.

Kaden glanced at Wesley. "There is little that escapes you."

"That's for sure," said Drew. "What about the rest of our group?" he asked. "Sir Adius and the rest of them?" he clarified. "Are they here?"

"They returned to Aloehan once Narin recovered," answered Kaden. "They wanted to stay, especially Sir Adius, but since there was no longer need for them here, they returned home."

"Oh, I wish they could have been here," lamented Anna.

"So do I," chimed another voice.

Anna turned her head and smiled. "Charmaine!"

The swordmaiden placed herself in the empty chair next to her apprentice. "You would not believe how vexing it is to try to speak with someone in a language you hardly know."

Anna cocked her eyebrows.

"I have been mingling with the elves, most of whom speak our language, but a few will not, I think simply to toy with us. I told one man, who was probably many centuries old, that I was a healer and swordmaiden. He was convinced that I needed their healing from a cut I had received from a sword." She rolled her eyes.

Anna couldn't help but smile. "I'm sorry."

Charmaine reached for a pitcher of cider to pour into her goblet. When she did so, Wesley noticed Faulburn sitting across from Charmaine. He saw them acknowledge each other and then Faulburn began speaking with Hwen.

"It's time to go," said Kaden.

Wesley nudged Drew and Anna and followed Kaden. Hadrian, Glenge, Hwen, and Faulburn also stood from their seats.

"What does he want?" Anna whispered as she and Drew followed the others.

Drew shrugged.

Sir Kaden led them to the base of a platform at the front of the courtyard where the elf king and his daughter were waiting for them.

Elaswén smiled at them, and King Elderair said, "This banquet is in your honor, and honor you we shall. Follow me."

He climbed the steps onto the platform where they tentatively followed. The monarch spoke a few words to summon the people's attention. Then the music ceased and all grew quiet.

The elf king stood near a blue lantern that cast a strange glow upon the aged man. He began to speak. He acknowledged the return of the Forsvárerne members and what a good thing it was to have regained them.

King Elderair turned so that he faced the three beside him. "Drew, Wesley, Anna, we are here to thank you for your service and courage. As a token of our gratitude, our gift to you is one that you may carry with you wherever you go." He emphasized the word *wherever*, and Wesley wondered if that was because they were unable to take things from Camnoel back to their world. "We give you our esteem. Such is a rare thing to receive from our race for we do not give it lightly. But to you three, we bestow this gift of honor. Your tale of courage will be told in the halls of this revered city wherever stories are preserved."

The three recipients bowed their heads in gracious acceptance.

"Thank you," said Wesley. "We won't treat it lightly."

King Elderair met his gaze and nodded.

They were dismissed from the platform, and the Forsvárerne members were called forth. King Elderair spoke of their fallen comrade, Ralphan, and of their imprisonment. He also expressed his thanks to the tracker, Faulburn, for his aid in the rescue.

The evening stretched long, as the elves were not ones who paid heed to the confines of time. They played their flutes late into the night and sang stories that recounted legends of old.

During the course of the evening, Kaden joined their table again and spoke to Wesley, Anna, and Drew. "You three would do well to get some sleep as you will be rising early tomorrow."

Anna agreed and covered her mouth with her hand to hide a yawn. "You're right."

"Remember to wear your garments from your own world tomorrow." Then he added quietly, "You should say good-bye. You will not be seeing them in the morning."

Anna bit her lip, unmasked grief on her face.

Somberly, they made their rounds to Hadrian, Glenge, Hwen, Faulburn, and Charmaine. The boys shook hands and Anna gave them all hugs.

"We shall look forward to seeing you again," Hadrian affirmed.

"Soon, I expect," grunted Glenge.

"Yes," said Drew, "Very soon."

Hwen hugged them each farewell.

Charmaine kept any emotion that she may have felt in check and commended them on their feats and said that she hoped to fight with them one day.

As they filed away from the perimeter of the banquet, Anna looked back one last time and started crying hard.

Wesley put his arm around her shoulder.

"We will see you soon!" called Hwen.

"Soon," Anna repeated.

"Come on," Drew spoke, "Let's go."

When the three reached their doors, Anna was about to enter her room, when Wesley stopped her.

"Wait, Anna," he said.

Anna looked at him.

"Do you know what day it is?"

Anna stared at him for a moment and then glanced at Drew and then back at Wesley. She shook her head. "No…should I?"

"Well, I'd say it's a pretty important day in your life," Drew replied, his eyes twinkling with a smile.

Anna looked to Wesley with a cocked head. "What is…" her eyes widened. "Is it my birthday?" she asked unsurely.

Wesley smiled and nodded. Drew disappeared behind the curtain to his room. He reappeared with his hands behind his back.

Anna's mouth parted in wordless form. Then a smile broke forth. "How did you know?"

"We were keeping track," Drew answered. "After Wes's birthday, we counted the days until yours. We wanted to surprise you."

Tears filled Anna's eyes.

Wesley shifted his weight awkwardly, not liking to see her cry. "We have something for you, but you won't be able to take it back home with you, since we got it here."

"But you can enjoy it whenever you're in this world," Drew added. He brought his arm around and displayed the gift.

A faint gasp escaped her. "It's beautiful." She reached forward and took the vase of blooming flowers from his hands.

Drew gestured to the vase. "The elves did something to the flowers so that they'll bloom for several years and stay fresh."

Anna admired the bouquet of peach and white flowers and touched her nose to one, inhaling its ambrosial aroma. She lifted her face. "Thank you."

"You're welcome," Wesley replied. He shrugged, "You're getting old."

Anna laughed and then stopped. A pensive look traced her eyes. "Time has really gone by, hasn't it?"

Wesley nodded. "Well, we'd better get to bed. Night."

Drew gave her a hug. "Happy birthday, Anna."

"Thanks, Drew."

"I'm gonna walk around for a bit," Drew told Wesley. Wesley nodded and didn't ask questions. He was too drained to ask.

45
PARTING WORDS

Colors flickered in a blurred arrangement. The picture was not precise. Then, something sharpened into focus. An object. It was a necklace made of intertwined leather, bearing at its center a white stone. Then, something else entered the picture. A tanned hand reached…and clasped the necklace.

"Wesley. Wesley, wake up!"

Wesley felt his shoulder being shaken. He opened his eyes and blinked, dazed from his dream. He turned over on his back and saw Drew above him.

Drew gave him a funny look. Wesley figured he must still look disoriented.

"You all right?" asked Drew.

Wesley nodded. "Yeah," he said as he propped himself up on his elbows. "Yeah, I'm okay."

Drew frowned. "You only look like that after you've had a dream."

"Uh-huh." He swung his feet over the edge of the bed, into a sitting position. He sunk his hands into the edge of the bed.

Drew crossed his arms. "Was it bad?" he asked quietly.

Wesley looked beyond Drew, recalling his dream. "No," he spoke distantly. "I don't think so."

"Well, come on. We need to meet Sir Kaden."

Wesley nodded and stood. He cast a second glance at Drew, noticing he was wearing his jeans and shirt from their own world. *"Ironic,"* he thought, *"it seems strange seeing those clothes back on him...It will be even stranger to wear them again."*

Moments later, Wesley pulled a t-shirt over his head, completing his native world outfit. Drew stared at him, apparently feeling the same thing.

"It doesn't really feel like we're going home," Wesley noted.

Drew simply nodded. "We'll be back soon."

Wesley followed Drew out of their room where they met Anna. She was tugging at her earth clothes.

Drew inhaled. "We better go."

***

Welcome," King Elderair spoke to the three young adults before him as they entered the room.

They greeted their elders and waited.

Wesley glanced around the room. Elaswén and Kaden stood next to King Elderair. Beyond them, a table set against a wall. On the table, a blue velvety blanket rippled in lush folds. Sitting upon the blanket and leaning against the wall was a pearly-framed mirror. *"Like Mr. Smith's mirror,"* Wesley thought. *"So much has changed since we first saw that mirror...our lives will never be the same."*

"I would have a word with you young men before you make your departure." The elf king's voice interrupted Wesley's thoughts.

Wesley and Drew gave the king their full attention while Anna remained silent.

"Sir Kaden informed me of the story of your travels," King Elderair began. "I admit I found it most remarkable. However, there is one thing of which I would speak to you. During your stay in Dradoc, you experienced a rather traumatizing event, that is, your separation from Anna," he glanced at Anna.

The king continued slowly, "When faced with that circumstance, you had a choice to make; family or duty. You chose family."

The king's eyes grew somber, as if his next words pained him. "If I were speaking to you as a friend, I would condone your actions. But I cannot speak to you as merely a friend, for I speak on behalf of many. I address you now as king of Revowen, and defender of the cause against Ratacin. I speak as a defender of justice. As such, I must tell you, as harsh as it may sound, I do not approve of you actions, Wesley and Drew.

"Although your circumstances, either by fate, luck, or providence, turned miraculously in your favor, there is no guarantee that will happen again. If ever you are presented with such a decision in the future, and if I am to entrust you with another quest, I must be able to depend on you to make a decision for the greater good. Many lives may depend upon it. That also goes for you, Anna."

Anna looked up and met his eyes with an aching expression.

Wesley's face knit in a pensive frown. Although he understood the king's position, he didn't like hearing it. He felt bad that Anna had to be present to hear it also.

"Do not be offended by this reproach," said the king, "After all, you were not completely at fault. Since your quest to rescue the Forsvárerne was an act of freewill, you were not bound fully to the duty given you. But, I want you to know, if ever you do make the decision to be ordained as knights of the Citadel, what will be expected of you. Do you understand?"

Wesley and Drew both nodded slowly, solemn expressions on their faces.

"Think upon my words," said the king.

After a brief silence, Kaden said softly, "You three should be going."

Elaswén stepped forward from where she had be standing quietly between her father and betrothed. She kissed each of their heads.

"We will see each other soon, Anna. Remember that."

"Thank you, princess Elaswén. I'll look forward to your wedding."

A giddy smile flickered across the elf's face and a look of joy passed between them.

Then Elaswén turned to Wesley. "Be strong, Wesley. Remember what I told you: the dawn will come."

Wesley nodded to express his gratitude.

Turning to Drew, the elf princess spoke quietly, "I look forward to seeing what the Maker has in store for you, Drew. I assure you it will be more than you can imagine."

Drew nodded.

Kaden stepped forward and laid a hand on their shoulders. For a moment he did not speak, but clamped his lips and seemed to be holding back emotion. Then he inhaled. "Come back as soon as you can. Josiah will see to that."

Drew shook his head confidently. "We will."

The knight tried to smile. "Very well." He ushered them to the mirror. "Touch the mirror," he instructed quietly.

Wesley felt butterflies in his stomach. Anna reached for her brother's hand and extended her other to the mirror. Drew stepped forward and lifted his arm.

"Farewell, my friends," said Kaden.

"For now," replied Drew.

Simultaneously, the three teenagers touched their hands to the mirror. King Elderair stepped behind them and laid a hand on it as well.

Their reflections rippled in the mirror until they altogether disappeared. Colors swirled dizzily on the glass surface until they appeared three-dimensional. Wesley thought he could see a blurry outline of a room. Then he realized it was Mr. Smith's attic. Suddenly, he was enveloped in living colors that wisped around him, so close that he thought he could taste them.

Blinding light surrounded him, blocking his view of everything else.

His senses prickled, as all was a blur of sights, sounds, and smells. He was aware of Anna's hands clasping his hand, but it was a struggle to hold on as he completely lost his bearings of everything around him. Then he felt something hard beneath him. Colors sharpened at an alarmingly fast speed. He moaned and felt body weights pressing on top of him.

They tumbled, rolled, and moaned. He opened his eyes, and looked around. Drew, Anna, and he were lying in a heap on the wooden floor next to the wooden table.

Drew was the first to stand. He gave Anna his hand and helped her up.

Wesley brought himself to his feet and brushed off his jeans and wiped his mouth with his sleeve. Somewhere in that tumble, he had caught dust in his mouth. He looked up to find the other two staring at him and each other.

A silent look passed among them and they glanced around the room. Looking back at the table they saw a looking glass in a golden frame. It looked like an ordinary mirror.

Anna reached and traced the glass with her fingers. Nothing happened. She tucked her lips into her mouth.

Without words, Drew turned and made for the door. Wesley and Anna quietly followed him down the narrow staircase and into the little den. They kept glancing at awkwardly at their old surroundings. Drew led them down the back stairway to the kitchen. There was no sign of Mr. Smith.

After a quick search around the house, they concluded he wasn't home.

"I'm hungry," said Drew.

Wesley shrugged dully. "We can eat while we wait for him."

Anna and Wesley followed Drew to the kitchen, where they sat around the dinning table.

46
THE UNRAVELING

Drew took a bite out of an apple and stared blankly into space. Few words had passed among them. None of them knew what to say. Drew was sure of one thing though.

"I'm going back...soon."

His attention was alerted suddenly at the sound of keys turning at the front door. The creak of the door, followed by footsteps, announced someone's arrival.

He craned his neck to see down the hallway and sighted the old man hanging his keys on a rack by the door. Josiah Smith shuffled down the hallway towards them. He entered the kitchen and abruptly stopped.

"Oh," his soft-spoken voice sounded slightly surprised. "Oh my." Then a gentle smile creased his face. "I was wondering when the three of you would return."

"You were expecting us?" asked Drew.

"Quite positively," replied Mr. Smith.

Drew scratched his face. "Um, Sir Kaden and King Elderair..." he began and then suddenly felt very foolish.

"I know them," Mr. Smith answered quietly. "Please, go on."

"They told us we need to talk to you," Anna finished.

Mr. Smith nodded. "We shall, indeed."

Leaning against the kitchen counter, Drew stuffed his hands into his jean pockets. He stiffened.

"What is it?" Wesley asked.

Drew brought a handful out of his pocket. He opened his hand and Wesley and Anna stood from their seats to look.

His heart started hammering a thousand beats per second. His voice was hoarse. "It's my coins from Aloehan."

Anna and Wesley stared at the coins and then looked up at Drew. Then all three looked to Josiah.

"They told us," Drew faltered, "that only those from Camnoel can take things from that world back to our world."

"You were informed correctly."

"You're joking, right," Drew's fingers fiercely clenched the coins and his jaw trembled. "Because...then...that would mean..." his voice trailed off.

A twinkle came to Josiah's eye, and a smile flickered across his face. "We need to talk."

To Be Continued in Book Two.

GLOSSARY OF CHARACTERS

Adius ~ (ADD-ee-us) A knight of Aloehan who trains Drew and Wesley

Aleron ~ (AL-er-on) The horse from Aloehan that Anna rides

Anna Connor ~ 14-year-old sister of Wesley

Austin ~ 15-year-old son for Sir Orson and Sairla, brother of Miraya, lives outside of the Citadel

Castonir ~ (cast-oh-NEAR) knight of Aloehan who accompanies Sir Kaden, the Connors, and Drew to Revowen

Charmaine ~ (shar-MANE) daughter of Sir Rowen, shieldmaiden of the Citadel who instructs Anna

Cleven ~ (CLEV-en, CLEV rhymes with Rev, as in Reverend) knight of Aloehan who accompanies Sir Kaden, the Connors, and Drew to Revowen

Cole ~ son of William and Elizabeth who discovers the first mirror on Earth

Delmore ~ (DEL-mor) knight of the Citadel who accompanies Sir Kaden, the Connors, and Drew to Revowen

Drail ~ knight of Aloehan who first discovers Wesley, Anna, and Drew; Miraya's suitor

Drew Vincent ~ 15-year-old orphan, Wesley's best friend

Elaswén ~ (ell-ess-WEN) Revowen elf princess, daughter of King Elderair, who is betrothed to Sir Kaden

Elderair ~ (Ell-der-AIR) Elf king of Revowen

Elizabeth ~ the first female human to enter Camnoel, married to William

Faulburn ~ (FAH-ool-burn, also pronounced FALL-burn) a tracker from Dradoc

Gallagher ~ (GAL-ag-er) the horse from Aloehan that Drew rides

Glenge ~ (GLENNGE) Kalegon dwarf, a member of the Forsvárerne

Hadrian ~ (HAY-dree-an) a man from Clavilier, member of the Forsvárerne

Hwen ~ a Miershire elf, member of the Forsvárerne

James Connor ~ Wesley and Anna's father who ran an orphanage in Europe but is missing

Josiah Smith ~ foster parent of Wesley, Anna, and Drew, has a mirror in his house

Kaden ~ (KAY-den) second of the guard at the Citadel (a knight)

Kate Connor ~ wife of James Connor, Wesley and Anna's mother who is missing

Lampwick ~ (LAMP-wick) a penman in Dradoc

Miraya ~ (mur-AY-uh) daughter of Orson and Sairla, sister of Austin

Narin ~ (NAR-in) knight of the Citadel who accompanies Sir Kaden, the Connors, and Drew to Revowen

Orson ~ (OR-son) Captain of the Guard of the Citadel (a knight), Austin and Miraya's father and Sairla's husband

Ralphan ~ (RALF-an) a member of the Forsvárerne who was killed

Ramee ~ (RAY-me) Kalegon dwarf who regretfully joined Ratacin, cousin of Rigórik

Ratacin ~ (ruh-TOSS-in, also pronounced rah-TOSS-in) Revowen elf who betrayed the elves to build his own army

Rigórik ~ (rih-GOR-ick) Kalegon dwarf, cousin of Ramee who started the Forsvárerne

Rowan ~ (ROW-an) steward of Aloehan while it is without a king, Charmaine's father

Sairla ~ (SAIR-luh) wife of Sir Orson, mother of Austin and Miraya

Wesley Connor ~ 15-year-old brother of Anna, Drew's best friend

William ~ first male human to enter Camnoel, father of Cole

GLOSSARY OF PLACES

Audrian Mountains ~ (ODD-dree-in) mountain range in northeast Camnoel, the north boarder of the Citadel.

Amil River ~ (uh-MEEL) river south of the Oakwood Forest.

Bengal Bur ~ (BANG-gul BUR) a large freshwater lake in northeast Camnoel.

Camnoel ~ (CAM-no-ell) a world originally inhabited by elves, dwarves, yorgons, vuls, and skyrogs, that is now also occupied by humans. It is almost entirely unheard of by those in Earth, but is accessible to those in Earth by passage of special mirrors.

Aloehan ~ (AL-oh-hawn) the city of the Citadel, the first human establishment in Camnoel, primarily a farming town, found on the east coast of Camnoel.

Citadel ~ the fortress of Aloehan where the first humans of Camnoel reigned.

Claverel ~ (clav-er-EL) a fishing and trading town consisting of mostly humans on the southeast coast of Camnoel, called the twin city of Clavilier.

Clavilier ~ (clav-ih-LEER) a fishing and trading town on the southern coast of Camnoel, called the twin city of Claverel.

Clavington ~ (CLAV-ing-ton) a sea and mining town consisting of mostly humans, located on the northeast coast of Camnoel, on the Eagle's Head.

Crill River ~ a large river in southeast Camnoel.

Dradoc ~ (DRAH-doc) a trading town in mid-west Camnoel, consisting mostly of humans.

Durim Wey ~ (DUR-im WAY) a small, hidden, rock city in the Grayback Mountains.

Eastern Sea ~ the vast body of salt water east of Camnoel.

Ellwood Forest ~ (ELL-wood) forest in northern Camnoel, marked by its smooth white and silver-barked trees, dominion of the Revowen elves.

Erin Dule ~ (AIR-in Dool) region in northern Camnoel covered with blue flames (deadly fires that emanate extremely cold temperatures).

Erion ~ (AIR-ee-on) a trading city in central Camnoel, one of the largest in Camnoel, composed of chiefly of humans, although there are various races represented there.

Flagin Gulf ~ (FLAY-jin) gulf on the east side of Camnoel, feeding into the Eastern Sea

Garshire Mountains ~ (GAR-shy-er) mountain range in northern Camnoel.

Golden Plains ~ undeveloped region (of plains and meadows) between the Garshire and Audrain Mountains.

Grourdon Desert ~ (GROR-don) hot, barren region enclosed by the Worrin and Grayback Mountains.

Hadis Shale ~ (HAY-dis SHALE, also pronounced HAY-dees SHALE) the two black mountain peaks that mark the entrance to Racin Dor.

King's Crown ~ a three-peak mountain range south of the Serrin Woods.

Kalegon ~ (KALE-gun, kale rhymes with pale) dwarvish city in the Garshire Mountains.

Kurgon Fort ~ secret fortress of Ratacin's in the foothills of the North Worrin Mountains.

Lake Farin ~ (FAIR-in) a small, freshwater lake in northeast Camnoel.

Leythairin Lake ~ (lay-THAIR-in, the 'th' in 'Thair' sounds like that in 'thimble', not 'there'.) the largest lake in Camnoel, feeds the Crill River, livelihood of Vladoc

Mereport ~ (MEER-port, also pronounced MAIR-port) elvin seaport city on the east coast, home of brown skinned elves.

Miershire ~ (MEER-shy-er) city of elves in southwest Camnoel, home of short elves

Miershire Woods ~ the dense forest that surrounds Miershire in southwest Camnoel.

North Worrin Mountains ~ (WOR-in) rocky mountain range bordering the north side of the Grourdon Desert.

Oakwood Forest ~ forest under the dominion of Aloehan.

Pal de Curr ~ (PAL day CUR) part of the South Worrin Mountains, region that is home to many vuls.

Pavin Forest ~ (PAY-vin) forest near the southeast coast of Camnoel.

Racin Dor ~ (ROSS-in DOOR) Ratacin's city and fortress behind Hadis Shale.

Revowen ~ (REV-oh-wen) city of elves in Ellwood Forest.

Serrin Woods ~ (SAIR-in) forest west of Aloehan inhabited by skyrogs.

Teardrop Lake ~ (also called the Lake of Sorrows) small, tear-drop shaped saltwater lake in northeast Camnoel.

The Vaildon Pass ~ (VALE-don) a valley through the Grayback Mountains, the easiest route through the range.

Vladoc ~ (VLAD-ock) large lake city in southern Camnoel, consisting of chiefly humans.

The Western Plains ~ extensive region of varied landscape in northwest Camnoel, inhabited by giants and yorgons.

Worrin Mountains ~ (also referred to as the South Worrin Mountains) the mountain range that borders the south side of the Grourdon Desert

Zjaldon ~ (ZJALL-done) a large city in southern Camnoel consisting chiefly of brown skinned humans.

A SNEAK PEAK INTO
BOOK TWO
OF
THE CAMNOEL TRILOGY

1
REVELATIONS

In the stillness of night, a solitary figure sat above the neighborhood streets of Ecklebridge on a house roof. With his knees bent in front of him, he clasped his hands around his legs. His jaw was tight, and his brown eyes stared fixedly ahead into the starry sky. His tanned face appeared even darker in the night's shadows. The sleeves of his long-sleeve T outlined muscular arms. His was a body marked by strenuous physical labor.

While the rest of the city slept, he sat alone on his perch, sleep eluding him. There wasn't a chance in the world he would be going to bed any time soon. He inhaled, and then let out a long, heavy sigh.

Drew Vincent, at fifteen, had received the biggest shock of his life. In one moment, his life had been undeniably and irrevocably changed. The world in which he had lived for fifteen years, no longer existed. All that he once believed to be true was now shaken, and it accosted him like a slap in the face.

Then it settled on him. Everything he had been seeking—purpose and an identity—he had now found.

Or rather, they had now found him.

Creases formed on his forehead and his eyes grew even more concentrated as he remembered the scene from the previous day.

***

Drew was standing in the kitchen with Wesley and Anna. Only moments ago they had returned to this world through the mirror. Now Josiah Smith stood with them as well.

Leaning against the kitchen counter, Drew casually stuffed his hands into his jean pockets. His fingers fished around, and a frown creased his face. *"It can't be,"* he thought.

Wesley noticed and tossed him a look. "What is it, Drew?"

Drew brought a handful out of his pocket. He opened his hand and Wesley and Anna stood from their seats to look.

Drew's mouth felt dry. "It's my coins from Aloehan."

Anna and Wesley stared at the coins and then looked up at Drew. Then all three looked to Josiah.

"They told us," Drew faltered, "that only those from Camnoel can take things from that world back to our world."

"You were informed correctly."

Drew's sweaty fingers fiercely clenched the coins and his jaw trembled. He hands and neck felt like they were burning. He tried to play it off but couldn't. "You're joking right. Because that…then…that would mean…" his voice trailed off.

Josiah looked him right in the eye. "We need to talk."

Josiah led the three of them down the hall to his office. On the other side of glass doors, the office was a small room thick with the musty scent of books. Shelves lined the walls and an oak desk filled most of the space in the center of the room, along with several chairs, all on an oriental rug.

Drew sat in a plush leather chair on one side of the desk while Josiah settled into a seat behind it. He was aware of Wesley and Anna sitting beside him.

"There is much I have to tell you," Josiah began, "but I would wait until you three have told me about your stay in Camnoel."

"That's not fair," Drew blurted. "What do you know about me?"

Josiah acknowledged Drew's outburst with silence.

"Drew," Anna said softly.

271

Drew tossed her an agitated look.

Wesley glanced at Drew. He complied with Josiah's request—of course he would.

Drew remained silent, his fingers battering away at his armrest.

When Wesley finished, Josiah nodded gratefully. "Thank you for sharing that." He inhaled, "You three have already been through quite a lot, but, to be perfectly truthful with you, there is still more to come."

Drew could feel his sweaty fingers pulsing. He felt ready to stand up and throttle the man, demanding he tell him what he knew.

"May I see your coins?" Josiah asked Drew.

Drew laid the coins on the desk. His palm had indentations from squeezing them.

Mr. Smith examined the currency. "These are indeed, genuine Camnoelian coins."

"Mr. Smith, I want to know right now…are you telling me…" he forced himself to say it, "are you telling me that I'm from Camnoel?"

Josiah stared back at Drew and replied evenly, "That is precisely what I am telling you."

ABOUT THE AUTHOR

Hannah Shoop is an English teacher from Birmingham, Alabama. When she's not teaching or writing, you can find her catching a good baseball game, sipping coffee with friends, hiking in the woods, or chilling with her family. Discover more of her writing at hannahshoop.wordpress.com or follow her on Facebook at HannahShoopAuthor.